CHAPTER ONE

Smith stopped at the reception desk. The man with the peculiar piercing in his left cheek was talking on the telephone. Smith smiled at him and waited. The man shrugged his shoulders to indicate that he would gladly end the awkward phone call but it was out of his control. "OK," he said eventually. "I'll let Doctor Grace know as soon as he gets in."

"Morning," he said to Smith. "You know the drill."

"Morning, Joe," Smith took out his phone and placed it on the tray Joe had put in front of him.

"Do you mind if I ask you something? You know she's a real whack job don't you?"

"That's a matter of opinion."

"It's been four weeks now," Joe said. "And you still keep coming back. Why?"

"I have my reasons. Can I go through?"

"You know the way," Joe said as the telephone started to ring again.

Smith walked down the corridor and nodded to the stocky woman standing by the first security door. She opened it and let him pass without saying a word. Smith continued down a long corridor that was badly in need of a coat of paint. The sound of singing could be heard from inside one of the rooms. Smith stopped to listen and smiled. The old woman who had shaved off half her hair was singing in a low voice. She was singing something about talking to the bees in the forest. Smith walked through the second security door and stopped outside a blue door. He knocked and waited. There was no answer. He opened the door and looked inside. The room was empty. A pencil drawing of a cat in profile was pinned to the wall.

That wasn't there before, Smith thought.

Jessica Blakemore was sitting by herself in the day room. She was reading a huge book. She stopped reading and turned to face Smith before he'd even approached her. Smith thought that she looked a lot healthier than she had done the last time he saw her - her cheeks had more colour in them and the bags under her eyes were less obvious.

"What are you reading?" Smith said. "The complete works of everybody who's ever written something? That book is enormous."

"It's a new bible of dreams," Jessica said. "Most of it is complete hogwash but there are a few interesting observations. Are you going to sit down?"

Jessica Blakemore was a psychiatrist Smith had only known for a few months. She had helped him and his team on a baffling investigation but she had paid the price for it - she had suffered a complete mental breakdown halfway through and had committed herself to the Crownside psychiatric hospital just outside York city centre. She'd committed herself for an initial period of three months and those three months were almost finished. Smith had started visiting her four weeks earlier and the visits had proved to be mutually beneficial - Jessica had come to realise that her condition wasn't as overwhelming as she first thought and Smith had opened up about his own demons.

"How are you?" Smith said. "You're looking much better than you did last week."

"Is that a compliment?" Jessica smiled. "Or does it merely imply that I don't look as ghastly as I did last time?"

"You'll be getting out of here soon," Smith ignored her. "Next week if I'm not mistaken."

"I'm thinking of sticking around, I like it here."

"What about your job?"

"I like to think of it as work experience. Do you know the doctors here are starting to come to me for advice? What an ironic world we live in. The shrinks are getting advice from a loonie."

"You're not a loonie. What about your husband?"

"Ian?" Jessica said and rolled her eyes. "He's been to see me once. Nearly three months and he's been here once. He reckons the people here freak him out. At least I have you. What's on the agenda today?"

"Agenda?"

"You're not here out of concern for me, what's bothering you?"

A young man with a shaved head entered the room and sat down opposite them. He stared blankly into Smith's eyes.

"Brian," Jessica said to him. "We're busy with a consultation here."

The young man didn't move. He continued to glare at Smith.

"Brian," Jessica said. "I said we're busy. We can speak later. Go back to your room."

The man stood up and left the room without regret.

"I'm impressed," Smith said. "They should be paying you a salary here."

Jessica stood up and looked out of the huge window that looked out onto a small cluster of trees.

"I'm thinking about a change," Smith said. "I'm thinking about doing something else. I've had enough."

"There you go - there's the rub, and what's brought this on all of a sudden?"

"I don't know. I'm not sure how much more I can take. What I do isn't exactly normal is it?"

"No," Jessica said. "Normal it isn't but essential it is. You're not normal detective sergeant. You never will be. Come on, look at this scenario - you're asking advice from a shrink who's been admitted to a mental institution."

"I'm sick and tired of death."

Jessica Blakemore appeared to be lost in thought for a moment.

"Are you still having the dreams?"

"Not as often as I used to. I seem to get them when I'm working on something nasty."

"They'll never stop you know."

"I'm getting used to them. The double awakenings are not freaking me out so much anymore."

"What about you and Miss Whitton? How's that all going?"

"Fine," Smith said. "I think."

"Hmm."

"I don't know what to do."

"Well," Jessica said. "The way I see it you have three choices."

"Three?"

"Choice one is to quit the job you're so brilliant at and do something else. I can promise you this, if you do that you'll be joining me in here before you know it. Choice two is to carry on like before. Who knows, people may even stop killing each other."

"I doubt it."

"Me too," Jessica said, "you carry on solving murders and sooner or later you'll probably end up losing your sanity."

"Great, and what's the third choice?"

"Take some time off. When was the last time you had any time off?"

Smith had to think hard. Each time he had tried to take some leave, it had been interrupted by work.

"I haven't had any real time off," he admitted. "I always seem to end up thinking about work."

"What are you working on at the moment?"

"Not much, there's a syndicate that keeps hitting the McDonalds in the city. It's obviously an inside job. It's not going to take a genius to crack that one."

"No murders?"

"Nothing. We haven't had a murder in the city since that Selene Lupei thing."

"Then what are you waiting for? I have a group therapy session in half an hour. If that's all, I'd quite like to do a bit of preparation for it."

Smith looked at Jessica Blakemore and shook her hand. Her hand was very cold.

"What's it like in here?" He asked.

"Peaceful. Sometimes I think that it's the wackos who are locked out there."

She pointed to the window.

"Not the other way round," she added. "Good bye, detective."

CHAPTER TWO

"Two weeks?" DI Bryony Brownhill said. "I don't think I can spare you for two weeks."
Brownhill sat opposite Smith in her office.
"I need a break," Smith said. "With respect, the city of York isn't exactly a hub of crime at the moment."
"These robberies at the McDonalds are causing us quite a problem," Brownhill said.
"Boss, my dog could figure that one out. It's an inside job. They know exactly when the cash gets removed from the premises and then they strike. They're out of there within two minutes. It's an inside job."
"How do you suggest we catch them then?"
"Set a trap. It's obvious. There are only five McDonalds in York. Speak with the managers and get them to change the cash drop times."
"And how will that help?"
"If these scumbags strike again, we'll know they've been tipped off by someone on the inside. That's how we catch them."
"I'll make you a deal. The Super is breathing down my neck. He's of the opinion that the McDonalds are an integral part of the city's heart and he's taking it personally."
"That moron would," Smith said.
"You clear up the robberies and you've got your two weeks."
"Boss, you do realise that I'm entitled to twenty seven days paid leave each year. I checked. Since I joined up I've always ended up losing most of my holidays. I want two weeks off."
"Detective sergeant," Brownhill stood up.
Smith had almost forgotten how imposing her bulk was. Even without the facial hair, she was a scary woman.

"And you realise," she said. "That I am your superior officer and as such, I am the one who approves your leave. At this moment, we have a gang of thugs who are intent on stealing the takings from the McDonalds in the city. So far, they have managed to get away with almost half a million pounds. As you have already pointed out, you have a plan to stop them. Bring them in and you've got your two weeks. End of conversation."

Smith was about to say something but he realised that any further argument would be futile. He stood up.

"Do we need to shake on it?" He offered Brownhill his hand.

Brownhill shook her head. Smith detected a slight smile on her face.

"Get out," she said.

The three DC's, Whitton, Bridge and Yang Chu were sitting in the canteen when Smith went inside. Whitton stood up and kissed Smith on the cheek.

"You two," Yang Chu said. "Could you please not do that at work?"

"What's wrong?" Whitton asked Smith.

Smith was obviously not happy.

"Haven't you lot got work to do?" He said. "The Super is breathing down Brownhill's neck about these McDonalds robberies and you know what he's like when he gets a bee in his bonnet. We all end up suffering."

"What's the big deal?" Bridge said. "Who cares if they steal money from McDonalds? Nobody has been hurt."

"They're breaking the law, and it's our job to stop them."

"I say let them get away with it," Yang Chu said. "They're only robbing from the Yanks."

"They're heroes," Bridge said. "We should be pinning a medal on every

one of them. There's even a Facebook page been set up for them.
They have over two thousand likes. They're modern day Robin Hoods."
"They're still armed robbers," Smith insisted. "And we're going to stop
them. The future of my sanity rests on it."
He put his hand on Whitton's shoulder.
"Can I have a word?" He said.
He walked out of the canteen. Whitton followed him.
"Looks like the day has finally arrived," Bridge said. "He's breaking up
with her. I knew it wouldn't last. The gospel according to DS Smith
'thou shalt not have relationships in the job'."

Smith and Whitton stood in the car park outside the station. Smith
took out a cigarette, lit it and inhaled deeply. A cloud of smoke flowed
out of his nose.
"I knew there was something wrong back there," Whitton said. "I could
see it on your face."
"There's nothing wrong."
He didn't know how to begin. He and Whitton had been in a
relationship for a few months. It was still early days but things seemed
to be going well for them.
"I went to see Jessica Blakemore again yesterday," Smith said.
"I see," Whitton said.
"She gave me an idea."
"Why do you keep going to see her? She's a complete psycho."
"She's not. She was sick, she got help and now she's getting better.
She suggested that I take some time off."
Whitton breathed a sigh of relief.
"How long have I been telling you that?" she said. "It's just what we
both need. We could do some island hopping in Greece. You could take

me to Australia; I'd love to see the places where you grew up. We could…"

"Time off by myself."

Whitton stared at him with her mouth wide open.

"By yourself? I thought we were doing ok."

"We were. I mean we are. I need to get away from this city. This job. I need a break away from everything."

Whitton didn't say anything. She looked at Smith with a mixture of anger and bewilderment.

"I made a deal with the DI," Smith said. "If we clear up these McDonalds robberies I can have two weeks off."

"Two weeks? Where are you going to go for two weeks?"

"I don't know. Somewhere I've never been before. Somewhere with no memories and somewhere as far away from the sea as possible. It's got nothing to do with you."

"Thanks a lot," Whitton said and marched back inside the station.

Maybe that came out wrong, Smith thought.

CHAPTER THREE

Smith parked his car outside the McDonalds on the High Street and turned off the engine. Whitton and Yang Chu had gone to one of the smaller McDonalds just outside the city centre.
"Have you and Whitton broken up?" Bridge asked.
Bridge was not known for his tact.
"That's none of your business," Smith said. "Besides, your taste in women is hardly anything to brag about."
Bridge had found himself involved with a woman who killed three men a few months earlier.
"Selene Lupei," Bridge mused. "It still doesn't seem real somehow. I'm thinking of going to visit her."
"Don't, it'll only end badly. What happened to her kid?"
"Maggie? Foster family. Her father gets killed and her mother get's locked up in a loonie bin. Life is shitty sometimes."
"She'll be fine," Smith opened the car door. "From what I remember, she was a tough one."

The McDonalds was surprisingly busy considering it wasn't yet lunch time. Smith and Bridge walked past the students who were busy putting away copious amounts of burgers and fries to soak up the previous night's alcohol. Smith pushed to the front of the queue and stood in front of a young man with the most pathetic excuse for a beard Smith had ever seen.
"Get to the back of the queue," the man said.
Smith saw from his name tag that his name was Steven Williams. He was the assistant manager.
"Police," Smith ignored him. "Can we speak to a proper manager?"
He showed Williams his ID.

"He's on a break," Williams said.

"Go and get him then," Smith turned to look at the people behind him in the queue. "These people can wait."

Williams sighed and walked towards a small door at the back of the counter. He returned shortly afterwards with another young man. The man eyed Smith and Bridge with obvious suspicion.

"John Burke," he said. "I'm the manager here. What can I do for you?"

"Not here," Smith said. "Is there somewhere we can talk in private? Somewhere away from these morons?"

He said it loud enough for most of the people in the place to hear. Bridge started to laugh.

"We can go outside," Burke said. "I was about to go out for a smoke anyway."

Burke led Smith and Bridge outside onto the street. A crowd of tourists carrying cameras shuffled past.

"Is this about the robberies?" Burke took out a packet of cigarettes. He offered the pack to Smith.

Smith shook his head. Burke took out a cigarette and lit the end.

"They've hit us twice now. I wasn't here the first time but the second time was terrifying. They were so calm about the whole thing."

"Do you have any idea who might be behind it?"

"No," Burke said straight away. "Why would I?"

Smith stared at Burke's face.

"Just thinking out loud," he said. "It's a terrible habit of mine. Tell me what happened."

"I've already spoken to the police," Burke threw his cigarette to the ground and lit another one.

"You haven't spoken to me," Smith said. "What happened?"

"It was Tuesday last week. We'd had a really busy weekend what with the bank holiday. We normally do the cash drop on Monday but because of the bank holiday it was moved to Tuesday."

"How much cash are we talking about?"

"About eighty thousand," Burke said. "Give or take a few hundred."

"Eighty grand?" Bridge said. "Eighty grand worth of burgers in one weekend?"

"Like I said it was a busy weekend," Burke said.

"When is the cash drop normally made?" Smith said. "Just one time a week?"

"Mondays and Thursdays."

"Can you run through the whole procedure? Where the cash is collected, everything."

"The money is kept in the safe in the back," Burke said. "Only me and the other manager have the combination and it changes once a month for security reasons. Once an hour the takings are deposited in the safe."

"The people who collect the cash on Mondays and Thursdays," Smith said. "Who are they?"

"A private security company - ADG security. They do a lot of the big stores in the city."

"OK, the money is kept in the safe. What do the security company do?"

"They come and collect it. They use the door at the back. Two of them stay outside by the van and two more come in to collect the money."

"Are these men armed?" Bridge asked.

"Of course not," Burke said. "Why would they be armed?"

"Because people with guns are stealing money," Smith said. "How was the robbery carried out?"

"They're good," Burke said. "I have to give them that and they're brazen."

"Brazen?" Bridge said.

"I opened the safe when the security company arrived. Those thugs were already inside waiting. They had guns. They told me to hand over the money. They were so calm and very polite. They said there was no need for anybody to get hurt as long as nobody did anything foolish. They walked out through the restaurant. There were loads of people eating at the tables but these people just calmly walked past them."

"Did you recognise any of these men?" Bridge said.

"They wore balaclavas," Burke said.

"How many of them were there?" Smith said.

"Three."

"So they walked out through the restaurant - if you can call McDonalds a restaurant. What did you do then?"

"The one who did the talking told us to wait in the back for five minutes, so I didn't see what happened inside the restaurant but one of the customers told me what happened as they walked through."

"Go on," Smith said.

"They had a full blown conversation with the customers. They pretty much bragged about the whole thing."

"How do you mean?"

"According to the woman who saw it all, one of them stopped in the middle of the restaurant and told everybody what they'd done."

"Do you have the name of this woman?"

"I can do one better," Burke said. "She's inside right now. She comes here most days; sit's there for hours with her lap top and drinks one coffee after another."

CHAPTER FOUR

"Can we have a word?" Smith said to a blonde haired woman typing frantically on a lap top computer.
"Of course," she smiled at Smith.
One of her top teeth was missing.
"Katie Young," she said. "Who are you?"
"Police," Smith sat down, "I'm DS Smith and this is DC Bridge."
"This is about the armed robberies isn't it?"
"I believe you were here on Tuesday."
"I'm here just about every day," Young said. "It was awesome."
"Awesome?" Smith couldn't believe his ears.
"It was like something out of the movies. Nothing like that ever happens in this dreary city."
"Go on," Smith said. "What happened?"
"The three of them walked through from the back. The one in the front was carrying the bag of money. He looked around and stopped. Everyone in the place was terrified. We didn't know what they were going to do to us. But then something happened. Even though the man was wearing a balaclava you got the feeling that he was smiling. You could just sense it."
"What did they do then?" Smith said.
"The one carrying the money told everyone to keep quiet. He told us to stay calm. He had something he wanted to say to us. He said that nobody was going to get hurt if we stayed in our seats. He told us they had just robbed the place - he said they had taken money from the greedy Americans and they no doubt had the money insured. It was surreal. He had such a calming voice. I shouldn't be saying this but I

could fall in love with that voice."

"What then?"

"Then he thanked us for our understanding. And then the weirdest thing happened. Somebody at the front started to clap and pretty soon everybody had joined in. It was addictive. It was the most amazing thing I've ever seen. The man carrying the money lifted the bag into the air, took a bow and left."

"This is quite disturbing," Smith said. "You applauded them for stealing money?"

"Modern day Robin Hoods," Bridge suggested..

Smith glared at him.

"Was there anything distinctive about the three robbers?" he asked Young.

"Distinctive?" Young said. "They were wearing balaclavas."

"Distinctive builds, unusual accents. Things like that."

"The man who spoke had a posh accent. He was definitely not from York. He spoke like he went to a public school or something. All three of them were average height but one of them was definitely a woman."

"A woman? Are you sure?"

"Positive," Young said. "The hips don't lie. Isn't that what they say?"

"Thank you, Miss Young," Smith said.

He turned to Bridge.

"We need to get going."

"Have you seen this?" Young opened up her lap top and turned it so Smith and Bridge could see the screen.

"There's a Facebook page been set up for them," she said. "They have over three thousand likes already. There are hundreds of comments. People are encouraging them to keep up the good work."

"Great, that's all we need. I'm starting to really dislike this Facebook thing."
He was beginning to think that his two weeks off were getting further and further away.

"I still think it's amazing," Bridge said as they drove away from the McDonalds.
"What's amazing?" Smith turned right onto Dene Street.
"They're not really doing any harm are they? They're stealing from a huge corporation. It's not like they're banging old ladies on the head and nicking their pension money."
"Bridge," Smith slammed on the brakes so hard that Bridge shot forward and almost hit his head on the windscreen. "These scumbags are armed robbers. Who they steal from is irrelevant."
"Look at the Facebook page, Sarge," Bridge sat back in his seat. "You can't argue with public sentiment."
"I've been going against public opinion my whole life. It happens to be our job to stop bastards like them. Don't you forget that."
"You're getting really boring in your old age, Sarge," Bridge said.
"Maybe."
"I still think it's quite romantic," Bridge carried on. "Robbing the rich to give to the poor."
"These idiots are not giving it to the poor. They're pulling the wool over everybody's eyes and this so called public opinion isn't going to make our jobs any easier."

"This is it here," Bridge pointed to the McDonalds on Glebe Street. It was much smaller than the branch on the High Street.
"Why rob this one?" Smith parked outside. "They can't make much money in this part of town."
He stopped the engine and got out of the car.

"You'd better lock the door, Sarge," Bridge warned. "I don't trust the people around here."

Smith locked his car door and they walked inside the McDonalds. The place was empty. An extremely bored looking woman was busy putting sachets of tomato sauce into a tray behind the counter.

"Morning," she said. "What can I get you?"

Smith took out his ID.

"I know that already. I've seen your photo in all the papers. I haven't seen you in there though."

She smiled at Bridge.

"Is this about the robbery?" She said. "I don't know why they bothered to knock over this place. The branch in the city centre turns over ten times what we do here. The people around here aren't exactly loaded."

"Were you here when the robbery took place?" Bridge decided to take the initiative.

"It's still a bit of a blur. There's plenty of crime in this neck of the woods but an armed robbery? That you don't expect."

"Can you tell us what happened?" Smith said.

"It was over so quickly. They somehow managed to get in the back. They were waiting when the security company arrived for the cash drop. They took the money and scarpered. Like I said before, I don't know why they bothered. There was only around two grand in the box. That's only a thousand pounds each. Hardly worth risking your freedom for is it?"

"There were only two of them?" Smith said.

"That's right."

"And this was on Tuesday?"

"I've already told your lot all of this."

"I'm just trying to get all the facts. Can you describe these two people?"

"They were wearing balaclavas," she said. "But one of them was a real tub."

"A what?"

"Lard arse, and short with it. He'd stand no chance if he was chased."

"That's interesting," Smith said.

"You won't catch them."

Smith smiled.

"What's so funny?" the woman asked him.

"Sorry, but if I had a hundred pounds for every time somebody's said that to me I wouldn't be standing here now. Is it always so quiet in here? It's almost lunch time and the place is dead."

"Sign of the times. The word around here is that old Phoenix might be closing the place down."

"Phoenix?" Bridge said.

"Jimmy Phoenix," she said. "Real bastard. He owns the franchises to all the McDonalds in York."

"Jimmy Phoenix," Smith repeated.

"I don't know what you think of me," the woman said. "But I'm not going to be working behind the counter in a dump like this forever. I only do it to help pay for my University fees. Some of us weren't born with a silver spoon in our mouths you know."

"What are you studying?" Bridge said.

"Economics. Third year. I know exactly what Jimmy Phoenix is playing at. Have you ever played Monopoly?"

"Never quite got to the end of a game," Bridge admitted.

"You never will. Anyway, Phoenix has the monopoly on every McDonalds in this city. To put it in terms of the game with York as the

board, sooner or later you're bound to land up on one of the arrogant bastard's McDonalds. Phoenix makes an absolute fortune out of it."
"So he has no reason to have someone steal the money to claim the insurance money?" Smith said.
"Excuse me?"
"Just thinking out loud. Thank you for your time."

CHAPTER FIVE

"Jimmy Phoenix," Smith said. "He owns all the McDonalds in the city.

Smith, Whitton, Bridge, Yang Chu and Brownhill sat in the small conference room at the station.

"He doesn't own them," Bridge said. "He owns the franchises. McDonalds still own the brand."

"He controls every McDonalds in York," Smith said. "We need to have a word with him."

"What for?" Brownhill said. "The way I see it, he's a victim in all of this. His businesses were robbed."

"He's just as bad as the McDonalds," Bridge said. "He's a part of these corporate thieves these people are trying to get at."

"We need to speak to him," Smith was adamant.

"Absolutely not," Brownhill said. "And I've been told in no uncertain terms that we are to leave him alone."

"By who?"

"Top brass," Brownhill said.

"Top brass? By that I assume you mean Smyth. Don't tell me that public school piece of plankton actually knows this guy."

"They play golf together. He's off limits. Have you got that?"

"This is bullshit," Smith said. "Phoenix is in the middle of all of this. We need to speak to the man."

"I agree," Whitton said.

"Me too," Bridge and Yang Chu said at the same time.

"This line of conversation is over," Brownhill said. "What did we find out from speaking with the people at the McDonalds?"

"The one on the High Street and the one on Glebe Street were hit by different gangs," Smith said. "The descriptions of the robbers were different."

"I thought there wore balaclavas."

"They did, but the woman at the Glebe street branch described one of the men. He said he was obese. The robbers on the High Street were of average build."

"And one of them was a woman," Bridge added.

"Good," Brownhill said. "Anything else?"

"The one who spoke had a posh accent," Bridge said. "A public school accent."

"Not unlike our retarded Superintendant," Smith said.

"That's enough," Brownhill said. "Whitton, what did you and Yang Chu find?"

"Pretty much the same. All of them were of average build. The leader of the gang - the one who spoke to the customers also had a rather posh accent. There was no mention of a woman though."

"Maybe there's a whole bunch of them," Bridge suggested. "Robin Hood and his merry men."

Brownhill scowled at him and shook her head. She turned to look at Smith.

"What next?" She said.

"It's an inside job. There's no doubt about that. We seem to have eliminated the managers at the McDonalds so that leaves just two more options."

"Two?" Brownhill said.

"Jimmy Phoenix," Smith said. "And seeing as though he's been granted temporary immunity that leaves the security company. ADG Security. Apparently they collect the cash from most of the shops in the city."

"That's our next move then."

"Hold on," Smith said. "I want to go over the chain of events first. Do we have the dates and times of all the armed robberies?"

"I've got them here," Yang Chu produced a sheet of paper and placed it on the table in front of them. "The first one was hit on the Thursday before last. That was the branch on the High Street. Twelve thirty two. Two more were hit the same day at two fifteen and three forty five."

"OK, what about the other three?"

"Tuesday this week. After the bank holiday. The High Street branch was robbed again, the one down the road from the football stadium and then the one on Glebe Street. The High Street branch and the Glebe Street branch were hit at roughly the same time."

"So it was different people," Brownhill said. "That's going to make things a bit more complicated."

"On the contrary," Smith argued. "I reckon it'll help us. The more people involved, the greater the odds that one of them will slip up and lead us to the others. Whitton, let's go and have a cup of crap coffee and then we're going to take a trip to this so called security company."

"They've changed the machine again," Bridge said. "The coffee machine in the canteen. You can get all sorts of fancy cappuccinos now."

"God help us all," Smith said.

"I thought you were heading up to the canteen," Whitton said as they left the conference room.

Smith had turned off towards the row of offices.

"I just need to speak to Chalmers. I'll see you there in five minutes."

Smith knocked on Chalmers' office door and went inside. The smell of cigarette smoke hit him straight away. Chalmers was standing by the window smoking a cigarette. He was gazing out over the car park.

"Afternoon, boss," Smith said. "Beautiful day."

"I'm beginning to really hate this place," Chalmers said. "Smoke?"

He handed Smith a packet of Marlboroughs. Smith took one and lit it. Smoking had been banned in the station for years now but Chalmers always seemed to get away with it.

"Stand by the window," Chalmers said. "What can I do for you?"

"Is Smyth in today?"

"He was," Chalmers threw his cigarette butt out of the window and lit another one. "But I think he has a meeting with the Chief Constable. Something about bloody immigrants again I think. This city is going to the dogs."

"Do you know what golf club Smyth is a member of?"

"This is about Jimmy Phoenix isn't it? You're going to talk to him aren't you?"

"I've been told not to, and it's bullshit. It's hindering the investigation. No, I'm going to follow orders for a change and leave Phoenix well alone but there's no harm in speaking to a few of his fellow golf buddies is there?"

"You're playing with fire," Chalmers said.

"Are you going to tell me or not?"

"Sandburn Hall. It's off the A64 on the way to Malton. Be very careful. Phoenix is going to know you've been snooping around. Jimmy Phoenix isn't someone you want to get on the wrong side of."

"Thanks, boss," Smith stubbed his cigarette out on a small plate on Chalmers' desk.

"Smith," Chalmers said. "You didn't hear that from me, OK?"

"Of course."

Smith realised he was smiling as he walked up to the canteen. The two weeks off are getting closer, he thought, I can feel it.

He went inside the canteen. Whitton, Bridge and Yang Chu were standing next to the biggest coffee machine Smith had ever seen. They appeared to be having a serious debate about something.

"What the hell is that thing?" Smith said.

"It's the new coffee machine," Bridge said. "I'm still trying to decide what to have."

"We can't seem to figure out how it works," Yang Chu said. "The instructions might as well be printed in Swahili."

Whitton stepped forwards, pressed a few buttons and a low gurgling sound could be heard. A plastic cup dropped out of a slot and was quickly filled with a dark brown liquid.

"It doesn't smell too bad," she said.

She picked up the cup and took a sip.

"I think you'll like this one," she handed the cup to Smith and pressed the buttons on the machine again.

"Let's sit by the window," Smith said.

Whitton took her coffee and followed Smith to the table. Bridge and Yang Chu seemed to get the hint and stayed where they were.

"I'm sorry," Smith said. "Sometimes my mouth works way before my brain has a chance to stop it."

"Sometimes? What exactly is going on with us?"

"I like what we have, but I really need to get away for a while. What I said before just came out all wrong. I didn't mean it was nothing to do with you, I meant it's nothing to do with anything you've done."

"I know, I just thought it would be nice for the two of us to get away together."

"It would," Smith said. "And we will but right now if I don't get away from all of this I'm afraid I might just lose my mind completely and then I'll be no use to anybody."

He smiled at her.

Whitton shook her head.

"Two weeks? I suppose that's not too long. I'm sure we can all benefit from not having you around for two weeks."

"Thanks," Smith said. "I need to ask a favour."

"Go on."

"Could you look after Theakston for me? I can't take him away for two weeks. He likes you."

"Where are you going to go?"

"I have no idea. Not far. Maybe somewhere in The Dales. Who knows, I'll probably get bored after a few days and come back."

Whitton finished her coffee and stood up.

"What's wrong?" Smith said.

"This McDonalds mess isn't going to sort itself out with us sitting around drinking coffee," Whitton said. "The sooner we crack this one, the sooner you can go off on your crazy sabbatical and the sooner we can all get back to normal."

CHAPTER SIX

"Where are we going?" Whitton asked. "The offices for AMG security are in the city centre.
Smith had turned right and was heading north up the A64 towards Malton.
"Slight detour," Smith said. "Do you feel like a round of golf?"
"You can't be serious? Brownhill will have both our arses when she finds out. Not to mention what the Super will do."
"Relax, I'm just going to find out a bit more about this Jimmy Phoenix bloke. Nobody will even know we were there. I have a plan."
"You'll never change will you?"

They drove in silence for a while. Smith stopped outside the impressive entrance gate to the golf club. An elderly man dressed in a suit emerged from a small brick structure and opened the gate. Smith watched as he looked at Smith's old Ford Sierra with obvious distaste. He approached the driver's side and Smith wound down the window.
"G'Day," Smith said in the most exaggerated Australian accent he could muster.
Whitton found it hard not to laugh.
"Beautiful day," Smith continued. "Me and the missus are gagging for a game of golf. We was thinking about joining the club. Can you help us?"
"Of course, sir," the man sighed. "Follow the road up to the club house and speak to Lorraine in reception. She'll be able to gauge if this club is for you or not. I have to warn you though, the fees are rather steep."
"No worries," Smith opened his wallet and took out a ten pound note. "Thanks, mate."

He handed the money to the man.

"That's not necessary," the man handed the banknote back to Smith and went back inside his shed.

"What was that all about?" Whitton said as they drove towards the huge clubhouse.

"What was what all about? We're just two prospective members. We'll ask a few questions about the place and maybe we'll be lucky. Maybe Jimmy Phoenix's name will crop up."

"You're asking for trouble."

Smith parked his car in the car park in front of the clubhouse. His old Sierra seemed out of place with all the SUVs and shiny Mercedes and BMWs.

"This is how the other half live," Whitton looked around.

The golf course was beautifully maintained. Elaborate water features were scattered randomly around the greens.

"This is my worst nightmare," Smith said. "Who ever came up with this stupid game?"

"They reckon that half the business deals in York are made on the golf course," Whitton said.

"We live in a mad world. Let me do the talking - you're a hopeless liar."

They went inside the clubhouse. A huge bar dominated one of the walls. Above it hung various trophies and awards. On the wall next to the bar was a photograph board showing golfing events from the past. The main room was empty apart from a table of four men who were eating something that looked very expensive. A tall woman with black hair tied in a tight bun approached them.

"Good afternoon," she looked Smith up and down. "Can I help you?"

"Are you Lorraine?" Smith said.

"I am. Who might you be?"

"Just having a look around," Smith said. "Me and the wife were thinking of joining. Bruce McClure's the name."

He held out his hand.

Lorraine looked at it as if it was something the cat might have brought inside.

"And this is the missus, Shelia," Smith added.

Whitton's face was starting to turn red.

"This is a very exclusive club," Lorraine didn't even try to hide her contempt.

"Just what we're looking for," Smith said. "Hey Sheila?"

He looked at Whitton.

Whitton wanted the ground to swallow her up.

"Maybe one of the golf clubs in the city centre would be more for you," Lorraine suggested.

"Nah," Smith said. "I'm getting a good vibe from this place. The golf pitch seems much bigger than the photos on the internet too. Is it alright if we just have a drink at the pub? We'll let you know what we think after a few cold ones."

He walked off without waiting for an answer.

"She wasn't going to tell us anything," Smith said to Whitton at the bar.

"She's probably terrified that you might want to join this club," Whitton said. "You're terrible sometimes."

"We might have a bit more luck with him though," Smith pointed to the young man working behind the bar.

He didn't look much older than eighteen. The barman approached them.

"Two pints of Theakstons," Smith said. "It's a bit quiet in here isn't it?"

"They're all on the golf course," the barman said. "It'll be packed in here in a couple of hours."
He poured the beers and placed them on the counter.
"Eight fifty," he said.
"How much?" Smith said.
"Eight fifty."
Smith handed him a ten pound note.
"Drink slowly," Smith whispered to Whitton.
"We shouldn't be drinking at all, Sarge," Whitton said.
"Keep your voice down - somebody might hear you."
"You're Australian aren't you?" The barman handed Smith his change.
"There's no flies on you," Smith said. "The name's Bruce. Bruce McClure."
"Pete," the barman said.
"How old are you, Pete?"
"Nineteen. I work here on the weekends. My Granddad got me the job. He works on the gate."
"We've met him. How long have you worked here?"
"Almost a year. The people are a bit snobby but the money's alright. You're the first Australian I've seen in here."
"Do you know many of the members here?"
"Quite a few. Most of them are filthy rich. They think they're something special but they're not."
"What about Jimmy Phoenix? Does he come in here much?"
"Jimmy?" Pete said. "He comes here a few times a month. Do you know Jimmy?"
"A bit," Smith lied. "We share some of the same interests if I can put it like that. What's he like?"
"Jimmy's alright, he's nothing like the others."

"How do you mean?"

"Most of the toffs we get in here were born with money. They didn't have to do anything to get it. Jimmy's different. He worked himself up from nothing to get to where he is today. He grew up with nothing and look how well he's done. He owns all the McDonalds in York, he has a few successful horse breeding stables and I heard he's looking at a few night clubs in town."

"He breeds horses?" Smith said.

"He doesn't breed them himself," Pete said. "He just owns the stables. He's had quite a few big winners out of it. Jimmy's alright. He doesn't treat me like the rest of them."

"We ought to get going," Whitton said.

She hadn't touched her beer.

"When was the last time Jimmy was in here?" Smith said. "Sorry about all the questions but I grew up in a small town where everybody knew everything about everybody else."

Pete was about to answer when his whole facial expression changed. "I have to get back to work," he said. "Davina Phoenix has just walked in. She's Jimmy's wife and she's not the most pleasant person to be around. I don't know how Jimmy puts up with her. As fast as he's making the money, she's spending it."

Smith turned round. A heavily made up woman in her late twenties was standing talking to two young men in the middle of the room.

"Come on, Whitton," he said. "Let's get out of here."

He cast a glance at Davina Phoenix as they walked past. She was obviously quite intoxicated - her blue eyes were very bloodshot and her gait was unsteady. She didn't appear to notice him staring at her.

Smith and Whitton were about to leave when Lorraine appeared as if from nowhere.

"Decided it's not for us," Smith said. "We were actually looking for somewhere a little more up market. No offence though."

He walked out leaving the secretary of the golf club standing with her mouth wide open.

CHAPTER SEVEN

The offices of AMG security occupied the whole of the top floor of the Cook building smack bang in the city centre. Bridge and Yang Chu stood by the reception desk waiting for the immaculately dressed woman behind the desk to end her phone call.

"Sorry to keep you waiting," she finished on the phone and smiled. "What can I help you with?"

Bridge took out his ID. Yang Chu did the same.

"We'd like to speak with someone regarding the cash drops at the McDonalds in town," Bridge said.

"Mr Green landed that contract personally," the woman said. "He's good friends with Jimmy Phoenix. Terrible business with those armed robberies. I'll just find out if he has time to talk to you."

She picked up the phone.

"Excuse me Miss..." Bridge said.

"Wright," the woman said. "Mrs Joan Wright."

"Mrs Wright, this is extremely important. We need to speak to Mr Green."

Joan Wright stared at Bridge for much longer than he thought was appropriate and pressed a button on the phone.

"Mr Green," she said. "There are two detectives at the front desk. They would like to talk to you."

A deep voice could be heard on the other end of the line.

"Thank you, Mr Green," Joan said and replaced the handset.

"Mr Green is extremely busy at the moment, but he has agreed to give you a few minutes of his time. His office is right at the end of the corridor."

The telephone started to ring again. Bridge nodded to Yang Chu and headed off down the corridor.

The name Adam Michael Green was carved into a brass plaque attached to a very expensive looking wooden door at the end of a row of offices. Bridge knocked and waited.

"Come in," a booming voice was heard from inside.

Bridge and Yang Chu went in. A huge man was standing by the window staring out at the impressive view over the city of York. The Minster dominated the skyline in the distance.

"Wow," Yang Chu couldn't hide the fact that he was impressed.

"Not a bad view don't you think?" Green said in a voice that any theatre troupe would be glad to get their hands on. "Take a seat. Would you like something to drink?'

"No thanks," Bridge said. "I'm sure you know why we're here?"

"Of course," Green sat down behind a huge desk. "I do hope you're here to tell me you've caught the reprobates responsible."

"Not yet, we just need to ask you a few questions."

"Fire away," Green said.

He sat with his hands clasped behind his head. He exuded the confidence of a man who was no stranger to stressful confrontations.

"Firstly," Bridge said. "Can I ask you what exactly it is that AMG security does? Sorry if I sound a bit stupid."

"Not at all. We provide security - security in all shapes and forms. AMG security, no job too big or small and all that bull."

Yang Chu smiled.

"Seriously," Green said. "I started this company twenty years ago. Not to be too defamatory to your lot but by the early nineties in the blur of post Thatcherism, the national security services, i.e. you lot had taken a bit of a knock with regards to public opinion. The police back then didn't exactly fill the law abiding citizens with confidence. That, plus the namby pamby policies of the so called Socialists who followed, meant that the power and respect you once had was all but obliterated. We filled a gap - provided a service that was lacking. We started with football matches, pop concerts, big events and then I stumbled on the cash drop business. Did you know that, only a few years ago a lot of the top businesses were still dropping off their takings at the bank in plastic envelopes? Sorry to babble on a bit - it's a really bad habit of mine. There you have it. That's my life. Anything else?"

Bridge was gob-smacked. Yang Chu continued to stare out the window. Rain clouds were forming in the east.

"Mr Green," Bridge said. "The people on your payroll. Where exactly do you find them from?"

"That's a very good question, and I can tell you it was a tricky endeavor. The vetting processes we use are not dissimilar to your own. No criminal records of course. You'd be surprised how many of our employees are former colleagues of yours. Retired policemen looking for a bit of an extra income. They already have a wealth of experience. Ex army too. We have a highly trained crew here at AMG."

Yang Chu was starting to get a headache.

This man certainly likes the sound of his own voice, he thought.

"Let's talk about the McDonalds robberies," Bridge said.

"I'm going to stop you there if I may," Green said. "As soon as I heard about them I ordered a very thorough internal investigation. That was my main priority. After offering my condolences and sincere apologies to Mr Phoenix of course."

"Jimmy Phoenix?" Yang Chu said.

"That's right. We've been dealing with the McDonalds for four years now. It's a very lucrative contract, I can tell you that."
"And this internal investigation," Bridge said. "What did you find out?"
"Nothing of course, and I didn't really expect to find anything. My security staff acted accordingly under the circumstances. There was nothing untoward going on."
"Your guards," Yang Chu said. "Do they carry guns?"
"Of course not," Green looked at Yang Chu as if he were an idiot. "That would be a completely different ball game son. We're talking all sorts of complications - firearms licenses, annual competency compliance, public liability insurance. It just isn't viable."

Bridge was unsure which direction to go next with the line of questioning. Green seemed to have all the answers.
"Mr Green," he said. "Five McDonalds were hit in the space of a week. One of them was robbed twice. AMG security handled all the cash drops on the days of the robberies. Don't you think that's a bit odd?"
"Odd?" Green stood up and walked over to an impressive teak book shelf.
He picked out a leather bound book and put it straight back again.
"I bought this book case and that desk when I landed my first contract," he said, more to himself than the two detectives sitting in his office. "Bootham Crescent. That was twenty years ago. We provided the security at the ground twenty odd weekends a year. I don't particularly like football but that's what started all of this. That was the building block on which we've built the company we have today."
He looked Bridge directly in the eye. For the first time, Bridge noticed he had one glass eye. He looked at Bridge as if he was waiting for him to say something.

"Sorry," Bridge said. "I didn't realise you'd asked me a question."
"I didn't," Green sat down again. "And the answer to the question on the tip of your lips is no. Absolutely not."
Bridge was confused. This man was talking in riddles.
"You're wondering. You're wondering if AMG were involved somehow in these robberies. That's why you're here isn't it?'
"Are you?"
"Let me explain something to you."
Yang Chu let out a huge sigh. His headache was getting worse.
"The money taken at the six robberies," Green continued. "Was a little under half a million pounds. Now that may seem like an awful lot of money. Let me break things down for you. The contract with Mr Phoenix and the McDonalds over ten years, two drops per week is worth ten times that. We have plenty of other contracts worth the same if not more. What I'm trying to explain to you is why would I risk all of that for that kind of money?"
"With respect, Mr Green," Bridge said. "It's not AMG or you personally we're looking at. How well do you know the people who work for you?"
"In a company such as this, I make it my business to know my employees. Most of them were handpicked by myself. I have nothing to hide here."
"Would you be able to provide us with a list of these employees?" Yang Chu said.
"Of course, and I'd also be happy to show you the results of the internal investigation. Like I said, I have nothing to hide. Integrity is tantamount to what we do here. Without integrity we have nothing. I'll have Mrs Wright prepare copies of everything you need."
He stood up again.

"Now," he said. "If there's nothing further, I have nine holes booked with Jimmy Phoenix. I'm sure you'll both agree, I have a few bridges to build there with the poor man. Gentlemen."

He gestured to the door. Bridge and Yang Chu stood up. Green put his hand in his pocket and took out a business card. He handed the card to Bridge.

"In case you ever feel like a career change," he said. "I've got a feeling you'd fit right in here."

CHAPTER EIGHT

"I don't know if that was a compliment or what," Bridge said to Yang Chu as they headed back to the station.
"That bloke can talk the hind legs off a donkey," Yang Chu said. "My head's still spinning. Do you think AMG has anything to do with the robberies?"
"We've got plenty to go through. What with the list of employees and the results from the internal investigation but I don't think we'll find anything."
"Me neither," Yang Chu agreed. "I think Smith's right again. I think this is all to do with Jimmy Phoenix."
"Step on the gas mate," Bridge said.
The car in front of him was driving so slowly that Bridge had to drop down two gears to avoid stalling.
"What's his problem?"
"Probably an old woman," Yang Chu said. "Or a man wearing a hat - they're the worst."
They were driving on a single lane road and there was nowhere for Bridge to overtake.
"Christ," he said. "If I go any slower I'll have to stick her in reverse. Old people shouldn't be allowed to drive on the weekends. I mean it's not like they don't have plenty of time on their hands is it?"
The car in front of them slowed down even more opposite the McDonalds and turned left into a side street.
"Thank God for that," Bridge increased his speed.
He crossed the river and headed in the direction of the station.
"Looks like rain," Yang Chu said.

Grey clouds were quickly merging above them. Rain was definitely on the way.

Bridge and Yang Chu made it inside the station just in time. The rain came down with purpose. Within minutes a small pool had formed outside the front door. They found Smith and Whitton upstairs in the canteen. They were talking to DI Brownhill at the table by the window.
"Summer's on the way," Brownhill said. "Look at that rain. That's a summer rain shower. It'll be dry again within an hour."
"Right," Smith said. "Down to business. We need to bring Jimmy Phoenix in right away."
Brownhill looked confused.
"What are you talking about?" she said.
"Phoenix is the key to all this, trust me."
"Have you not been listening? I've already told you that Phoenix isn't to be bothered. Please don't tell me you've already spoken to him?"
"No, I actually followed an order for once but me and Whitton did do a bit of digging in one of his domains."
"Domains?"
"His golf club," Smith said. "Gruesome place. If that's how the rich folk like to live then let me be poor for the rest of my life."
"I told you to leave him alone."
"Yes you did, and we did leave him alone. We spoke with a rather chatty barman there. We also met Phoenix's wife briefly. Lovely woman by the sound of things. As quickly as Phoenix makes his money, she spends it. That's the key to all of this."
"I don't follow you."
"Phoenix's wife," Smith said. "Davina. I reckon that Phoenix couldn't keep up with her so he arranged the robberies to earn a bit of extra cash. A lot of extra cash."

"I've never heard such rubbish in my life. Do you know how much the man's worth? He's a millionaire many times over. I assume you have evidence to back up these preposterous insinuations?"

"Not yet," Smith admitted. "But it'll turn up and when has evidence ever stopped us from badgering a suspect before? Phoenix is a suspect - it's time to bring him in."

"Absolutely not. In case you haven't forgotten, he is a good friend of Superintendant Smyth's. He is not to be questioned without good reason."

"Are you telling me he has immunity? Just because he happens to knock a few little balls around with our sorry excuse for a boss?"

"No," Brownhill looked for an escape route.

She turned to Bridge.

"What did you find out from the security company?" She asked him.

"I don't think they were involved," Bridge replied. "In my opinion, they didn't act like they had anything to hide. They also stood to lose a lot more than they gained if they were found out. They gave us all the information we asked for. It's going to take us hours to go through the file containing the info on the staff and the results of their own internal investigation."

"You'd better get started then," Brownhill said.

"But it's almost six," Bridge looked like he was going to cry. "And I'm supposed to have a day off tomorrow. I have a sort of a date tonight."

"Cancel it. We're going to get to the bottom of all this."

"What about the insurance company?" Whitton said. "Has anybody spoken to them?"

"I talked to the investigator myself," Brownhill said. "They have their own investigators in matters such as this. They have to follow certain procedures. They employ people specifically to root out irregularities in insurance claims. It appears there was nothing untoward here. They've already paid out the money."

"I still say we have a look at Jimmy Phoenix's bank accounts," Smith said. "That bloke is hiding something."

"That is one of the first things the insurance investigators do in cases such as this," Brownhill said. "Jimmy Phoenix is financially very healthy. Please remember that the man is still a victim here. Bridge, you and Yang Chu get onto the security company file. With any luck, you may be finished before your day off tomorrow."

Bridge stood up. He looked extremely annoyed. He picked up the heavy file and stormed out of the canteen.

"I'll see you all tomorrow," Brownhill stood up and walked through the cloud of steam that Bridge had left in his wake.

"Poor guy," Whitton said. "He hasn't been on a date since that Selene Lupei thing. He told me he was looking forward to getting back on the horse."

"Back on the horse?" Smith said. "That's just like something Bridge would say."

"I feel sorry for him anyway."

"Come on, Whitton," Smith said.

"Where are we going?"

"Working supper. I've got plenty of beers and I'm sure there's a frozen pizza in the freezer at home. Let's help Bridge to get back on that horse."

CHAPTER NINE

The file that Smith and Whitton had relieved Bridge and Yang Chu of was much thicker than Smith had expected. AMG security had done a very thorough job in their investigation.
"This is going to take all night," Whitton sighed. "Is this your idea of a romantic Saturday evening?"
"It's not that bad," Smith said. "Besides, I have an ulterior motive."
"I didn't bring my toothbrush."
"Get your mind out of the gutter for once. What I mean is, the sooner we sort this mess out, the sooner I get my two weeks off and sort my shit out. Then we can get back to normal. Two weeks in the middle of nowhere is getting closer. I can feel it. Let's get started."
He walked through to the kitchen and returned with two bottles of beer. He handed one of them to Whitton.

"There are sixteen full time employees at AMG security," Smith read through the file. "Twelve men and four women. All the security personnel are men apart from one. Petra Redshaw. Ex army according to this. Call me old fashioned but why would a woman want to join the army?"

"Probably for the same reason a woman wants to join the police," Whitton slapped him on the shoulder. "To serve and protect and all that bull."
"OK, you take eight and I'll take the other half. See if anything jumps out at you."
"What do you mean?"
"You'll know when you see it," Smith turned the page in the file.

Two hours and three beers later, Smith and Whitton were none the wiser. None of the people who worked for AMG security seemed to have any reason for getting involved in the armed robberies. Most of the staff were ex-armed forces or police. Smith had even worked with two of them when he had first joined up.

"Did I remember you mentioning something about a frozen pizza?" Whitton finished her beer and handed Smith the bottle. "Another beer would go down well too."

"I'll see what I can do. You can make a start on AMG's internal investigation."

"Thanks," Whitton said.

The secretary at AMG security had been very methodical in her chronicle of the McDonalds cash robberies. Each individual incident had been scrutinised thoroughly - no stone had been left unturned. There were step by step accounts of how the robberies had been carried out, witness statements and statements from all the personnel on duty at the time. Whitton thought they couldn't have done a better job themselves. There was nothing to suggest that AMG were involved in any way. Whitton skimmed through the pages again. Nothing struck her as suspicious. Everyone had acted in accordance with the guidelines stipulated by AMG. These guidelines were also included in the file. Whitton sighed and stretched her arms.

What a total waste of a Saturday night, she thought.

Smith placed the pizza on the table and handed Whitton a beer. "Anything?" he asked.

"Nothing, this has been a complete waste of time."

"Oh well, at least we've ruled out a whole load of possible suspects. Tomorrow we can throw that file on Brownhill's desk and tell her to organise and interview with Jimmy Phoenix."

"I wonder how Bridge's date is going," Whitton took a slice of pizza from the plate. "I bet he's having more fun than we are."

"Come on," Smith stood behind her and gently massaged her neck.
"It's not that bad. We haven't spent much time alone in ages."
"What?" Whitton said. "Beer, pizza and a case file longer than War and peace. That's my dream of a perfect Saturday night. Don't stop."
Smith pressed harder on Whitton's shoulders.
"Sarcasm doesn't suit you," he said.
"People in Yorkshire are born sarcastic. Are we finished for the night? Can we relax for a bit now?"
"Almost," Smith said.
He removed his hands from Whitton's shoulders and walked over to the makeshift desk he had put up in the corner of the room. He turned on his computer.
"What are you doing now?" Whitton said.
"Just one last bit of research. I want to see what my good friend Google has to say about Jimmy Phoenix.
He typed in his password and opened up the search engine.
"Then can we chill out a bit?"
"Yes, I promise. Could you get me another beer first though?"
Smith typed in 'Jimmy Phoenix' and pressed 'search'. There were not many Jimmy Phoenix's to choose from.
"Bingo," Smith found what he was looking for.
A Wikipedia page had been set up for Phoenix.
"Find anything?" Whitton placed a beer on the desk next to him.
"Thanks. Not yet."
He looked at the Wikipedia page. Jimmy Phoenix had been born in 1960 in Foveran, a small village a few miles north of Aberdeen on the Scottish east coast. He had graduated from the University of Aberdeen in 1982 with a degree in Economics. After that there was a gap until 1989 when it stated that Phoenix had made it onto the Forbes rich list

in the under thirty category. He had acquired his wealth by a series of shrewd land purchases in Glasgow, Edinburgh and Dundee. Phoenix had bought up dilapidated buildings for a bargain, renovated them and turned them into low cost student accommodation. By 1989, at the age of twenty nine, Phoenix was reported to have assets worth well over six million pounds.

"He likes his horses," Whitton was standing behind Smith. "It says here he owns three top stables. Two in Scotland and one just up the road from us in Skipton."

"Thoroughbreds," Smith said. "Whatever that means."

"It's big business. I read somewhere that some of these horses have bloodlines going back years. They're like royalty. People pay huge amounts of money just for the sperm from these horses."

"Yuk," Smith said. "The world's gone crazy."

Smith carried on reading.

"Look at this. Our friend Phoenix is a bit of a philanthropist. It says here that between ninety five and two thousand and five he reportedly gave away over five million to various charities."

"Tax write offs," Whitton said. "All the rich people do it. It's got nothing to do with generosity. It costs them bugger all and it makes them look like saints. What about after two thousand and five? Why did he stop giving away his cash then? What happened?"

Smith scrolled down the page.

"The donations stopped. Do you want to know what happened?"

"What happened?"

"Davina Cole happened," Smith said. "Poor Phoenix got married. Davina Cole. It says here that he met her while he was staying in a hotel in Edinburgh. It must have been love at first sight. She worked as a cleaner there."

"The plot thickens," Whitton said. "How old is she?"
"She was nineteen when they met," Smith did some quick mental arithmetic. "That means Phoenix is twenty six years older than her. They were married within two months."
"Love at first sight," Whitton mused. "That kind of money makes it easy to fall in love. What else does it say?"
"Not much. It doesn't mention the McDonalds franchises. This Jimmy Phoenix is a bit of an enigma."
Whitton sat back down on the couch. Smith carried on reading. There wasn't much more to read. He started again from the beginning. He had missed a part about Phoenix's children from a previous marriage in 1990. Two daughters. Charlotte, aged twenty one and Sophie who was eighteen.
His eldest daughter is not much younger than his wife, Smith thought. He closed the Wikipedia page and switched off the computer.
"We need to talk to this man," Smith said. "We need to find a way to get him to the station.
Whitton didn't reply. Smith turned around. She was sitting on the sofa with her eyes closed. From the low breathing sounds coming from her mouth, Smith knew she was asleep.

CHAPTER TEN

Smith's wishes came true the following morning. He had barely stepped inside the station when he was leapt upon by a very angry looking DI Brownhill.
"What have you done?" Brownhill asked him.
"I've been here two seconds," Smith said. "What do you mean what have I done?"
"Jimmy Phoenix is waiting for you in your office. He's been here for over an hour. He's asked to speak with you specifically. What's going on?"
"I have no idea," Smith said.
Brownhill glared at him. Her eyes were full of suspicion. Smith noticed that the fine growth of hair on her upper lip was back.
"Really, boss," Smith said. "I have no idea what he wants."
He walked past her and headed towards his office.

The man who sat on the chair behind Smith's desk wasn't what Smith had expected. Jimmy Phoenix was a short, balding man who clearly didn't have any kind of fitness regime in his life. An impressive beer belly hung down onto the top of his flabby thighs.
"Morning," Smith said. "Mr Phoenix?"
"DS Smith," Phoenix stood up. "We meet at last. I've read all about you."
Smith didn't know what to say. Here he was face to face with the man he wanted to talk to most and he couldn't find the words.
"You wanted to speak to me," Phoenix's accent was a peculiar blend of Eastern Scottish and something Smith couldn't put his finger on.

"How did you know that?" Smith said. "Please sit down."

Phoenix shuffled his bulk back down on the chair. Smith sat opposite him.

"Detective," Phoenix said. "I didn't get to where I am today without keeping my eyes and ears open. You were at my golf club yesterday. You're not exactly unknown in these parts."

For the first time ever, Smith realised this was true; his photograph had been in the papers more times than he cared to remember.

"Sorry," he said. "And thank you for coming in."

"Bruce and Sheila from Australia? I may be rich but I still have a sense of humour. Love it."

"What do you want to tell me?"

"I want to tell you that I know nothing about the robberies at my McDonalds. Why would I? It was my money that was stolen after all."

"The insurance money was paid out almost immediately wasn't it?"

"And what would that suggest to you?"

"I don't know."

"Then let me tell you how insurance companies work," Phoenix smiled a smug smile. "They are incredibly reluctant to pay out. They're famous for it. They will look for any pathetic excuse to renege on their promises to pay the policy holder. When the claim is settled promptly it can mean only one thing - there was nothing suspicious about the claim."

"I believe the payout was close to half a million pounds altogether."

"After their exorbitant excess and admin charges, I managed to recoup about eighty percent of what was stolen. Even a non-business minded person can see I didn't exactly get a good deal."

"OK," Smith realised he was running out of questions to ask. "Do you have any idea who might have done this? Do you have any enemies?"

"Plenty," Phoenix said without hesitation. "You show me a successful businessman who claims to have no enemies and I'll show you a liar. I've trodden on so many toes on my way up that I've kept a whole bunch of chiropodists in business."

He smiled as if he had told this joke many times before.

"But I can't imagine anybody who would go to such extremes to get back at me," he added. "It doesn't make sense."

"Forgive me if I sound rude," Smith said. "But I heard a rumour that your wife is a bit careless with money."

"Davina? If she's got it, she'll spend it. It doesn't matter if it's ten pounds or ten thousand. I'm not stupid, detective. I mean look at me. I know very well that if it weren't for the money she wouldn't have even looked in my direction but she married me. I have no pretenses about why she married me. What's this got to do with all of this?"

"So she does have expensive tastes?"

"Yes," Phoenix said. "In fact it was starting to get a bit out of hand. I may be well off, but the way Davina was carrying on it was like I had an endless supply of money. That's why I had to do something about it."

"What did you do."

"Let's say I put her on rations."

"Rations?"

"Davina has her own bank account. She no longer has access to any of mine. I pay a generous allowance into her account each month and once that's gone she's on her own. She needs to learn to budget. It's not a meager amount either. If Davina can't survive on twenty thousand each month then she has a serious problem."

Twenty thousand pounds a month? Smith thought, I'd have to work almost a whole year for that.

"Thank you for coming in," he said. "If you think of anything else, please give me a call."

He handed Phoenix one of his cards. Phoenix stood up and offered his hand. Smith shook it. It was cold and clammy.

"One more question," Smith said. "How did your wife react when you told her you were denying her access to your bank accounts?"

Phoenix started to laugh.

"How do you think?" he said. "How do you think?"

He was still laughing when he walked out of the office.

CHAPTER ELEVEN

"Anyone feel like a round of golf?" Smith burst into the canteen. Bridge and Yang Chu were sitting in the corner quietly. Smith walked over to them. Bridge looked like he'd had a very rough night. His eyes were half closed and his face was a strange grey colour.

"I thought you were off today," Smith said to him.

"I was," Bridge said. "But Brownhill called me in. She said I might be needed. I don't know for what - there's bugger all going on."

"What's this about a round of golf?" Yang Chu said.

"I have a theory," Smith said. "One that might get me a step closer to my two weeks off. Come on, we'll go in my car."

DI Brownhill was standing by the front desk talking to PC Baldwin when they walked through.

"How did it go with Jimmy Phoenix?" She asked Smith. "I hope you haven't upset him."

"He's innocent. Why would I upset him? Anyway, he's given me an idea."

"I don't like the sound of this. What's going on in that head of yours?"

"Give me a few hours," Smith walked out before she had a chance to argue.

Bridge and Yang Chu followed quickly behind him.

"What's this idea of yours?" Yang Chu said.

Smith drove out of the car park and turned left. Bridge was already half asleep on the back seat.

"I have a feeling that Jimmy Phoenix's wife is behind these McDonalds robberies."

"What?" Yang Chu said.

"It all makes sense, she knew all about the ins and outs of the business. She knew when the cash drops were to take place and from what I've just heard her expense account has just taken a bit of a knock."

"But she's loaded," Yang Chu said. "Jimmy Phoenix is worth millions."

"And he wants to keep it that way. He's cut her allowance. She's used to having endless funds and now that's all stopped. Anyway, let's find out shall we. I spoke to the chatty barman at the golf club a while ago and he informed me that the lovely Mrs Phoenix is, as we speak chairing a meeting for the junior golfers at the club. Apparently, she's very active in that sense."

"I don't follow you, Sarge."

"I reckon the meeting is just a front for something else. Young impressionable, upper class rich kids. They fit the witness accounts for the robberies. One of the witnesses said a woman was involved. Davina Phoenix organised the whole thing. I must admit it was a brilliant idea. I mean, who would suspect a bunch of toffs?"

Bridge was now snoring loudly on the back seat.

"I hope she was worth it," Smith said to him.

Smith parked his car in the car park at the golf club and stopped the engine. The car park was almost full.

"Sunday golfers," Yang Chu said. "I still can't figure out what the fuss is all about. It's a stupid game."

Bridge started to stir.

"Where are we?" He rubbed his eyes.

"Golf club," Smith said. "How was the date."

Bridge smiled an inane smile in lieu of a reply.

"Don't you think we should phone for back up?" Yang Chu said.

"Not yet," Smith got out of the car. "I just want to find out what's going on first."

"Where's Whitton today?" Bridge asked.

"Day off," Smith said. "This is what we're going to do. We'll go inside the clubhouse and have a drink at the bar. Keep your eyes and ears open."

"Don't you have to be a member to get in?" Bridge said.

"I learned a long time ago, if you act like you belong somewhere nobody will ever doubt whether you do or not. Just walk up to the bar and sit down."

They went inside and approached the bar. Pete, the barman was working alone. The place was deserted.

"Where is everybody Pete?" Smith said. "The car park is almost full."

"They're on the golf course," Pete said. "Can I get you a drink?"

"Three cokes," Smith looked at Bridge. "You'd better give him two."

A woman and five young men entered the bar area. Smith recognised the woman straight away. It was Davina Phoenix. He was hoping she wouldn't remember him from the previous day. Their group walked straight past and sat at the opposite end of the bar. Pete placed four cokes in front of Smith.

"Barman," Davina Phoenix bawled. "Are you even working today? We need two bottles of Moet. Our meeting is due to start again in ten minutes."

Pete looked absolutely terrified.

"What's up with you, squire?" A short fat youth with a red face looked directly at Smith. "Are you lost? Do you even know how to play golf?"

"What's your handicap?" Another young man asked.

"I'm unable to tolerate arseholes," Smith said. "It's a handicap I was born with."

Pete started to laugh.

"Where's the toilet, Pete?" Smith said.

"Out of the door to the left," Pete said. "Next to the conference room."

Smith stood up.

"Come with me," he said to Yang Chu.

They headed towards the door.

"Need someone to hold it for you do you?" the fat youth called after them.

Smith stopped in his tracks for a second then carried on walking.

Smith opened the door to the conference room and looked inside. The lights were on but the room was empty.

"What are you doing, Sarge?" Yang Chu said.

"Those idiots at the bar are up to something. They'll be coming back in here in a few minutes. Go back to the bar and wait for them to leave. When they're gone, you and Bridge stand outside this door and make sure none of them leaves."

"What are you going to do?"

"I'm going to find a place to hide and try to hear what they have to say."

"I don't like this, Sarge."

"Me neither," Smith said. "You'd better call for back up just in case."

Yang Chu walked back to the bar. Smith took a look around the conference room. It was a similar size to the large conference room back at the station. He tried to find somewhere to hide. He could hear the low murmuring of voices which meant Davina Phoenix and her gang were coming back from the bar. Smith spotted a large cupboard in the corner of the room. He opened it up but it was full of old trophies and medals. There wasn't enough room for him. The voices were getting closer. He rushed to the window and slid behind the curtain just as the door to the room opened.

"Right," Smith heard Davina Phoenix say. "We don't have much time."

The room went quiet as everybody sat down. Smith's hiding place had obviously not been discovered.

"Firstly," Davina said. "I'd like to congratulate you all. You've done an amazing job."

"Hear hear."

Smith heard the sound of glasses clinking together.

"Our Facebook page has over ten thousand likes," a boy with a high pitch voice said. "I checked this morning."

"Well done, but that's not why I brought you all here. I want to do one more."

The room fell silent.

"One more," she said again. "And then we'll call it quits."

"No," the chubby youth said. "You said it was all over. Let's quit while we're ahead."

"I don't have to remind you who I am, and what I've done for you boys. You'd be nothing without me."

"Mrs Phoenix," a tall man with a pasty complexion said. "It's too risky. We'll never get away with it. They'll be watching the McDonalds like hawks from now on."

"I never expected you all to turn chicken," Davina said.

"We're not chicken," pale face said. "But we're not stupid."

The curtain that Smith was hiding behind had obviously not been cleaned for a very long time and a thick layer of dust had built up. The dust was making Smith's eyes water. He desperately wanted to wipe them but he didn't want to risk moving the curtain. A speck of dust made its way inside his nose and he sniffed it up instinctively. He couldn't help what happened next. He let out the loudest sneeze he had ever sneezed.

"What the hell?" Davina Phoenix screamed.

Smith pulled the curtain aside and smiled.

"Sorry," he said. "I must have got lost. You ought to have a word with the cleaner. Those curtains are filthy."

Everybody stared at him in disbelief.

"While I have you all here," Smith continued. "You are all under arrest for armed robbery. Please don't try anything stupid. Half the York police department is standing outside this room."

Nobody in the room said a word. They looked as though they didn't believe what Smith was saying.

Then all hell broke loose. Davina Phoenix made a dash for the door. As she did so, she tripped over a chair leg and fell to the ground. The chubby youth stood up and, with a turn of speed that didn't seem possible, he rushed to the other side of the room. Two golf clubs were attached to the wall in a crossed swords position. The boy ripped one of them off the wall and approached Smith with the club raised in the air.

"Yang Chu," Smith shouted. "Bridge, it's alright if you come in now."

The youth swung the club at Smith's head. Smith ducked and the number six iron missed his head by a few centimeters. The youth raised the club and came in for a second time. This time Smith wasn't quick enough. The club missed his head but landed with a crack on his right shoulder. Smith felt a shooting pain rush down his arm.

"Yang Chu," Smith screamed again.

The door to the room opened and Bridge and Yang Chu stood there wide eyed. Three uniformed officers stood behind them. Davina

Phoenix had got to her feet and was now looking for an escape route. She slumped down on one of the chairs - it was all over. There was nowhere to run. Smith sat down next to her and held his hand to his shoulder.

"Get them out of here," he said to Yang Chu.

CHAPTER TWELVE

Davina Phoenix sat on the chair in interview room four. She hadn't said a word since she had been brought in an hour earlier. She had refused the offer of a drink and had scoffed at the idea of free legal representation. She jumped when Smith and Brownhill entered the room. They sat down opposite her. Smith's shoulder was still throbbing from the blow from the golf club.

"Mrs Phoenix," Smith switched on the recording device. "We know everything. We know you were involved in the armed robberies. It doesn't matter whether you choose to talk or not, we have plenty of evidence to charge you."

Davina stared at him defiantly.

"You don't know anything."

Her voice was very hoarse.

"Would you like something to drink?" Brownhill asked her.

"Not unless you've got a bottle of Bollinger hidden away somewhere in this dump."

"Your husband has been informed," Smith said. "He should be here shortly."

This information seemed to bring about a change in Davina Phoenix's whole demeanor. Her facial expression changed.

"The great Jimmy Phoenix," she said. "The hero of the working classes. You don't know the half of it. He cares more about his bloody horses than he does about me."

"I still don't understand," Smith said. "Why did you do it? From what I've gathered you didn't want for anything. You were well provided for."

"Well provided for?" Davina started to laugh. "A few measly grand a month? I can spend more than that on a ten minute shopping spree. Jimmy made ten times that each time one of his stupid nags squirted into a jar if you know what I mean."

"So it was all about the money?"

"What do you know about money?" Davina looked Smith up and down. "What will the likes of you ever know about real money? That bastard husband of mine has ruined my life."

"By giving you more than enough money to get by on?" Brownhill said.

"You wouldn't understand. I happen to have very exclusive tastes. When Jimmy cut my allowance, I just couldn't keep up. Do you know what that's like for someone who travels in the circles I do?"

"So you arranged the armed robberies?" Smith said. "How did you persuade the kids at the golf club to help you?"

"That was easy," Davina smiled. "They worship the ground I walk on. They would do anything for me. After the first one, Simon came up with the idea of the Facebook thing. This whole ideology crap. The rich getting robbed by the poor and all that nonsense. It worked. The idea was brilliant."

"But it wasn't the poor robbing the rich was it?"

"Of course not - that's what made it so perfect. Nobody would ever think a bunch of rich kids were responsible. Those kids don't need the money. They got a thrill out of it, it's as simple as that. They became modern day heroes overnight and I got to keep the money. It was flawless."

"Until you got caught," Brownhill said.

"What about the gun?" Smith said. "Where did the gun come from?"

"It wasn't a real gun. Any nine year old could see it was a Playstation accessory. So it wasn't actually an armed robbery."

"I'm afraid it was," Smith said. "Real gun or not - it's still classed as armed robbery. You and your band of merry men are going to be locked up for a very long time."

Davina Phoenix started to laugh.

"Constable," she said. "You've got a lot to learn haven't you? People like us don't go to jail. That's just the way it is."

"I believe you were working as a cleaner in a hotel when you met Jimmy?" Smith said.

It was a dirty trick but it seemed to have the desired effect. The smug grin on Davina Phoenix's face vanished.

"I'd like to speak to my solicitor now," she said.

"That's your right, and if you can't afford one, one will be provided for you. I think we're done here. It's out of our hands now. I need some fresh air. Something smells bad in here."

He opened the door and left the room.

Jimmy Phoenix was talking to Superintendant Smyth by the front desk when Smith walked through. Smith braced himself for a barrage of abuse.

"DS Smith," Smyth said. "Mr Phoenix would like a word with you."

Here goes, Smith thought.

"Detective," Phoenix held out his hand.

Smith stared at him.

"I must admit," Phoenix said. "I'm as shocked as everybody else about this whole business. Gob smacked is the word. Davina of all people. It still doesn't seem real."

Smith didn't know what to say.

"Mr Phoenix," he said eventually. "I'm afraid your wife is going to be charged with six counts of armed robbery. There's nothing any of us can do about it now."

He glanced over at Superintendant Smyth who was standing with an inane grin on his face.

"I don't quite understand what you're implying," Phoenix said.

"I'm not implying anything," Smith said. "I'm stating a fact. She's admitted everything. She's going to jail. All the money in the world won't change that."

"Of course," Smyth said. "But people like us still have to stick together don't we?"

He winked at Phoenix. Smith felt a sudden urge to punch the retarded Superintendant on the nose.

"I'm sure there are still avenues open," Smyth added. "I'll see what I can do."

"No," Phoenix said. "What's done is done. There will be no special treatment here."

Smith could not believe what he was hearing.

"Davina will be dealt with like anybody else," Phoenix continued.

"She'll get no help from me."

"Let's not be rash," Smyth said.

"Jeremy, please go away."

Smyth opened his mouth to say something but he was interrupted by the sound of his phone ringing in his jacket pocket. He took it out and looked at the screen.

"Must dash," he said. "I'll see you at the club Jimmy."

He turned and walked off down the corridor.

"Thank you," Phoenix said to Smith. "Thank you for getting to the bottom of all this."

"It's my job."

Two weeks, he thought, two weeks away from all of this madness.

"I'd better get going," Phoenix said.

"Aren't you going to see your wife?"

"What's the point? I'd say that part of my life is over wouldn't you?"

"You know the press are going to be all over this don't you?"

"Oh yes, that lot are probably thinking up all kinds of dirt to write about me as we speak. I'm used to it and you know what they say? Any publicity is good publicity. Who knows, McDonalds might even get a boost out of it. Thank you again detective."

He held out his hand. This time Smith accepted it.

"Good luck, Mr Phoenix," Smith said.

"Well that's it then," Bridge said.

Bridge, Whitton and Smith were sitting at their usual table in the canteen.

"How's the shoulder?" Whitton said.

"Sore as hell, but nothing a hot bath and a massage from a pretty DC won't cure."

"Sarge," Bridge said. "There are other people in here you know. I suppose now we just have to wait for something else to crop up. There's always something."

"Not for me," Smith smiled. "I'm officially on leave for two weeks. The DI has cleared it - I'm a free man for two weeks."

"Where are you going to go?" Bridge said.

"Somewhere quiet - somewhere where nothing much happens. There's a place up in the Dales that looks perfect. There are areas up there with no cell phone reception for miles."

"Sounds awful," Bridge said.

Whitton seemed miles away. She was staring out the window. Two swallows darted past the window and settled on a nearby telegraph pole. Summer was definitely on the way.

"I need a break," Smith said. "I've had nothing but dead people and scum for as long as I can remember."

CHAPTER THIRTEEN

The sun appeared from behind a large fluffy cloud as Smith drove out of the city and headed west on the A59 in the direction of Harrogate. Smith smiled.
It's an omen, he thought, a good omen for what lies ahead.
He suddenly remembered there was something he needed to do. He performed an illegal U-turn and drove back towards the city. As he drove he thought about the expression on Whitton's face that morning when they had said their goodbyes. Whitton had assured him that she was happy with his decision but the look on her face told a different story. Smith wasn't sure he was doing the right thing but he did know that he had to get away. He turned into the small lane that led to the hospital and parked the car next to a cluster of trees.

The young man behind the front desk looked surprised to see Smith as he approached.
"Back so soon?" he said. "I'm starting to worry about you. You know what to do."
Smith placed his phone on the tray on the counter and walked off down the corridor without saying a word to the man. The place seemed different - it was too quiet. Smith made his way to Jessica Blakemore's room and knocked on the door.
"Who is it?" A voice was heard from inside.
"It's Smith," Smith said, "can I come in?"
"I'll come out."
The door opened and Smith gasped at the woman standing in front of him. Jessica Blakemore had shaved off all her hair. It made her eyes even more striking.

"What do you think?" Jessica asked him. "I decided that seeing as I'm going to be a full time loon, I might as well look like one. Let's go to the day room."
Smith followed her down the dreary corridor. He noticed that there were a few wisps of hair on the back of her head she had missed but he decided not to mention it.

They sat down on the sofa next to the window and looked out onto the lawn outside. Two men were playing badminton on the grass. One of them was clearly better at it than the other - each time the shuttlecock came near the shorter man, he ducked and let it fall to the ground. Smith watched as the other man walked over, picked up the shuttlecock and hit it back to the short man. This carried on for some time before the taller man threw his racket on the grass and walked off.
"You got your two weeks," Jessica said.
"How do you know that?"
"I'm a shrink, remember. I can see it all over your face. You look like you've had a weight lifted from your weary soul. But there's still something troubling you isn't there?"
"I'm not sure I'm doing the right thing."
"Whitton obviously wasn't pleased."
"You're in a very telepathic mood today," Smith said. "I tell you what, why don't I just sit here in silence and you can carry on reading my mind."
"Don't be pedantic. You came to visit me remember."
"Sorry, how are you anyway? And why is it so quiet here today?"
"Quiet? What do you mean?"

"There's normally something happening," Smith said. "Where's the woman who usually sings all day about freaky stuff?"

"She's dead," Jessica said casually.

"Dead?" Smith said. "What happened?"

"She killed herself. It was bound to happen - she's tried it a few times before but this time she was lucky."

"Lucky?"

"They had her on suicide watch. They took away everything she might use to kill herself but they didn't bank on the human will."

"You've lost me there."

"The will to die can be as strong as the will to live sometimes," Jessica said. "The poor lady bit open her own wrists. Do you know what kind of strength of character that must have taken?"

"That's awful, how could they let that happen? They were supposed to be looking after her."

"It was her choice," Jessica started chewing at her left thumb nail.

"They ought to have given her that at least."

"When are you getting out of here?" Smith decided to change the subject.

"I'm not ready," Jessica said. "My initial assessment period is almost over but I'm going to recommend they keep me here for another three months."

"The shrink in the loony bin. You're an all round weirdo Mrs Blakemore."

"Soon to be Miss," Jessica sighed. "Ian has asked for a divorce. Can you believe it? Bloody architects - they're just so logical."

Smith started to laugh.

"It's his loss," he said. "I just came to say thank you and good bye."

"So that's it then, you're cured?"

"Hardly," Smith said. "Ask me the same question in two weeks time. I'll come and see you when I get back."

"Where are you going to go?"

"A small village in the Dales - a quiet, charming place where nothing ever happens and people don't go around butchering each other."

He stood up.

"Take care, Jessica," he said. "Oh and you might want to check the back of your head in a mirror; you missed a few spots there."

CHAPTER FOURTEEN

Clouds were forming in the sky above Smith as he drove away from the hospital and headed west towards Harrogate. Rain was definitely on the cards. Smith opened the glove compartment and took out a cassette tape. He slotted it into the tape player and smiled.
I must be the only person left in the world who still plays cassettes in the car, he thought.
The sound of the barking dogs in the introduction to Jane's Addiction's 'Being caught stealing' came over the speakers and Smith turned up the volume. The road that led out of the city was almost deserted on this Monday May morning and Smith increased his speed. He wanted to get away as quickly as possible. A drop of rain hit the windscreen. It was followed by a few more and then the heavens opened. Smith slowed down and switched the windscreen wipers on full. They were finding it hard to keep up and Smith had to slow down even further - he was finding it hard to see the road in front of him. He almost missed the Skipton turn off but managed to slow down just in time and turn off onto the A65. As he drove further west, the rain stopped and Smith could see the Forest of Bowland on his left hand side. The sun made an appearance through the clouds and cast an eerie glow over the treetops. He drove on for a few miles and turned onto a road that was obviously seldom used. He'd memorised the route and he smiled when he stopped the car outside the Dove Inn in the tiny village of Scarpdale.

There was only one other vehicle parked outside the Inn - a red Range Rover. A huge sticker depicting a phoenix rising from the flames covered almost all of the back windscreen. Smith got out the car, stretched his arms and looked around.

This is perfect, he thought, I'm in the middle of nowhere. Nobody knows who I am and nothing ever happens here.

He went inside the Dove Inn and walked up to the small reception desk. An elderly woman was knitting something behind the counter. She reminded Smith of Marge, the owner of the Hog's Head, Smith's favorite pub.

"Morning," the woman looked up from her knitting. "Can I help you?"

"I booked a room here," Smith said. "Jason Smith."

"Of course, the Australian. We don't get many Australians around here. Are you on holiday in the country?"

"Something like that," Smith didn't feel like explaining further.

"I'm Mrs Killian," she said. "But you can call me Ethel. Me and my George bought this place twenty two years ago when George retired. He's gone now though, God rest his soul. I'm seventy eight you know."

"Nice to meet you, Ethel."

Ethel Killian sat behind the desk and stared at Smith. It made Smith feel slightly uneasy.

"Oh yes," she said. "I suppose you'll be wanting to get to your room."

She plucked a key from a wooden key holder behind her desk.

"Number one," she handed the key to Smith. "It's quiet at the moment. The room's nothing special but it's clean. Two weeks. We don't normally have people staying that long - they normally just stay for a day or two."

She looked at Smith quizzically.

"Two weeks," Smith said. "I need some peace and quiet."

"Well, you'll certainly get that around here. I suppose you must have your reasons. First door on the right. We have a dining room here for the guests. It's open from six to nine, morning and evening and there's a pub next door if you're that way inclined."

"Thank you, Ethel," Smith smiled at her.

"Anything you need," Ethel said. "Just shout."

Smith opened the door to his room and went inside. The smell of lavender hit him in the face straight away. He walked to the large window and opened it as wide as it would go. The sickly smell started to fade. Smith put his bag on the floor and sat on the bed. He took out his phone and smiled. There was no cell phone signal.

Perfect, he thought, this place is perfect.

He spent the next few minutes getting acquainted with his home for the next two weeks. He lay on the bed and closed his eyes. The smell of the lavender had almost disappeared altogether. His eyelids felt heavy and he was just about to doze off when he heard a commotion outside in the street. A car engine was being revved too high and a man was screaming. Smith heard the screech of tyres and ran to the window. The red Range Rover was hurtling down the road at an alarming rate of knots. A man around Smith's age was trying to run after it. He stopped when he realised it was pointless. Smith shook his head and lay back on the bed. He'd just closed his eyes when there was a knock on the door. He got off the bed and opened it.

"I thought you might be hungry," Ethel was standing in the doorway. She was holding a plate with a sandwich on it.

"I've also got a map of the area. There are some lovely hikes around here. You really ought to get out and see the tarns."

She placed the map and the sandwich on the bedside table and left the room. Smith picked up the map and unfolded it. He took a bite out of the sandwich. It was beef and mustard - not his usual choice but he was hungry and finished it in less than a minute. He looked at the map. The area around Scarpdale was littered with small lakes. Most of them were within walking distance from the village.

It was early afternoon when Smith set off, armed with the map and a packet of cigarettes. He walked the short distance to the edge of the village and followed the marked path towards Whooton Tarn, the closest of the lakes. The sun was high in the sky and by the time Smith reached the halfway point the sweat was pouring off him.
I'm unfit, he thought, and I'm going to get burnt if this weather stays like it is.
He laughed at the idea. An Australian getting sunburn in North Yorkshire. He reached the lake and sat down on the bench at the water's edge. He lit a cigarette and rubbed his forehead. It was extremely hot now and he was tempted to jump in the lake. He cast the thought aside, somebody might see him. He finished his cigarette and stubbed it out in the dirt below the bench. He suddenly felt very thirsty. He made a mental note to remember to bring something to drink next time he went for a walk. He gazed across the lake. There was no wind and the surface was like a mirror. Smith wondered how deep it was. His thirst was now getting unbearable. He stood up and walked along the edge of the lake. He suddenly realized that the water must have come from somewhere.
This can't all be rainwater, he thought.
He followed the lake around until he came to a gradual slope that appeared to end at a rocky outcrop about a hundred metres above. He scrambled up the hill and found what he was looking for. A small brook was flowing over the rocks down to the lake below. Smith scooped some water in his hands and took a tentative sip. The water was freezing cold but it tasted fresh. He took a longer sip and felt instantly refreshed. He scooped up as much as he could and drenched his hair and face. He felt more awake than he had done in weeks.

CHAPTER FIFTEEN

It was almost six by the time Smith returned to the Dove Inn. He had lost all track of time by the lake. For four hours, he'd had the place to himself and he had made the most of it. He had already made his plans for the evening. A quick meal in the dining room of the Inn and a few beers in the pub next door. Then he was intending to sleep like he had never slept before.

"Do I have to book a meal?" He asked Ethel behind the reception desk.
"No love," Ethel said. "Just go through. We can just add it to your bill at the end. You were out for ages. It seems to have done you good though. You've even got a bit of colour in your face."
"Thanks, Ethel."

He walked through to the dining room. An old man was sitting in the corner of the room. The ugliest dog Smith had ever seen was sitting on the chair opposite him. It appeared to be a cross between a Pug and a toad. Its eyes were on the verge of bulging out and a trickle of drool was hanging from its mouth.

Smith sat with his back to the old man and the hideous dog and took out his phone. There was still no signal.

"That thing's useless in here," a man in his forties stood at the table. "If you want signal you have to drive back towards Skipton. You'll get maybe one bar after about three miles. What can I get you? Tonight we've got either lamb shank or steak pie cooked in stout."
"I'll have the pie," Smith said without thinking.

He hoped it would be as good as Marge's steak and ale pie at the Hog's Head.

"Do you want something to drink? I can get you something from the Quail next door.

"Quail?" Smith was puzzled.

"The pub, The Quail's Arms. It's quite funny don't you think? I mean, who's ever seen a quail with arms?"

"I'll have a pint of beer please. Theakstons if they have it."

"Quail's Arms," the waiter sniggered. "I'll organise your order."

He walked off giggling like a small child.

Quail's Arms? Smith though.

He didn't even know what a quail was.

"Are you here on holiday?" the man with the dog shouted across the room.

"Yes," Smith said.

"Nowt ever happens round here," the man said.

"What kind of dog is that?"

"I've got no idea. I found it up on the moors. He's an ugly bugger isn't he? He looks just like my first wife."

He started to laugh and a chronic coughing fit followed. Smith was afraid he was about to have a heart attack.

"I'm alright," the man said.

He stood up.

"Come on Fred," he said to the dog.

The gruesome specimen of a dog fell off the chair and followed him out of the room.

The waiter returned with the pie and the beer.

"There you go," he put them on the table. "On holiday are you?"

Smith wondered how many more people were going to ask him the same question.

"I just thought you might be one of those horsey types," the waiter said. "We get a lot of them staying here."

"Horsey types?" Smith had no idea what he was talking about. "I don't know anything about horses."

"Me neither. Enjoy the meal."

When Smith had finished eating he realised he was exhausted. This country air is making me tired, he thought.

He debated whether to go straight to bed. He looked at his watch. It was only seven thirty. He left the Dove Inn and headed next door to the Quail's Arms. The red Range Rover was parked outside again. He was quite shocked when he went inside - the place was reasonably busy. The old man with the repugnant dog was reading a newspaper at a table by the window. He nodded to Smith in acknowledgement. Two young women and an older man were sitting at the bar. Smith was sure the man was the same one he had seen chasing the Range Rover earlier in the day.

"Pint of Theakstons," Smith said to the angry looking barman.

The barman shrugged his shoulders and poured the beer. He slammed it down on the counter so hard that Smith jumped.

"Two fifty," he said.

Smith paid him and decided he would have one drink and leave. Tomorrow, he thought, I'll find somewhere else to drink.

Smith took a sip of the beer and was instantly aware that he was being observed. It was a feeling he had felt many times before. He looked across the bar. The man sitting with the two young women was glaring at him. The younger looking of the two women smiled. Smith turned his attention back to his beer. He was in no mood for a confrontation. He could still feel the man's eyes boring into his head.

"Hey pal," the man shouted at Smith even though he sat a few feet away. "Are you here for the horses or what? If you are, you're wasting your time."

Smith ignored him and took a long swig of beer.

"I'm talking to you."

Smith turned and looked at the man again. He was short but very stocky. His eyes were very bloodshot - he was obviously quite drunk. The two women sitting with him seemed scared. Smith finished his drink and stood up to leave.

"I said I'm talking to you," the man stood up and took two steps towards Smith.

"Leave it, Lewis," the younger looking of the two women said. "Leave him alone."

"Shut it," the man called Lewis said.

He shoved the woman so hard that she almost toppled backwards. That was it. Smith couldn't ignore him anymore.

"Lewis," he said. "I suggest you leave right now before it's too late."

"Too late for what?"

The ugly dog started to bark at him. Its eyes popped out even further.

"Too late," Smith said. "Too late to wonder if you're going to spend the next few days in hospital."

Smith realised how ridiculous he sounded but it seemed to do the trick. Lewis retreated a few steps.

"Come on, Sophie," he said. "Let's get out of here."

"I'm not going anywhere with you," the woman he had shoved said.

"You'll regret this," he said to her.

He turned to look at Smith.

"Both of you."

He staggered out of the bar.

Why does this sort of thing always happen to me? Smith thought as he turned to leave for the second time.

"You can't go now," the woman called Sophie said. "I believe I owe you a drink. Lewis can be a nasty bastard sometimes."

"No thanks," Smith said. "I'm tired."

"But I insist, and I'm used to getting my own way. Theakstons wasn't it?"

Smith was too tired to argue.

One beer, he thought, one beer and I'll leave. What harm can one beer do?

CHAPTER SIXTEEN

The harm that one beer can do became apparent the next morning. Smith was woken from a dreamless sleep by an incessant banging noise. He opened his eyes and winced. The sliver of light shining through a gap in the curtains felt like it was piercing his brain. His mouth was dry and his head was throbbing. The banging noise wasn't going away. Smith realized it was coming from outside his room. Somebody was banging on the door.
"Who is it?" He shouted.
The sound of his own voice made his head throb even more.
"Police," a man's voice said. "Open up."
Police? Smith thought, What do they want?
"Open the door," the man said.
Smith tried to remember what had happened the night before - it was all still a bit of a blur. He recalled asking the obnoxious man to leave the Quail's Arms and he remembered having a few too many drinks with the man's girlfriend. After that, he had returned to the hotel and gone straight to bed.
"What do you want?" He shouted.
"Open the door," the man said again. "We'd like a word with you."
Smith got out of bed and put on a pair of shorts and a T shirt. He rubbed his eyes and opened the door. Three policemen in uniform were standing in the hallway. They all seemed very nervous.
"What's going on?" Smith said.
"Jason Smith?" One of the policemen said.
"That's right, what's wrong? Has something happened back in York?"
"York? No, we'd like to talk to you. We'll need you to come with us."

"I'm not going anywhere until you explain to me what this is all about," Smith said.

"How well do you know Sophie Phoenix?"

"Sophie Phoenix? I don't know her at all."

"She's dead," an older looking PC informed him. "She was found by one of the tarns this morning."

"My God, that's terrible but what's it got to do with me? Are you asking for my help?"

"Help?" the short PC said. "Why would we ask you for help?"

"Then why are you here? What has it got to do with me?"

"That's what you're going to tell us," the tall PC said. "You were seen drinking with Miss Phoenix last night in The Quail's Arms."

"Oh her," Smith said. "We had a few drinks and then I left. This has nothing to do with me."

This isn't happening, he thought, a woman is found dead and I haven't even been here for twenty four hours.

"We'd like to ask you a few questions down at the station," the older PC said. "This is not up for debate."

Smith realised it was pointless arguing. The sooner he got these annoying policemen off his back, the sooner he could get back to his holiday.

Twenty minutes later, Smith sat opposite a man by the name of Sergeant Wilkie in the tiny room that served as the interview room at Skipton police station.

"Name?" Wilkie said.

"Jason Smith," Smith said. "You already know that."

"Don't be impertinent. I have to do this properly. Name?"

"Jason Smith."

"Occupation?"

"Detective Sergeant," Smith looked Wilkie in the eye. "I work for the York police department."

"You're not helping your case with this attitude, Mr Smith. This is a very serious matter. You're in big trouble."

Smith was starting to get a headache. The hangover from last night was now in full force.

"My name is DS Smith. I've been a DS in York for five years."

"Do you have any ID to prove that?"

"I didn't bring it with me. Why would I? I'm on holiday."

"I don't believe you. What are you doing in Scarpdale?"

"I told you, I'm on holiday and I'd like to get back there if it's alright with you."

Wilkie scratched at a scab on his nose and shook his head.

"Right Mr Smith," he said. "If that's even your real name. Tell me what happened last night."

"Nothing happened last night. I had a meal in the hotel and then I went to the pub next door for a drink. This moron was getting a bit out of hand so I asked him to leave."

"Then what?"

"He left. The woman he was with insisted I stay for a few drinks so I did. A few hours later, I went back to my hotel room."

"Alone?" Wilkie said.

"Alone."

"And now a woman is dead," Wilkie had a very grave expression on his face.

"Do you know how she died?"

"Not yet, but that's not really any of your business is it? How well did you know Miss Phoenix?"

"I've already told you," Smith was starting to get annoyed. "I met her for the first time last night. Her boyfriend was getting a bit obnoxious so I asked him to leave. If you ask me, it's him you should be speaking to right now."

"Lewis Van Camp?" Wilkie said. "Do you know who his father is?"

"No, and I don't care. When he left the pub last night he said something about me regretting what I'd done. He would be the first person I'd drag down here if I was heading up the investigation."

"Mm," Wilkie said. "But you're not are you? You say you asked Mr Van Camp to leave and stayed to have a few drinks with Miss Phoenix?"

"That's right."

"And then you went back to the hotel?"

"How many times do I have to tell you?"

"I don't believe you."

Smith's headache wasn't getting any better.

"Sergeant Wilkie," he said. "Am I a suspect here?"

"You were one of the last people to see Sophie Phoenix alive."

"As was this Van Camp idiot. As well as the barman at The Quail's Arms, not to mention Sophie's sister."

"Mr Smith," Wilkie adopted a more condescending tone. "I've been doing this a very long time and my gut is telling me that something's not right here. Stop me if you don't understand. A stranger walks into town and that very night a very prominent member of our community is found dead. Don't you think that's a bit more than a coincidence?"

"I don't believe in coincidence," Smith said.

The door opened and a very timid looking police constable entered the room.

"Sarge," he said. "Can I have a word?"

Wilkie stood up and followed the nervous PC out the room. He returned a few minutes later and smiled at Smith.

"Your story checks out," he said. "PC Fielding took the liberty of phoning York. They confirmed that they do have a DS Smith working there."

Smith stood up.

"Thank you, I'm going to catch up on some sleep."

"I haven't finished," Wilkie said.

"But you said you confirmed I am who I said I was."

"You may be a detective sergeant, but that doesn't mean you're above the law. Please sit down."

Smith thought hard for a moment. The first holiday he had taken in years was being ruined by a pedantic little village sergeant.

"Then arrest me," he said.

He kicked the chair across the room and opened the door. He walked down the short corridor and headed for the exit. He had just put his hand on the handle when he felt a hand on his shoulder.

"Jason Smith," sergeant Wilkie's grating voice said. "You're under arrest for the murder of Sophie Phoenix."

CHAPTER SEVENTEEN

Chalmers took the phone call thirty minutes later. He was just about to leave his office to attend a meeting with the Superintendant.
"Chalmers," he said.
"Boss," Smith said. "Are you missing me yet?"
"What do you want? I thought you were on holiday."
"I am. I was having a great time until I was arrested for murder."
The line went quiet.
"Boss?" Smith said. "Are you still there?"
"I'm still here. What are you babbling on about? Are you drunk?"
"They've arrested me for the murder of Jimmy Phoenix's daughter. I need your help. These country police are a bunch of incompetent idiots."
"Christ, what's wrong with you?"
"It's all a big mistake. I didn't kill her."
"Alright," Chalmers thought for a moment. "I'm going to be in meetings for most of the day. I'll arrange for Whitton to get over there and see if she can smooth things over."
"No," Smith said. "Not Whitton. Send Bridge or Yang Chu."
"Why not Whitton? I thought you two were getting on alright."
"We are, and I'd like to keep it that way. This is a bit delicate. I sort of had a few drinks with the dead woman last night. Whitton will only jump to the wrong conclusions."
"You'll be the death of me. Where are you?"
"At the police station in Skipton. I've never met such a bunch of retarded policemen in my life."

"Yang Chu will be there in an hour or so. In the meantime, don't do anything stupid. What is it with you? You've been gone for less than a day and you're already in trouble."

"Thanks, boss," Smith said and rang off.

Smith sat down on the bed in the only holding cell at Skipton police station and stared at the wall. Somebody had carved the name Jethro in the plaster above the bed. There was a strange musty smell in the room - it had obviously not been used for a very long time. Smith thought about whether he ought to contact a solicitor but decided against it straight away. He hated solicitors. The door to the room opened and the nervous PC came inside. He was holding a tray of sandwiches and a mug of coffee.

"I thought you might be hungry," he looked at Smith as though he was about to be attacked.

"Thanks," Smith said. "And relax. I'm not a vicious murderer. It's PC Fielding isn't it?"

"Yes, I've read all about you. You're a legend."

"I'm not a legend, I just seem to be in the wrong places at the right times. How on earth did sergeant Wilkie manage to become sergeant? The man's a real moron."

"He's alright," Fielding put the tray of food on the bed. "Have they organised a solicitor to come in for you?"

"That won't be necessary. How long have you been working here?"

"Two years," Fielding said.

"How many murders have you had?"

"None," Fielding said. "Nothing much happens around here. This is the first murder. Although we don't know yet if it was murder. They haven't finished examining the body."

"PC Fielding, let me tell you a few things about murders. The first thing you look for is motive. Motive is everything. Why would somebody want to kill Sophie Phoenix? What was the motive? Love? Hate? Jealousy? Money? It's almost always one of those four."

"Aren't you scared?"

"Why would I be scared? I've been arrested for a murder I didn't commit. I have no motive for it and you have no evidence to suggest I was involved. If I'd conducted a murder investigation the way your dimwitted sergeant has I'd be on my way to a disciplinary right now."

"I'd better get back," Fielding said. "I'm very sorry about all of this."

"Worse things have happened to me than this. I'll be out of here in no time."

Smith lay back on the bed and closed his eyes.

Sophie Phoenix, he thought, Jimmy Phoenix's daughter. Why would somebody want to kill Sophie Phoenix?

He thought back to the robberies at the McDonalds. Jimmy Phoenix's wife had been behind all of them and now Phoenix's daughter has been killed.

Coincidences, he thought, Chalmers had always drummed it into him that there were no such thing as coincidences.

He lay further back on the bed and was asleep in seconds.

CHAPTER EIGHTEEN

Smith didn't know how long he had been asleep when he was shaken awake by a very smug looking sergeant Wilkie.
"Wake up," Wilkie said. "It's time we had a little chat."
"What's going on now?" Smith rubbed his eyes and sat up in the bed.
"This is what's going on," Wilkie rubbed his impressive beer belly. "My gut feeling is what's going on. It's never let me down yet. You're a smoker aren't you?'
"That's amazing, and here's me thinking you were a third rate country bumpkin sergeant. Did your amazing detective gut help you to deduce that or was it the packet of cigarettes I handed in with the rest of my stuff when you brought me in here?"
"You're not as clever as you think, we have evidence."
"No you don't."
"Oh but we do," Wilkie's grin widened. "We've searched the area around where Sophie Phoenix's body was found this morning and we found a whole load of evidence. Cigarette butts. They're the same brand that you smoke."
"Benson and Hedges," Smith said. "The same brand that half the smokers in this country smoke. That's not exactly what I would call evidence."
"We'll need to take your fingerprints, and you'll have to give us a DNA swab but my gut is telling me that those fag ends are yours."
Smith sighed.
"You're wasting your time," he said. "Have you spoken to that Van Damme bloke yet?"
"Lewis Van Camp? No we haven't. Mr Van Camp is very distraught at the moment. His girlfriend has just been killed. The doctor will be here

in half an hour. If the DNA taken from the cigarette butts found at Whooton Tarn matches yours then…"

"Whooton Tarn?" Smith said.

"That's where Sophie Phoenix's body was found."

"Then I can save you the effort. I was there yesterday afternoon. I smoked a few cigarettes by the lake."

"That's very convenient all of a sudden. Is there anything else you want to tell me?"

"Nothing complimentary. How was Sophie Phoenix killed? You said she was found by the lake. How did she die?"

"We're not at liberty to say."

"You haven't a clue have you? Do you know what I think? The daughter of a multimillionaire is found dead on your patch. You have no idea what happened but you have to be seen to be doing something so you find out a stranger walked into town the day she was murdered and you bring him in. You've got no real evidence but it looks like you're on the ball. Am I getting warm?"

"About as warm as my testicles in the middle of January," Wilkie said. "I'll get one of my officers to take your fingerprints."

The sound of Wilkie slamming the door behind him reverberated in Smith's head for a very long time. Smith lay back down on the bed and closed his eyes. He tried to get back to sleep but too many thoughts were spinning round in his mind. The question that kept coming back to him was why was Sophie Phoenix killed? Who would want to kill a young woman in the prime of her life? It didn't make sense - something was going on that Smith didn't understand. His detective brain was having trouble putting the pieces together.
Why can't I just switch off? He thought, this is none of my business.

He then realised how wrong he was. When the cerebrally challenged sergeant had arrested him for her murder, it had become his business.

The door to the holding cell was opened and PC Fielding walked in. "You've got a visitor," he said. "He's asked to speak to you in the interview room. We don't normally allow it but he was very insistent."
"Yang Chu?" Smith said. "That was quick."
"I'll escort you through."
He seemed very agitated - something was clearly bothering him. Smith opened the door to the interview room and gasped. The man sitting in the chair facing him wasn't Yang Chu but a very self satisfied looking Lewis Van Camp.
"Take a seat," Van Camp smiled. "I trust they've been treating you well in here?"
The smug grin on Van Camp's face made Smith instinctively clench his fists by his side. He'd taken an instant dislike to this obnoxious man in The Quail's Arms and now he could feel the blood boiling in his veins.
"I said sit down," Van Camp said.
Smith took a deep breath and sat down opposite him.
"What do you want?" He said.
"I want to give you some free advice. You've got yourself in a bit of trouble haven't you?"
"I'm not scared of you. I've dealt with the likes of you plenty of times before."
"The likes of me?" Van Camp started to laugh.
It was a childish laugh. He sounded like a little girl.
"What do you know about the Van Camps?"
His facial expression had changed. He looked very serious.
"Rich folk," Smith said. "You think you can buy everything. You think you're above the law. Well, you're not."

"My father owns this place. He owns just about everything around here. Including the police. And that is exactly why..."

The smile had returned to his face.

"That is exactly why," he repeated. "You're in here on a murder rap and I'm not."

"What happened to Sophie Phoenix?"

"You tell me, you were the last person to see her alive. What did you do? Did she spurn your advances? Did you just see red? Sophie has a natural talent for making the blood boil."

"You're not going to get away with this," Smith stood up and took a step closer to Van Camp.

"Yes I am. What are you going to do now. Hit me? Go ahead, I won't even try to defend myself. That'll look even better won't it? You kill Sophie Phoenix and the very next day you beat up her grieving boyfriend. Be my guest."

Smith realised that Van Camp was right and sat down again.

"What do you want?" he said. "What are you doing here?"

"I told you, I came to offer you some advice. Go home. Get as far away from here as you can. I can make your problems go away but what happens around here is no concern of yours."

"Go to hell," Smith said.

"You're going to regret this," Van Camp stood up.

"I'll take my chances. I'll be coming for you."

Van Camp started to laugh again.

"Are all Australians as naïve as you?" he said. "Maybe I'll come and visit you in jail if I have the time."

He opened the door and walked off down the corridor.

CHAPTER NINETEEN

Smith was sitting with his head in his hands in the interview room when Yang Chu came in.
"Sarge," Yang Chu said. "What the hell is going on?"
He sat down in the chair Lewis Van Camp had been sitting in minutes earlier.
"Money," Smith sighed. "Money is what the hell is going on."
"What happened?"
Smith told Yang Chu about the argument with Van Camp at the Quail's Arms and how Sophie Phoenix's body had been found by the lake that morning.
"They think I killed her," he said. "I was one of the last people to see her alive."
"They can't hold you here without evidence," Yang Chu insisted.
"These people don't live in the real world. This Van Camp family seem to run the whole show around here and the Skipton police department are as incompetent as they come. Does Whitton know you're here?"
"No, Chalmers made it very clear that she isn't to find out."
"That's something at least," Smith said.
"We'll get you out of here," Yang Chu said. "Have you spoken to a solicitor?"
"No, and I have no intention of calling one. I'm innocent - I don't need some rat faced lawyer telling me what to do."
"Who's in charge of the investigation?"
"Sergeant Wilkie, a fossil of a policeman and as stubborn as they get. He won't listen to reason."
"Don't worry, Sarge, we'll have you out in no time. Do you want me to do a bit of digging around?"

"Thanks," Smith said. "But you'd better not. This lot are all in the Van Camp's pocket. You'll probably end up joining me in here."
"This isn't right. I didn't think this kind of thing still went on."
"This isn't York, and these Van Camps are very big fish in a very small pond. Money talks in places like these."
"I still think it stinks."
The door opened and sergeant Wilkie barged in the room. He was very red in the face.
"Mr Smith," he said. "It appears that you're free to go."
"Just like that?"
"Just like that," Wilkie said. "And if you know what's good for you, you'll get straight in your car and go back to York. It would be best if you'd forget all about this."
Smith stood up.
"You can collect your belongings at the front desk," Wilkie added.

"So that's that then," Yang Chu said outside the station. "It's all over. Back to York it is then."
"Not a chance in hell," Smith said. "I'm not having my holiday ruined by a retarded village sergeant. I've still got nearly two weeks of my leave left and I intend to make good use of it. I like it here. I'm going to go back to my room, have a shower and then I'm going to do a bit of rambling or whatever they call it around here."

Smith wasn't prepared for the scene that met him outside the Dove Inn. A large crowd of people had gathered. Smith didn't need to look too closely to know they were journalists. Their beaklike noses and inquisitive piggy eyes gave them away immediately.
"Detective," a man with such bad halitosis, Smith could smell him three metres away said. "Are you out on bail?"
News spreads fast even in this neck of the woods, Smith thought.

"No comment," he said.

He headed for the front door of the hotel.

"DS Smith," a particularly tall woman said. "What's the story with you and Sophie Phoenix? Do you have any idea who her boyfriend is?"

"Me and Miss Phoenix had a couple of drinks together. End of story."

He regretted it immediately.

Whitton is probably going to read all about this, he thought.

By the time he got inside the Dove Inn, Smith's head was spinning. He got his key from reception and went up to his room. He turned on the shower and got inside. He turned the temperature down as low as he could tolerate. The freezing jets of water blasted down on his head and gooseflesh spread across his entire body. By the time he'd turned off the shower and got dressed, he had decided what he needed to do. He would drive towards Skipton and find an area that had cell phone coverage. Then he'd phone Whitton and tell her everything before she read about it in the newspapers. Smith was certain that the story would make the evening papers that day.

The journalists were still camped outside the Dove Inn when Smith emerged into the sunlight. He ran to his car and opened the door.

"Are you leaving town?" Smith heard just before he closed the door and drove off.

Maybe I should leave, he thought, maybe I should get the hell away from this nightmare.

He decided to wait and see what Whitton had to say before making any rash decisions. He drove in the direction of Skipton. He glanced at his phone on the passenger seat every thirty seconds or so to check whether there was any reception. One bar appeared on the phone as he reached the top of a steep incline. Smith stopped the car and dialed Whitton's number.

"Hello," Whitton answered almost immediately. "Are you missing me already?"

"Whitton," Smith said. "I need to tell you something. Please let me finish before you speak."

He told her everything that had happened since he arrived in Scarpdale - the argument with Lewis Van Camp and the murder of Sophie Phoenix. When he was finished there was silence on the other end of the line. Smith wasn't sure if the signal had been lost again.

"Whitton, are you still there?"

"I'm still here," Whitton's voice sounded different.

The cheeriness in her voice was gone.

"What do you think I should do?"

"Why are you asking me?"

"I don't know," Smith said. "Maybe because you're probably the only person in the world whose opinion counts for me."

"If I tell you to come back to York, what will you do?"

"I'll come back to York. I've been thinking along those lines anyway."

"Then come back," Whitton said. "You know you can't stick around there after everything that has happened."

"That's what I thought. I just needed to hear it from someone else. I have to go back to the hotel to fetch the rest of my stuff and I'll be on my way."

"I'll see you later then."

"Nothing happened," Smith said. "Nothing happened between me and Sophie Phoenix."

"I know," Whitton said. "I'll see you later."

She ended the call.

The crowd of journalists had gone by the time Smith parked outside the Dove Inn. The road was empty apart from a racing green

Jaguar. It was parked badly outside the Quail's Arms. It was identical to the car owned by Superintendant Jeremy Smyth.

What the hell is Smyth doing here? Smith thought.

Before Smith reached the Dove Inn, a man emerged from the pub next door and Smith realized who the owner of the green Jaguar was. It was Jimmy Phoenix.

CHAPTER TWENTY

"Detective," Phoenix held out his hand. "Can I have a word?"
"Mr Phoenix," Smith shook his hand. "I'm so sorry about Sophie."
He didn't know what else to say.
"I came here as soon as I found out. I need a drink. Let's go inside the pub. There's something I need to talk to you about."
The Quail's Arms was empty so early in the day. The surly barman had been replaced by an equally angry looking woman. She looked Smith up and down as they approached the bar.
"Judy," Phoenix said. "Double scotch and whatever my friend here is having."
"Pint of Theakstons please," Smith said.
They took the drinks to the table in the corner of the room and sat down. Smith took a long swig of the beer.
"I'm really sorry about your daughter," he said again. "She seemed like a really nice young woman."
"She was," Phoenix sighed. "Sophie was one in a million. She was the naïve one - she would see the good in everyone. I shouldn't really be saying this but Sophie was always my favourite. Charlotte is a bit of a wild one you see. She get's that from her mother."
He stopped abruptly. Smith hoped he wasn't going to break down and cry. Phoenix drained his glass and winced.
"Judy," he shouted towards the bar. "Same again."
They sat in silence while they waited for the drinks. Smith wanted to get out of there as soon as possible.
"I believe you saw Sophie last night," Phoenix said.

"We had a few drinks," Smith said. "Her boyfriend was getting a bit out of hand so I asked him to leave."

"Lewis?" Phoenix seemed surprised. "And how did he take that?"

"He left."

"Just like that?"

"Just like that."

"You were lucky. I've known that stuck up toff to start a fight over much less. He's a bit hot headed at times. He's just like his father."

"Who are these Van Camps? Everyone around here talks of them like they're some kind of gods."

"New money. Basil Van Camp made a fortune on the New York stock exchange. He had New York in his pocket. Manhattan apartment, summer house in The Hamptons. He had everything but then something happened and the family ended up here."

"What happened?"

"Nobody knows," Phoenix said. "And Basil refuses to talk about it. The Van Camps own a substantial amount of land around here, not to mention the horses."

"What's so special about the horses around here? People keep asking me if I'm one of the horse people."

"There are more stables in a thirty mile radius around here than anywhere else in the country," Phoenix said. "Top class stables at that. I own one of them myself but Van Camp owns more than anybody else by far."

"I don't know much about horses," Smith admitted.

"I don't either, but I do know a few things about making money and I've learned that people are prepared to pay handsomely for exceptional horses. Another drink?"

"I'd better not, I've still got to drive back to York. You know what bastards the police can be on the roads these days."

Phoenix started to laugh.

"That brings me to why I want to talk to you," Phoenix said.

"I don't understand."

"You're an exceptional police detective. I've done a bit of research and your career makes for very interesting reading."

"I've been lucky at times," Smith said.

"Don't be so modest - nobody can be that lucky. The police around here are different. It's all very well sorting out drunken brawls and the odd livestock theft but when it comes to murder, they're way out of their depth."

"What about the police in the outlying areas? Can't they get some help from them?"

"They won't, I know sergeant Wilkie all too well. He'll want to keep it local. He won't appreciate any outside interference."

"I don't see how I can help," Smith finished his second beer in one go.

"You're one of the best there is," Phoenix said. "I want you to catch the bastard who killed my little girl."

CHAPTER TWENTY ONE

Jimmy Phoenix's words were still fresh in Smith's head when he closed the door to his room and sat on the bed.
'I want you to catch the bastard who killed my baby girl'.
Smith had no idea what to do. He knew that sergeant Wilkie wouldn't appreciate him digging around on his patch and he was sure the Van Camps would feel the same but Jimmy Phoenix had been very insistent with his request. He was of the opinion that the Van Camps and Lewis Van Camp in particular were involved somehow. Smith lay back on the bed and closed his eyes. His peaceful holiday was turning into the vacation from hell. All reason was telling him to pack his things and get as far away from Scarpdale as possible but his curiosity and his detective brain were telling him otherwise. He could still picture the expression on Jimmy Phoenix's face when he asked his to find out who killed his daughter. He had almost pleaded. Smith didn't know what to do. He went to the bathroom and splashed some water on his face.
"What's the logical thing to do?" He asked his reflection in the mirror.
"Get the hell out of this place of course."
Phoenix had persuaded him to stay in Scarpdale overnight and give him his decision in the morning.

Smith changed his clothes and left the room. He went down to the dining room and sat down at the same table he had sat at the previous evening.
"If it isn't the famous detective," the man with the repulsive dog shouted across the room. "You're a dark horse aren't you?"
The toad-like dog stared right at Smith. Its eyes seemed to bulge out even further today.

"I knew those bloody Van Camps were trouble," the man added. "The likes of them always bring trouble."

"What do you mean?" Smith said.

"They think they can come out here and bring their city ways with them. Well, it always ends badly. I'm surprised you got away with putting that snot nose down a peg or two last night."

"Do you live around here?"

"Aye," the man said. "Have done for sixty years. The names Jethro." Jethro? Smith thought about the name carved in the wall in the police holding cell.

"What did you mean when you called Lewis Van Camp a snot nose?" he said.

"Lewis Van Camp. Nasty bastard that one. That's what money does to you, I can tell you that. Anyway, I've said enough; I'm not one to pry. I keep myself to myself most of the time. Fred, stop drooling on the tablecloth."

The dog had left a pool of dribble on the red tablecloth. More saliva was dripping from the side of its mouth.

"What can I get you tonight?" the same waiter who had been on duty the evening before asked. "We have braised lamb chops or vegetarian lasagna. Vegetarian lasagna. Have you ever heard of anything more ridiculous? Bloody city folk are ruining this place."

"I'll have the chops then please," Smith said.

"And a pint of Theakston?"

"That would be great."

"Now, Jimmy Phoenix," Jethro hadn't finished yet. "He's a different kettle of fish altogether. Ok, he's also one of those horsemen but he's alright. He doesn't think that just because he has money he has the right to do whatever he pleases. Terrible business with his daughter though. Murdered by the lake they say. If you want my opinion, I'd say those Van Camps were involved but, like I say, I don't like to pry. It's none of my business really. Come on Fred, it's time for your walk and a few pints in the Quail."

He stood up, nodded to Smith and left the dining room. The dog followed behind him, grunting all the way.

Thank God for that, Smith thought.

His head was spinning from the verbal diarrhea that had just come out of the mouth of the man who doesn't like to pry.

The waiter approached and placed the lamb chops on the table. He put the beer next to them.

"I'd stay out of the Quail tonight," he said.

"Why's that?"

"Lewis Van Camp and a few of his toffs are in there, and they're already a bit worse for wear. They can get a bit out of hand sometimes. Just offering a bit of advice that's all."

"Thanks," Smith picked up his knife and fork and made a start on the lamb chops.

I have no intention of setting foot inside that place tonight, he thought.

Smith finished his meal and sat back in the chair. He thought again about what Jimmy Phoenix had asked him. Every ounce of reason he possessed was telling him it would be a bad idea. Everybody he had spoken to had cryptically warned him off too. He would be stepping on the toes of just about everybody - the local police, the Van Camps and probably a few more of these so called horsemen too. He made up his mind. He would go straight up to his room, get a good night's sleep and leave for York first thing in the morning.

CHAPTER TWENTY TWO

Smith was about to open the door to his room when his phone started to beep in his pocket.
I thought there was no signal around here, he thought.
He took the phone out and looked at the screen. The light was flashing to indicate that the battery was about to die. He'd forgotten to bring the charger with him. He remembered he kept a spare in the glove compartment of his car. He went outside and walked towards he had parked his car. He opened the door and found the charger. He was about to go back inside the Inn when the door to the Quail's Arms opened and a woman ran out. She was screaming on the top of her voice. Smith recognised her - it was Charlotte Phoenix, Sophie's elder sister.
"He's gone crazy," Charlotte shouted. "He's got a knife."
She ran off down the street. Smith didn't know what to do.
Who's gone crazy? He thought. Anyway, it's none of my business.
He was about to go onside the Dove Inn when he heard another scream. This time it was coming from inside the pub. Smith ran inside and braced himself for an attack.

Jimmy Phoenix had one hand around Lewis Van Camp's throat. In the other hand he held a long knife. The woman behind the bar looked absolutely terrified. The man with the Pug was sitting reading a newspaper as if nothing was happening.
"Jimmy," Smith said. "Let him go."
Phoenix glared at Smith. His eyes were glazed over – he'd obviously carried on drinking when Smith had left.
"Jimmy," Smith said again. "Please. This isn't going to help anybody."
Lewis Van Camp was very red in the face. For the first time since

Smith had met him, he looked genuinely scared. Phoenix seemed to snap out of some kind of trance. He dropped the knife on the floor and slumped onto a chair. Lewis Van Camp put his hand to his throat and took a deep breath.

"You saw that," he said to Smith. "I want him arrested."

"I'm on holiday," Smith said. "Besides, I didn't see anything. I think you've had too much to drink."

"That maniac tried to kill me. He would have killed me if you hadn't come in."

"I think you'd better leave."

"I'm not going anywhere until you've arrested him," Lewis was adamant. "I want that animal locked up."

He pointed to Phoenix. Phoenix was sitting with his head in his hands.

"Get out of here," Smith said.

"You're going to regret this," Lewis said.

He looked around the bar. The man with the ugly dog shrugged his shoulders.

"I saw nowt," he said and returned to his newspaper.

"All of you," Lewis said. "You're going to pay for this."

"That's the second time you've said that. Please leave."

Lewis Van Camp shook his head and walked towards the door.

"Jimmy," Smith sat down next to Phoenix. "What happened?"

"She was my baby. My whole world and that bastard took her away from me."

Smith didn't know what to say.

"We nearly lost her when she was a baby," Phoenix carried on. "Pneumonia. Her little lungs nearly gave up but she was always a fighter. She hated Davina you know. Right from the start she knew that woman was evil. I should have listened to her then."

"I think we should get you out of here," Smith said.

"Are you going to help me?"

"I don't know. The people around here are not going to appreciate it."

"Please, you need to find out who did this to my little girl. You'll be well looked after."

"It's not about money. I don't want your money. I'm supposed to be on leave. Anyway, I can't just start digging around without anybody noticing. The police around here won't let that happen."

"I'm begging you," Phoenix said. "You'll get all the help you need. I know a lot of people."

Smith regretted the words that came out of his mouth as soon as they left his lips.

"OK," he said. "I'll help you."

CHAPTER TWENTY THREE

Smith shot up in bed and ran to the window. It was still dark outside but the sun was starting to appear behind the hills in the distance. Something had woken him. He looked out over the road that led to the tarns. There wasn't a soul in sight. He heard a strange noise. It sounded like it was coming from the roof above his room - it was an eerie scraping noise like something was being dragged across the tiles. Something flew past the window and landed with a dull thud on the grass outside the Inn. Smith peered down. It seemed to be the body of a woman. She was lying on her back and her eyes were open. They were staring right up to his room. It was Whitton.

Smith gasped and sat up in the bed. He was absolutely freezing. Somehow, he had managed to throw all the blankets onto the floor in the night. He picked them up and wrapped them around his shivering body. There was a knock on the door to his room. He held the blankets closely around him and stood up to answer it. The door handle felt hot to the touch. He turned the handle and it seemed to get warmer. As the door opened, a hot blast of air gushed into the room and nearly knocked him off his feet. He looked down the corridor. There was nobody there. He could smell smoke. Something was on fire further down the hallway. The heat it was giving off was unbearable. There was a sudden explosion and Smith was thrown through the window out into the street outside. He shot up in bed. The blankets were still on the floor.

What the hell was that about? he thought.

He hadn't had a double awakening dream for quite some time now and he'd forgotten how unnerving they were. He closed his eyes but all he could see in his head were Whitton's cold, dead eyes staring up at him.

He knew he wouldn't be able to get back to sleep. He got out of bed,
went to the bathroom and turned on the shower. He stepped inside
and felt the blood rushing to his extremities as the hot water warmed
up his body. As the warm jets hit the top of his head, he thought
about the conversation he'd had with Jimmy Phoenix the night before.
He'd agreed to help Phoenix find the person responsible for killing his
daughter.

Whitton will never forgive me for this, he thought, that's probably
what the dream was trying to tell me.

Smith got out of the shower and dried himself off. The sun was
now above the hills and bright light was being reflected off the mirror
in the bathroom as he got dressed. He went to make the bed and
noticed something on the floor next to the door. It looked like a file.
Someone had pushed it under the door while he was in the shower.
Smith picked up the file and sat on the bed. He opened it up and saw
it was a pathology report from the hospital in Leeds. The name Sophie
Agnes Phoenix was printed in block capitals at the top of the report.
What am I getting myself into? Smith thought as he read further down
the page.

The apparent cause of death was drowning. A large amount of water
had been found in the lungs. Smith had read countless autopsy reports
before but the information in this one made him shudder. Dr Aneka
Svenburg, the pathologist had noticed certain irregularities that only
confirmed what Smith already suspected. Sophie Phoenix had been
murdered.

Smith carried on reading. Dr Svenburg had found bruising on the
neck and back of the head which, in her opinion suggested that the
victim had been held under the water against her will. Her blood
alcohol level was very high but it was what Smith read further down

the report that disturbed him the most. Sophie Phoenix's uterus was unusually enlarged and on further examination, Dr Svenburg had confirmed that she had been seven or eight weeks pregnant when she died. Smith put down the report and sighed.

Pregnant, he thought.

He remembered a murder investigation a few years earlier. A young student had been killed in her bed. She had also been pregnant. Smith felt the same terrible feeling in the pit of his stomach now as he had done back then.

Smith read through the report again. His mind started to work at twice its normal speed. Sophie Phoenix had been down at Whooton Tarn in the middle of the night. What she was doing there is still a mystery. Two thoughts immediately entered Smith's head. Either she was there with somebody she knew or somebody followed her there with the intention of killing her.

"She was with somebody," Smith said out loud. "She knew the person who killed her. She knew them well."

Somebody forced her head under the water until she was dead, Smith thought, and then placed her on the grass next to the lake. Why not leave her in the water?

Smith went to the bathroom, splashed some water on his face and brushed his teeth. He sat back down on the bed and went through the report a third time.

Sophie Phoenix was two months pregnant, he thought, did the killer know this? Is that why she was murdered?

There was a knock on the door. It was so loud that Smith jumped. He put the autopsy report on the table next to the bed and opened the door. Jimmy Phoenix was standing there with another man. He was much taller than Phoenix and the mop of blond hair on the top of his head was definitely not his own.

"Good morning," Phoenix said. "I trust you remember our conversation last night?"

He glanced at the autopsy report next to the bed.

"Good," he said. "You got it. Like I said, I know a lot of people around here. Are you hungry?"

"Not really," Smith said.

"You will be when you smell the bacon and eggs they cook where we're going. Let's get out of here. There are prying eyes and ears everywhere."

CHAPTER TWENTY FOUR

Jimmy Phoenix opened up the back door of the green Jaguar and Smith got inside. Phoenix climbed in the back next to him. The man with the ill fitting blond wig started the engine and drove away from The Dove Inn.

"Sounds like nothing you've ever heard before doesn't it?" Phoenix said.

"Sorry?" Smith was confused.

"The Jag. Five litre V8. Real beast of an engine. Hardly cheap to run and not very environmentally friendly but she's a joy to behold."

"I don't know much about cars," Smith admitted. "I don't even know what engine I've got in my car. Where are we going?"

"For breakfast, and a bit of a chat. There's this place I know just outside Darley. We won't be disturbed there."

"Who's your driver?"

"Driver? That's Keith. He's not my driver - he's my right hand man. We've known each other since school."

"Can he talk?"

Phoenix started to laugh. Keith hadn't said a word since Smith had met him.

"Only if there's something important to say," Phoenix said. "It takes Keith a while to trust people."

They drove in silence for the rest of the journey. The purr of the engine was making Smith feel sleepy. Keith turned off onto a gravel road and Smith noticed a sign for The Black Horse. Keith parked the car in the small car park and stopped the engine.

"Not many people know about this place," Phoenix said. "And I'm happy to keep it that way. They do the best breakfast in the whole of Yorkshire."

The Black Horse was an old fashioned English pub. A strange green plant, Smith had never seen before covered the whole of one side of the building. Phoenix opened the door and gestured for Smith to go inside. Keith followed closely behind them.

"Jimmy," a loud voice was heard before they had even closed the door behind them.

"Morning Frank," Phoenix approached the bar.

An old man was washing cups in a small sink. He was wearing an old fashioned monocle.

"Private table for breakfast," Phoenix said. "Three of us."

"No problem," Frank said. "Your usual room is free."

Phoenix led Smith to a separate room at the end of the bar. Keith had mysteriously disappeared.

"Weak bladder," Phoenix noticed that Smith was looking to see where the strange blond man had gone. "He's had it for years. That's why I let him drive most of the time - it takes his mind of it. Take a seat."

Smith sat down on a very expensive looking wooden chair. Phoenix sat opposite him.

"We won't be disturbed in here," he said.

Frank appeared with a large tray containing coffee and tea. A bottle of Macallan single malt was also on the tray.

"Old habits die hard," Phoenix said. "My Grandfather took a nip every morning with his coffee. He lived to be ninety eight."

"I'll leave you in peace," Frank said and left the room.

"How did you manage to get the pathology report so quickly?" Smith poured himself a large cup of coffee.

"I know the right people," Phoenix said.

"Have you seen it yourself?"

"Of course not, that's your department I'm afraid."

Smith didn't know how he was going to tell him that his daughter was carrying his grandchild.

"I've organised some assistance for you too. PC Fielding will be working with you. He's young but he's very keen."

Smith almost spat out a mouthful of coffee.

"PC Fielding? Sergeant Wilkie isn't going to allow that."

"He's got no choice. I went right over his head. I happen to play golf with York city police's superintendant."

"Old Smyth?" Smith said. "Please don't tell me you got Smyth involved."

"Jeremy may be a complete idiot, but he's also a high ranking police officer and that gives him certain powers."

Smith finished the coffee in his cup and poured himself another.

"Have a tot to warm you up a bit," Phoenix pointed to the single malt.

"No thanks," Smith said. "I'd prefer to keep a clear head."

"Good idea. You don't mind if I have one though?"

Smith shook his head. He was amazed at how upbeat and calm Phoenix was so soon after losing his youngest child.

"You probably think I'm cold as hell," Phoenix seemed to read Smith's thoughts. "Joking and talking as if nothing has happened but I'm not. It's killing me inside. I'm boiling up as we speak but this is my way of coping with it all right now. I can't let my heart get in the way - we have matters to attend to. It's just my way of dealing with things I'm afraid."

"It's a man thing," Smith said. "Blokes are just built like that I suppose."

"I like you, DS Smith," Phoenix poured a large measure of the single malt into his cup. Frank entered the room with Keith in tow. Frank placed the biggest plate of food Smith had ever seen onto the table. There was bacon, eggs, sausages, mushrooms and tomatoes.

"Eat up," he said. "There's plenty more if you run out."

"Are you not hungry?" Phoenix asked Smith fifteen minutes later. Smith had barely eaten anything. The outcome of the autopsy was sitting heavily on his mind and gnawing at his insides. He couldn't face food. How would he be able to tell Jimmy Phoenix that his daughter was carrying his grandchild when she died?

"I don't usually eat breakfast," Smith said. "A cup of coffee and a cigarette is normally enough for me."

"How long have you been in the country?" Keith said out of the blue.

"See," Phoenix smiled. "I told you he could speak."

"Since I was sixteen," Smith said. "It's a long story."

"I went to Australia once. I didn't enjoy it one bit. The weather was too hot and the people were rather odd."

"You're dead right there."

He turned to Phoenix.

Here goes, he thought.

"Do you want to know what they found out from the autopsy?" he said.

"Not now," Phoenix said. "I have a story to tell you first. You need to know everything about those Van Camps."

"I'm listening."

"Lewis is the oldest," Phoenix began. "He has a sister. She's still in America with their mother."

"You mentioned something about a brother too."

"I'm getting to that. Something happened while they were in New York - something terrible if you believe the rumours and Lewis and his father came to England in a bit of a hurry."

"What happened to the brother?"

"Nobody knows," Phoenix poured himself a large measure of whisky. "Apparently, he vanished into thin air. Nobody seems to know what became of him. Of course, the tongues have been wagging; you know what gossip mongers people are. Some say he ended up in Canada, some say Mexico but nobody really knows."

"What happened that was so terrible?"

"I told you, nobody knows. It's all a mystery. All I know, whatever it was, it tore the family apart. It's all hush-hush. And I know this much - Lewis and his father came back here faster than a hare with a fire cracker up its arse."

"Why here? Why Yorkshire of all places?"

"Van Camp senior knows the place. Even when he was in the US, he still owned a substantial amount of land around here. It's the perfect climate for breeding certain types of horses."

"Do you still think the Van Camps had something to do with Sophie's death?"

"I'd stake all the money I have on it," Phoenix stood up. "I have matters to attend to. I'll drop you back at Scarpdale and you can start doing what you do best."

He took a business card out of his jacket pocket and handed it to Smith.

"My mobile number is on the back," he said. "Phone me anytime, day or night."

CHAPTER TWENTY FIVE

Smith closed the door of the Jaguar and watched as Jimmy Phoenix and his strange associate drove away. The sun was beating down on the road and it was promising to be a scorching day. Smith still couldn't believe what was happening. His much needed two weeks of peace and quiet was turning out to be the opposite - it had turned into a particularly disturbing murder investigation. He realised that he ought to phone Whitton and let her know what was going on but he didn't know how to explain it to her. He tried to figure out where to begin.

Sophie Phoenix was last seen at the Quail's Arms, he thought, she had an argument with Lewis Van Camp and the next day she's found dead next to a small lake. I need to start at the beginning.

Smith set off in the direction of Whooton Tarn. On the way he stopped at the small village store and bought two bottles of water and a packet of cigarettes. The weather was getting even warmer as he walked and sweat was making his shirt stick to his back. He followed the same path he'd taken the day he arrived in Scarpdale and reached the lake in less than half an hour. He looked around. The Tarn was exactly as it had been the other day - there was no sign that a terrible crime had been committed there. There was no indication that the scene had even been investigated - no tape to cordon off the murder scene, nothing.

Smith approached the lake. He took off his shoes and socks and rolled up his jeans. He waded in and winced as the rocks on the bottom of the lake stuck in his feet. He waded in a very long way - the lake was very shallow. A thought suddenly hit him.

It would be very difficult to drown somebody in such a shallow lake.

He carried on walking until the water reached his folded up jeans.

"If it's a swim you're after, you'd be better off trying Robber's Tarn," a loud voice was heard from the shore.

Smith turned around. It was Jethro. His grotesque dog was lapping the water from the edge of the lake.

"Morning," Smith started to walk back to the shore. "I'm just cooling my feet off a bit."

"Poppy Cock," Jethro said. "I know what you're doing. I wasn't born yesterday. Find anything yet?"

"Nothing," Smith reached the edge of the lake. "Do you know this area well?"

"Like the back of my hand. I've been hiking these trails since I was a lad. They didn't have these namby pamby paths back then though."

Smith looked around.

"How many paths lead to the lake?"

"Just the one," Jethro pointed towards the path. "And it's a tarn, not a lake."

"So there's only one way in and out?"

"Unless you want to do a bit of scrambling," Jethro looked up to the ridge. "You can get down here from up there. Tatters Ridge. But you use that at your peril - the rocks are devilish slippery up there, especially in the spring when the snow on the hills melts. Quite a few folk have found that out the hard way."

Smith gazed up at the overhanging rocks far above the lake.

No, he thought, Sophie Phoenix and whoever she was with didn't go up there.

Smith sat down and put his shoes and socks back on. The ugly Pug jumped on his lap and within seconds it was asleep. It began to snore very loudly.

"Well I'll be buggered," Jethro said. "I've never seen Fred do that before."

"I have this thing with dogs," Smith said. "I've got a Bull Terrier."

"Brilliant dogs - stubborn as hell. Hearts of gold though."

He shook his head at the dog grunting on Smith's lap.

"Fred," he shouted. "Wake up. It's time for a pint."

The dog shot up and they walked back down the path.

Smith stood up and sat on the bench facing the lake. He lit a cigarette and gazed out across the flat water. He tried to picture what had happened that night after Sophie Phoenix had left the Quail's Arms.

"Why did she come here in the middle of the night?" He said out loud. Had she arranged to meet someone here? he thought, or was it a place she often came to be alone. Did someone follow her? Who could possibly have wanted to kill Sophie Phoenix?

He lit another cigarette and closed his eyes. The sun beating down on his face was invigorating.

Maybe Sophie and her killer sat on this very bench, he thought, maybe she'd just found out she was pregnant and arranged a meeting here to break the news to the father. Is that what all this is about? Did the father of the baby react badly and kill her?

Smith stood up. He realised he now had a starting point. He needed to find out who was the father of Sophie Phoenix's unborn child.

As Smith walked back into the village, he wished he had eaten something at the breakfast with Jimmy Phoenix. His stomach was growling. It was too late to catch breakfast at the Dove Inn. He decided to take a drive around the area and see if he could find a place to get something to eat. He walked over to where he had parked his car. He knew straight away that something was wrong. His car was sitting far too low on the ground. He looked closer and saw that all four tyres were flat. On further inspection he realised that somebody had slashed them open.

CHAPTER TWENTY SIX

Smith walked round his car. All four tyres were damaged beyond repair. They'd been torn to pieces. He took out the card Jimmy Phoenix had given him and looked at the number on the back. He took out his phone but the display on the screen told him there was no signal.

"Crap," Smith said.

He went inside the Dove Inn and approached the reception desk. A man he hadn't seen before was playing solitaire on a computer.

"Morning," Smith said. "Do you have a phone I can use please? I'm staying here. I'll pay for the call."

"No mobile phone reception plays havoc on your love life doesn't it?" The man said.

"Do you have a phone I can use?" Smith was getting impatient. "This is urgent."

"You can use this one," the man pointed to the phone behind the desk. "I hope you're not phoning home though."

"Home?"

"Australia," the man said. "Then you'll definitely have to pay."

"No, I'm phoning a mobile number. I'll be thirty seconds."

"Be my guest," the man handed Smith the phone.

Smith dialed Jimmy Phoenix's number. Phoenix answered on the third ring.

"Mr Phoenix," Smith said. "This is DS Smith."

"Have you found something already?" Phoenix asked.

"I've found out that somebody doesn't like me very much. All four tyres on my car have been slashed."

"I see," Phoenix didn't sound very concerned. "Where are you?"
"Back at the Inn, my cars been parked there since yesterday."
"Wait there. I'll be there within the hour. I just need to pick up something that might help you first."

He ended the call. Smith replaced the handset.

"Thanks," he said to the receptionist. "How much do I owe you?"
"Nothing," the man said. "Someone slashed your tyres did they?"
"That's right."
"Kids - little bastards these days."

Smith went back outside and looked at his poor car. He had only replaced the tyres a few weeks earlier.

Why would somebody want to do this? He thought.

He turned and looked at the Quail's Arms. The door was open and the smell of food cooking was wafting out onto the road. He decided to kill two birds with one stone. He went inside and walked up to the bar. Jethro was sitting reading a newspaper at a table next to the window. There were a couple of tourist looking people in the pub but apart from that it was empty. The angry looking barman appeared to be fighting with the beer pump behind the bar. He had obviously recently changed the barrel - the beer was spitting out of the pipe in fits and bursts. A pint glass full of mostly froth was standing next to the pump.

"Morning," Smith said. "Having a bit of trouble there?"

The barman scowled in way of a response.

"You might want to turn the tap back for a few seconds," Smith suggested. "Then quickly flip it forwards again."

He'd seen the skilful way Marge had dealt with a stubborn beer pump before at the Hog's Head. The barman didn't reply but, even so, he appeared to take Smith's advice. After a few seconds, the gurgling sounds stopped and the beer started to flow in a more even fashion.

"Thanks," he said reluctantly. "Are you a barman or something?"
"No," Smith said. "But I am thirsty and seeing as though you've already poured a beer, I'll have that one."
He pointed to the almost perfect pint in the barman's hand.
"No charge I suppose," the barman shrugged. "We normally chuck the dregs."
"What's on the menu today?"
His stomach was really growling now.
"On the board," the barman pointed to a blackboard displaying the day's specials next to the bar.
Smith scrutinised the blackboard and settled on the gammon and chips. He walked to an empty table next to the window and sat down. From there he could see his car quite clearly.
"Hiking makes you thirsty doesn't it?" Jethro said.
The Pug was fast asleep on the chair next to him.
"It certainly does," Smith took a long sip of his beer. "You didn't happen to see anybody messing around by my car earlier did you? It's the red Sierra parked out the front."
"Nope," Jethro said. "I've had my eyes glued to the paper since I came in here but I can tell you the tyres were flat when I got here if that's what you're going on about."
"It is. Someone slashed all four. With what looks to me like a razor blade."
"Kids. No respect these days. In my day, the worst we got up to was a bit of apple thieving. Nothing serious and we always ended up with a clip round the ear afterwards. No, kids are animals these days."
"I don't think it was kids," Smith said. "Something's going on here - something that's not quite right."

"You're not wrong there pal. Ever since those bloody horsemen arrived, this place has changed and it's not for the better, I can tell you that."

The barman placed the gammon and chips on the table.
"Enjoy it," he said. "I hope you don't mind but I couldn't help overhearing you back there. You're wondering who might have slashed your tyres?"
"Did you see something?"
"You didn't hear this from me," the barman looked nervously around the room. "But I'm sure I saw old Johnny Grouse lingering earlier. He was up to no good, I can tell you that."
"Johnny Grouse?"
"Johnny's a halfwit," Jethro chipped in.
"He follows Lewis Van Camp round like a puppy," the barman said. "He does whatever Lewis Van Camp tells him to do. You didn't hear this from me, OK?"
"Fair enough," Smith cut into his gammon. "Thank you."

Smith had just finished eating when Jimmy Phoenix walked in the pub. His associate Keith was standing behind him. Phoenix approached Smith's table and sat down.
"Come on Fred," Jethro stood up and shook the dog awake. "It's time we made ourselves scarce."
Jethro nodded to Phoenix and left the pub.
"I tend to have that affect on people," Phoenix smiled. "I have something for you outside."
He stood up again. Smith followed him out. Parked next to Phoenix's Jaguar was an old green Land Rover. Smith was confused.
"Beautiful isn't she?" Phoenix said. "I bought her at an auction about ten years ago and she hasn't given me a day's trouble since. The

moron who sold her to me didn't know what he had. She's one of the first stage one V8s to come off the production line in seventy nine. She's yours for as long as you need her."

"I don't know what to say," Smith said. "I don't even know if I'll be able to drive it."

"You drive it like you would a car, although that lady can go places most cars only dream of going. Get in, take her for a spin. Just watch the gear box; it takes a bit of getting used to."

Smith didn't know what to do. He didn't particularly want to drive Phoenix's old bone shaker but he could see that he didn't have much of a choice. He suddenly thought of something.

"Do you know a man by the name of Johnny Grouse?"

"Johnny?" Phoenix said. "Of course, everybody around here knows Johnny. He's a bit of an idiot. His brains not wired properly. Why?"

"I need to have a word with him. Do you know where he lives?"

"He stays on the Russell's farm," Phoenix said. "He works for them. He lives in a caravan in one of the fields. What's Johnny Grouse got to do with any of this?"

"I want to ask him what he knows about slashing tyres."

"Be careful," Phoenix warned. "Johnny Grouse may be simple but he's as strong as an ox. Try not to upset him."

"I'll do my best."

"Do you want Keith to go with you?"

"I'll be fine," Smith said. "How do I get to the farm?"

"Take the road out of Scarpdale, and turn left towards Wigton. About four miles down the road there's a road on the right. The Russell's place is right there. You can't miss it. Enjoy the Landy."

"Do you have the key?"

"It's in the ignition," Phoenix said. "This is Yorkshire. Folk around here are honest. You should know that by now."

CHAPTER TWENTY SEVEN

Smith managed to start the old Land Rover and maneuvered it around Jimmy Phoenix's Jaguar without incident. A crowd of people had gathered - probably hoping for him to make a fool out of himself but they ended up disappointed. Smith crunched the gear stick into second and drove off slowly in the direction Phoenix had told him to go. The Land Rover's engine began to over-rev but Smith couldn't seem to manage to get it into third gear. He looked closely at the gear stick and in doing so he veered onto the other side of the road. He looked up, just in time to avoided colliding with a blue tractor. He swerved and missed the tractor by inches. The driver of the tractor seemed unperturbed and continued on driving in the opposite direction.
This thing must have more than two gears, Smith thought.
He slammed his foot down on the clutch as hard as he could, pushed the gear stick where third ought to be and felt a satisfying click as the gear was engaged.

Smith turned left and carried on driving towards Wigton. The sun was high in the sky and a warm breeze was drifting in through the window that wouldn't seem to close. Smith smiled - he was actually starting to enjoy the experience of driving an old 4x4 through the countryside. After around four miles a small signboard informed him he had reached the farm - 'Albert Russell Smallholdings'. Smith slowed down and turned off onto a poorly maintained dirt track. Two magpies seemed to be having an argument in the middle of the road. They waited until the last minute to get out of the way and carried on where they had left off. Smith drove further on. He passed a field where

twenty or thirty cows were taking cover from the sun under a small
cluster of trees. He spotted a small caravan next to the field.
This must be where Johnny Grouse lives, he thought.
He stopped next to the caravan. An old bicycle was leaning against a
tree next to it. It was an old chopper style bicycle - one of the ones
popular in the eighties. Smith parked the Land Rover and got out.
There wasn't a soul in sight. He approached the caravan and banged
on the door so hard that it swung open. One of the hinges was broken
and the door rocked to and fro from it. Smith pushed it aside and
stepped inside. The smell hit him straight away and he winced. The
stench was a combination of body odour, stale cigarette smoke and
something he didn't want to think about. A small television set lay on a
table next to one of the windows. There was nobody inside; whoever
stayed there wasn't at home.

   Smith stepped outside into the fresh air and stood face to face with
the barrel of a double barreled shotgun.
"What the hell are you doing sneaking around Johnny Grouse's
caravan?" the owner of the shotgun said.
He was a short, slightly built man with a red bulbous nose. Smith
thought he looked around sixty years old.
"I'm looking for Johnny Grouse," he said. "I need to have a word with
him."
The man eyed Smith with suspicion.
"And what are you doing driving around in Mr Phoenix's Landy?" He
said.
He still had the shotgun pointed at Smith.
"Jimmy Phoenix let me borrow it. My car is out of action at the
moment. That's actually what I came to speak to Johnny about."

"You're that policeman," the man finally lowered the gun and made sure the barrel was pointing at the ground. "I've heard all about you. I'm Albert Russell. This is my place. Johnny is just seeing to one of the calves. Dumb thing got snagged in some barbed wire. It's a right mess. It's going to have to be put out of its misery I'm afraid. Johnny seems to think he can save it. What's he done?"

"Where can I find him?"

Russell looked at his watch.

"He'll be here in ten minutes. Johnny watches Sesame Street without fail every day. Johnny's a bit slow I'm afraid - he has the brain of an eight year old but he's as strong as an ox and I can tell you, he wouldn't hurt a gnat."

"I'll wait then. How long have you had the farm?"

"Twenty nine years, and it's not really a farm. We have a few cows, some sheep and the odd goat every now and then. It's small compared to some of the places around here."

"Do you know the Van Camp family?"

"Everybody knows the Van Camps. Old man Van Camp is intent on buying everything he can around here. I tell you, he won't be satisfied until he owns the whole of Yorkshire."

"So you're not exactly a fan of his then?"

"I've said enough. I've got work to do. Johnny will be here shortly." He nodded his head and walked off towards the field of cows.

Smith spotted Johnny Grouse when he was at least fifty metres away - he was a large lumbering figure who seemed to shuffle along slowly. Grouse stopped when he spotted the Land Rover. He appeared to be trying to figure out whether the old vehicle was dangerous or not.

"Johnny," Smith shouted to him. "My name's Jason. Can I talk to you please?"

Grouse shrugged and ambled closer. He stood a few feet away from Smith and looked down at the top of his head. Johnny Grouse had to be almost seven feet tall.

"Do you like Sesame Street?" He said in an unusually deep voice.

"Of course," Smith said. "Who doesn't? Can I ask you a few questions before it starts?"

"It's on in five minutes."

"There's plenty of time then. Do you know Lewis Van Camp?"

"Lewis is my friend. He buys me things. He bought me a television for my caravan. I watch Sesame Street on it. I like Elmo the best. Elmo's mad."

"Does Lewis ask you to do things for him?"

"Sometimes," Grouse scratched his unusually large nose and shuffled from side to side.

"What kinds of things does he ask you to do for him?"

"He's not very strong," Grouse started to laugh. "He said I'm the strongest person he's ever met."

He smiled a proud smile. He had quite a few teeth missing.

"He's probably right," Smith said. "There was a red car outside the Quail's Arms in Scarpdale. Have you seen it?"

"No," Grouse said.

Smith could tell straight away that he was lying. His piggy eyes darted from side to side.

"Somebody cut the tyres," Smith said. "Looks like they did it with a razor blade. Did Lewis ask you to do that?"

"No," Grouse shouted so loudly that Smith took a step back.

"It's alright, Johnny, you're not in any trouble. It was my car you see - I'm just trying to work out why someone would cut my tyres. Did Lewis Van Camp tell you to do it?"

"No," Grouse said again. "It wasn't a razor blade. It was a knife. It has the sharpest blade in the world. Do you want to see it?"

"Not at the moment," Smith said.

"Can I watch Sesame Street now? I like Elmo the best. Elmo is mad."

CHAPTER TWENTY EIGHT

Smith realised he wasn't going to get anything else out of the giant simpleton. Johnny Grouse seemed to live in a world of his own. He thought about his next plan of action as he drove back to Scarpdale. Nothing made any sense. Sophie Phoenix had been killed – she'd been pregnant and the identity of the father was still a mystery.
Why did Lewis Van Camp get Johnny Grouse to slash my tyres? Smith thought, was it supposed to be some kind of warning? If so, what was it warning me against?
Smith was no closer to getting to the bottom of this than he was the day he was arrested for Sophie Phoenix's murder.

As Smith pulled up outside the Dove Inn, he noticed a police car parked further up the road.
Here we go again, he thought.
He got out of the Land Rover and walked up to the police car. PC Fielding got out and Smith sighed.
"Hello, sir," Fielding said. "Can I have a word?"
Smith saw that Fielding wasn't wearing his uniform. He was dressed in a pair of black jeans and a plain black T shirt. His face seemed very pale against the black clothes.
"Fielding," Smith said. "What's going on?"
"Not here - there's eyes and ears everywhere. I want to show you something. We'll go in Mr Phoenix's Landy if that's all right with you."
"Fine," Smith said. "Where are we going?"
"To see how the other half live," Fielding looked around nervously. "Let's go. Basil Van Camp's place is about ten miles past the Russell farm on the Skipton road."

They drove away from Scarpdale and Smith increased his speed.

"You drive this thing pretty well for a city boy," Fielding said. "I hope that didn't sound too rude."

"Not at all, I've been driving since I was fifteen."

"I've always wanted to go to Australia. I've always been fascinated with the outback."

"It's just like the moors," Smith said. "Only bigger, hotter and everything that moves there is capable of killing you. This has got to be the place here."

He slowed down and turned onto a road that looked like it had recently been tarred. A six foot fence had been erected on either side of it. Horses stared at them vacantly as they drove past.

"Old Van Camp bought this land ten years ago," Fielding said. "I was still at school then. It was all just open moorland. It must have cost a small fortune to build this place."

Smith stopped the Land Rover next to a long row of stables. To the left was a huge enclosure containing various equestrian hurdles and obstacles. A figure on a horse was galloping at unbelievable speed around the course. The horse cleared the last jump, slowed down to a canter and trotted over to the Land Rover. Smith got out and stared in amazement at the mere size of the beast in front of him. Its muscles were bulging and its flank was glistening with sweat. Flies buzzed around its face. The rider of the horse deftly jumped off and removed the riding hat. Smith recognised her from his first night in Scarpdale. It was Charlotte Phoenix.

"What do you want?" She was obviously not pleased to see them.

"Miss Phoenix," Smith said. "We just need to ask you a few questions. That's a beautiful horse you have there."

"He's not mine," she spoke with the same tone a child does when an adult has said something patronising. "He's a Percheron. He's still pretty wild. I'm trying to break him in. What do you want? I have a lot to do. We're burying my sister tomorrow in case you didn't know."

"I'm sorry," Smith didn't know. "This won't take long."

"Don't pat her," Charlotte screamed at PC Fielding.

Fielding was stroking the head of a much smaller, white and grey horse in one of the stables.

"They're not dogs," Charlotte added. "They're thoroughbred animals. The less contact they have with outsiders the better."

"Sorry," Fielding said. "She seemed to like it. I love horses."

Charlotte glared at him.

"Miss Phoenix," Smith said. "I know this is difficult. That night at the Quail's Arms - the night I had an altercation with Lewis Van Camp, where did Sophie go after she left the pub?"

"How should I know? I'm not her keeper."

"Had Sophie and Lewis been seeing each other for a while?" Fielding chipped in.

"About a year. On and off. Mostly off if I can remember."

"I see," Smith said. "So it wasn't what you'd call a happy relationship?"

"They were madly in love. At least they were this time last year but I always knew it was just a holiday infatuation."

"Holiday infatuation?"

"You know how it is, you get lost in the moment. The sun and the parties. It isn't real. Summer in The Hamptons has that effect on you."

"The Hamptons?" So Sophie was in New York last summer."

"There's no flies on you."

"How long have you known the Van Camps?" Smith ignored her sarcasm.

"Ages," Charlotte said. "Me and Sophie went to the same God-awful school as Lewis, Sebastian and their sister Matilda"

Smith thought hard for a moment.

"Were you also in New York last summer?"

"For a while," Charlotte rolled her eyes. "I got bored of it all to be honest. I mean, nobody can possibly tolerate that kind of bullshit for too long."

"What do you mean?"

"Have you ever been to The Hamptons?" Charlotte said.

"No."

"I didn't think so. Well, let me put you in the picture. Party after party - endless bragging and bitchiness you wouldn't believe. I've got a bigger house and bigger yacht than you'll ever have. I'm sure you get the gist. It bored the pants off me to be honest."

"So you came back here?"

"I'd rather spend time with horses than the so called prime specimens of society that call New York home," Charlotte said.

"Something happened in New York last year didn't it? Something that prompted Basil and Lewis Van Camp to come back here in quite a hurry. Do you know anything about it?"

"I heard about it," Charlotte said. "Mostly rumours. I'm sure Sophie knew what it was all about but she never wanted to talk about it and she's not likely to spill the beans now is she?"

Smith didn't know what to say.

"Sorry," Charlotte said. "I have this habit of letting my tongue work before my brain has time to think. I miss Sophie, I really do."

"What were these rumours?"

"You know," Charlotte said. "Idle gossip. Crap on Facebook and Twitter. It was something to do with Lewis' brother Sebastian."

"What did he do?"

"Something terrible. Something so terrible that he was shipped off to Mexico or Canada, never to be seen again."

"What about the mother and the sister?" Fielding asked.

"They're still in New York as far as I know, but I can tell you this - they've kept a very low profile since the scandal."

"Where are Basil and Lewis now?" Smith asked.

"The old man's in China. The Chinese are going crazy for thoroughbred horses at the moment."

"Did Lewis go with him?"

"No, he was around earlier. He must have gone out somewhere."

A short, fat woman in her twenties approached them. She was almost as wide as she was tall. Smith hoped she wasn't allowed to ride the horses.

"Miss Phoenix," she said. "Sorry to bother you but Victor is in a bad way. He's not eating and his eyes don't look right to me."

"Get the vet out from Skipton," Charlotte said. "I'll sit with him in the meantime."

She turned to Smith.

"Victor's my baby. He's an Arab but he doesn't know it. If you don't mind, I have a very valuable horse to look after."

"Can I ask you one more thing?" Smith said.

"Shoot."

"Your father also owns horses doesn't he?"

"He's got three very well established stables," Charlotte said.

"Why don't you work for him then? Why work here for the Van Camps?"

Charlotte started to laugh.

"Sorry," she said. "I don't work here. The likes of us don't have to work. Don't get me wrong, I love my Dad but working for him wouldn't seem right. I like the independence I have here. Basil gives me free rein if you'll pardon the pun. Now, if that's all, I need to check on Victor."

CHAPTER TWENTY NINE

"What do you think?" PC Fielding asked as they drove back to Scarpdale.
"What do I think about what?" Smith's brain was trying to process a thousand thoughts at the same time.
"Now that's money," Fielding said. "That's more money than the likes of us will ever see. If only I had a tenth of that money, I'd never have to put on a uniform again. Just imagine it - never having to kiss the arses of jumped up rich kids like Charlotte Phoenix again."
"Sorry?" Smith was miles away.
Something had clicked in his brain but he couldn't quite figure out what it was.
"There's trouble in paradise," he said without thinking. "Something's not quite right in the affluent world of these horsemen."
"If I had their money I wouldn't care," Fielding said.
"Fielding," Smith slammed on the brakes so hard that PC Fielding was almost jettisoned through the windscreen. "Money isn't real - it doesn't give you instant happiness."
"So the brakes on this thing work then," Fielding sat back in his seat. "What are we going to do now?"
"I need to think, but first I have to make an important phone call. Where's the best place to find a signal around here?"
"Top of Maggie's Moor. Take the next left and drive to the top of the ridge."
"Maggie's Moor?"
"You definitely don't want to find yourself up there alone at night,"

Fielding said. "They say the ghost of a woman walks the moor by moonlight. All dressed in black she is."

Smith shook his head and turned left. The road to the ridge was steep but the old Land Rover made short work of it.

Smith turned off the engine and got out of the Land Rover. The wind had picked up and a cool breeze washed across the heather. He took out his phone. The signal was at full strength. He dialed the number.

"Hello," Whitton sounded angry.

"Whitton," Smith said. "Sorry I haven't been in touch sooner but a lot has been happening around here."

"You said you were coming home."

"I know, I'm sorry. I'm going to be stuck here for a while longer I'm afraid."

"What's going on?"

"Something sinister," Smith said. "Something I can't let go of."

There was silence on the other end of the line. Smith thought the signal had been lost.

"Whitton," he said. "Are you still there?"

"I'm still here, do you need some help?"

Smith told her everything that had happened. Whitton listened without saying a word.

"You know where you need to start looking don't you?" Whitton said when Smith was finished.

"I think so," Smith said.

"You need to find out what happened last summer in New York."

"Thanks, Whitton, I just needed someone else to say it."

"Just get to the bottom of all this," she said. "And come back home."

"You're an amazing woman. How's Theakston?"

The line went dead.

"It does that sometimes," Fielding said when Smith got back in the Land Rover.

Smith was staring at his phone.

"Sometimes the signal disappears for no reason," Fielding added.

"Welcome to deepest, darkest Yorkshire. What now boss?"

"Back to Scarpdale," Smith said. "I need to get my car fixed. This bone shaker is giving me back ache, and please don't call me boss."

He started the engine and slowly maneuvered the Land Rover down the hill.

"Was that your girlfriend?" Fielding asked when they reached the main road again.

"You should be a detective. What about you. Are you married?"

"No, there's not much choice in these parts. All the good ones either get snapped up or leave to seek more exciting lives. Anyway, I like being single."

"I used to think that," Smith mused.

A surprise was waiting for Smith when they got back to Scarpdale. His car was parked outside the Quail's Arms complete with four new tyres. Keith, Jimmy Phoenix's sidekick was standing next to it. He was beaming from ear to ear.

"Looks like you have friends around here," Fielding said.

"Keith," Smith said. "How did you manage that?"

He pointed to his car.

"You've got Mr Phoenix to thank for that. He had four new tyres brought in from Skipton. You'd better get the wheel alignment checked though - the mechanics changed the tyres on the side of the road."

"Thanks," Smith said. "Where is Jimmy?"

"I haven't seen him all day. He's probably getting ready for the funeral tomorrow."

"Of course, how's he doing?"

"Remarkably well under the circumstances, but he's tearing himself to pieces inside. It must be the worst thing in the world having to bury your child. What did you find out at the Van Camp stables?"

Smith was shocked.

How does he know we were there? He thought.

"We need to know everything," Keith seemed to read Smith's mind. "It's better that way. We are working together after all."

"I spoke to Charlotte Phoenix, but she didn't give me much to go on. We talked mostly about what happened in New York last summer."

"New York," Keith said. "Terrible business."

"Do you know what happened?"

"Only what I've heard in the rumours. Something to do with Lewis Van Camp's brother."

Is there anybody who really knows what happened over there? Smith thought.

Sophie Phoenix seemed to be the only person who knew and now she was dead. Whether Smith liked it or not, he knew what he had to do. He was going to have to take a trip across the Atlantic.

CHAPTER THIRTY

The day of Sophie Phoenix's funeral dawned grey and bleak. A low, thick mist clouded the top of the moorland in the distance. Smith stood with Keith and Jimmy Phoenix outside the old church half a mile from the village centre. Smith fidgeted in the suit he had borrowed from PC Fielding. Something was making him incredibly itchy. The field next to the church that was being used as a temporary car park was slowly filling up with vehicles Smith had only seen in TV lifestyle programs before. Mercedes, BMWs and top of the range SUVs soon made the small field resemble an up market car showroom. Smith felt out of place as he watched the owners of these vehicles walk towards the church. He suddenly realised what a cold, unemotional lot these affluent funeral guests were. Greetings were limited to sympathetic nods of the head and insincere half-smiles.

"That's the way we are," Phoenix said, noting the look of surprise on Smith's face. "You don't make money by letting your emotions get the better of you. We lead a miserable existence really, don't we?"
Smith didn't know what to say.
"Are you a religious man?" Phoenix asked him.
"I'm afraid not."
"Me neither," Phoenix admitted. "And Sophie thought it was a load of old crock too but I've always liked the old church and the rector doesn't tend to preach too much."
"We'd better go inside," Keith said.

Smith followed them inside the church. Phoenix and Keith sat on either side of Charlotte at the front. Smith found a seat at the back

next to an old lady whose perfume smelled like rotting lavender. He
scanned the room. Most of the funeral party were middle aged men.
Friends of Jimmy Phoenix's, he thought.

Lewis Van Camp was nowhere to be seen. The door to the church
opened and a red faced Jethro shuffled in. He took the empty seat
next to Smith, much to the obvious distaste of the elderly woman with
the rancid smelling perfume. For once, Jethro was without his
repulsive dog.

"Thought it only right," he whispered to Smith. "To show my respects
to Mr Phoenix."

Smith nodded. The man in the seat in front turned round and glared at
them both.

"Please stand," the rector indicated he was ready to begin.
The opening bars of 'Amazing Grace' were played over a loudspeaker
and the most awful singing Smith had ever heard filled the church. The
old lady sitting next to him was in possession of a particularly
unpleasant voice. Her high pitched monotone could be heard over
everybody else. Smith was glad when the music stopped and
everybody was told to be seated.

The rector related stories of Sophie Phoenix's short life and Smith
listened with interest. She'd been a star pupil at school and had taken
to the equestrian life with ease. She had represented Yorkshire in
dressage and show jumping and her future in the field seemed bright.
A short prayer was followed by a few words from her sister Charlotte
which mostly centered on their childhood. Smith thought the words
were touching but the lack of any emotion on Charlotte's face was
quite disturbing. He looked around the church. A woman in her thirties
was dabbing the corner of her eye with a handkerchief but she seemed
to be the only one affected by the somber occasion.

These people are a bunch of cold hearted bastards, Smith thought.

To Smith's horror, the rector announced they would finish off with another hymn and he was forced to endure the old woman's off key monotonous shriek again while she murdered 'Onward Christian soldiers'. He was glad when the music stopped and Jimmy Phoenix invited everybody back to the Quail's Arms for food and drink. Smith's ears were ringing. He needed a drink. He waited for the guests to file past and joined the line at the back. Jimmy Phoenix was talking to the rector at the front of the church. Smith was sure he saw Phoenix hand the rector a wad of banknotes in an ill-disguised handshake.

A grand total of five people accepted Phoenix's offer of refreshments. Smith, Charlotte, Keith, a man Smith did not recognise and Jethro stood at the bar in the Quail's Arms. Smith knew that Jethro was merely taking advantage of the free drinks. Charlotte, Keith and himself were there out of loyalty to Phoenix and the other man didn't seem to belong there somehow.

"Obligations," Phoenix said. "Everybody else had prior obligations. Can you bloody believe it?"

"Dad," Charlotte said. "What did you expect? Nobody cares about anybody else anymore. It's all about the money. You should know that by now. I need a drink."

She looked over at Smith and for a split second, Smith thought she was smiling at him.

"That suit's terrible," she said. "It looks like something you'd find in a second hand shop."

"It's itchy as hell," Smith said. "I borrowed it from PC Fielding."

"What are we drinking?" Phoenix said. "It's on me."

Smith, Phoenix, Keith and Charlotte sat at the table by the window. The fog had lifted and the sun was poking through the clouds. Jethro sat at his usual table in the corner. He was busy finishing off his third free pint in the space of half an hour.

"I don't mean to sound rude," Smith said. "But I thought Lewis Van Camp would have been at the funeral."

"He knows to keep well away," Phoenix drained a large glass of single malt whisky in one go. "Another drink?"

He nodded to the woman behind the bar.

"Same again," he said.

They sat in silence while they waited for the drinks. Smith stared out of the window. He had the strange feeling he was being observed. He looked over and saw that Charlotte Phoenix was staring at him.

"Sorry," she broke eye contact. "You have a very unusual face."

"I was born with it," Smith said. "My folks had a warped sense of humour."

The drinks arrived and Smith took a large gulp of his beer. The first one had already made him feel light headed.

"You're funny," Charlotte said. "I imagine there's a Mrs Smith back there in York."

"Charlotte," Phoenix glared at her. "That's enough. This is neither the time or the place for your games."

"Dad," Charlotte rolled her eyes. "I'm just trying to make conversation. To lighten the mood."

She looked back at Smith.

"So," she said. "Mrs Smith. Is she waiting for you in York?"

"No," Smith said. "No Mrs Smith but there is somebody."

"I knew it. All the best looking ones are either gay or spoken for."

"Charlotte," Phoenix said.

PC Fielding burst through the doors of the pub. He was very red in the face.

"Fielding," Smith said. "What's wrong?"

"He's dead," Fielding said. "Dead."

He sat down next to Smith with his head in his hands. He was shaking quite badly.

"Who's dead?" Smith said.

"Lewis Van Camp," Fielding looked up at Smith with bloodshot eyes. "An old man driving past found him up on the moors this morning. It looks like he killed himself. His brains were all over the window."

CHAPTER THIRTY ONE

Smith put a large measure of brandy in front of PC Fielding and asked him to repeat what he had said.
"He killed himself," Fielding raised the glass to his lips with shaking hands. "His head was splattered all over the window of the car. I've never seen anything like it in my life."
"Where was this?" Smith had sobered up in an instant.
"Maggie's Moor, not far from where we were yesterday."
Phoenix and Charlotte hadn't said a word. Charlotte was very pale in the face but otherwise she showed no reaction to the news.
"The old man who found him," Smith said. "Where is he now?"
"Wilkie's busy with him now."
"I'll need to talk to him."
"Wilkie won't allow it. He had no choice with Sophie Phoenix but this is his patch and he's going to defend it with everything he has."
Smith thought hard for a moment.
"OK," he said. "This is what I want you to do. Go back to the station. Wilkie can't hold the old man for long. I want you to find out who he is. I need to speak to him."
"I'll see what I can do," Fielding finished the brandy in his glass and stood up.
"Fielding," Smith said. "Why does this suit make me itch so much?"
"It must be my cats. I've got four cats."

Cats, Smith thought as he drove to Maggie's Moor, no wonder Fielding's single.
The wheels on his car were not balanced properly and he had to concentrate to stay in a straight line. The Sierra kept veering off to the left. He reached the top of the ridge and looked around. About a

hundred metres in the distance he spotted a commotion. An ambulance was parked next to the road. Two police cars and a black saloon car were parked behind it. A silver Range Rover was standing about fifty metres from the road in the middle of the heather. Smith thought about what he was going to do. Sergeant Wilkie was still interviewing the old man back in Skipton but he still had to be careful. He parked behind the black car and got out.

"Sorry, sir," a woman in uniform approached him. "You'll have to leave. This area is off limits."

"Then why hasn't someone ensured it's off limits?" Smith asked her. Her mouth opened wide.

"A man is found dead in his car," Smith continued. "The circumstances are suspicious. This is a potential crime scene. You need to block off the road in both directions and you need to seal off a perimeter of at least a hundred metres around the car."

"Who are you?"

"DS Smith," Smith decided to tell her the truth. "York city. I was in the area and I've been given the go ahead to assist. Now, will you please do as I say before the scene is contaminated any more than it already is?"

"Looks like he killed himself, sir," the woman said.

"What's your name?"

"PC Swift, sir."

"Listen to me PC Swift," Smith said. "You'll soon learn not to assume anything in this job. Who's in charge here?"

"Sergeant Wilkie, but he's busy talking to the man who found the body."

"I know Wilkie. Me and him are good friends. I want you to stop anybody coming up here and I need to take a look at Van Camp's car myself."

"It's not a pretty sight, sir," Swift said. "They've taken the body away but most of his head is still spread over the window."

Smith walked over to Lewis Van Camp's Range Rover. He wished he had changed into something else before he left. Fielding's suit was becoming unbearable. As he approached the vehicle he realised that PC Swift had been right. The whole of the passenger window was caked in dry blood and pieces of what could only be brain matter were stuck to the glass. Smith noted that all four windows were open. The passenger side window had been shattered. He peered inside the driver's side and spotted a double barreled shot gun in the seat. The gun had an unusually long barrel. Something struck him straight away - something wasn't right.

"What the hell are you doing here?" A familiar voice interrupted his thoughts.

It was Sergeant Wilkie.

"This one's mine," Wilkie said. "Now piss off before I have you arrested again."

"Where's the body been taken?" Smith ignored him.

"That's none of your business. You've got until the count of ten. One…"

"There's just one thing," Smith said.

"Two," Wilkie said. "Three…'

"I'm no expert on guns," Smith said.

"Four…"

"But that shotgun has a longer barrel than most if I'm not mistaken."

"You're not from around here," Wilkie said. "The long barrel is better for hunting grouse. Five, six…"

"If I recall," Smith was not shutting up. "Lewis Van Camp was a short, stocky man. His arms were thick and short."

"Seven," Wilkie said. "Eight, nine…"

"And I'm sure the forensics guys will do the measurements, but even somebody like me can see that, with the longer barrel, it would have been impossible for him to have pulled the trigger and put the end of the barrel against his head at the same time."

Wilkie's jaw dropped. The word he was looking for refused to come out.

CHAPTER THIRTY TWO

"Murder?" PC Fielding said.
Fielding and Smith were standing in the small car park outside the Skipton police station.
"Looks like it," Smith said. "It hasn't been confirmed one hundred percent but I'm pretty sure of it."
"Lewis Van Camp made a few enemies - he was a bit of an arrogant bastard but I can't think of anyone who would want to kill him."
"Now you experiencing real detective work," Smith took out his cigarettes and offered one to Fielding."
"I don't smoke, but I suppose one cigarette isn't going to kill me."
He took a cigarette, put it in his mouth and Smith lit the end. Fielding inhaled deeply and started to cough. His vision went blank for a few seconds then he seemed to relax. Smith lit one for himself and shook his head.
"I've seen this plenty of times before," he said. "A murder made to look like suicide. It's almost impossible to get away with. Something always gives them away. Some tiny detail they overlook. This one's different though."
"What do you mean?"
"The shotgun," Smith said. "I know nothing about guns but I knew straight away that it would have been impossible for Lewis Van Camp to blow his brains out with that particular weapon."
"Why not just use a pistol?" Fielding suggested.
"Good thinking. That was my first question too. Where's the shotgun now?"
"All Wilkie would say was it's in safe hands," Fielding said.
"How many people around here own a shotgun?"

"Pretty much everybody," Fielding sighed. "This isn't the city. They use them for shooting grouse and the farmers use them to keep the foxes at bay. What do we do now?"

"I've been told in no uncertain terms to stay away from this one, but I think Wilkie is out of his depth here. Something strange is going on."

"Do you think whoever killed Lewis Van Camp also killed Sophie Phoenix?"

"I'm almost certain," Smith said. "And that means we're back to square one."

"What do you mean?"

"My odds on favourite for the killer of Sophie Phoenix is now missing a head. We'll have to go right back to the start again. Something sinister is going on around here and I haven't a clue what it is. There is something you can do for me though."

"I'll try," Fielding said. "What is it?"

"This isn't common knowledge, so I don't want you to mention it to anybody, but Sophie Phoenix was pregnant when she died."

"Pregnant?"

"I thought I had it all figured out. I was sure Lewis Van Camp was the father. He finds out and loses it. That's why he killed her. This new murder changes everything."

"What is it you want me to do?"

Smith tore a strip off his cigarette packet, took out a pen and wrote a number on it.

"Phone this guy," Smith handed Fielding the paper. "He's a bit of a social misfit but he's the best forensics officer I've ever met. His name's Grant Webber."

"I can't just invite an outsider to join the investigation. Wilkie will have my bollocks for it."

"This isn't Wilkie's party anymore. You'll probably be in for a bit of grief but Webber will give us something to go on. He has years of experience."

"What do I say to this Webber bloke?"

"Tell him you need him here in an advisory capacity," Smith said. "You're short staffed Make something up. Nobody will even question it. Webber get's called away all the time."

"I'll try," Fielding said.

"Just one thing though," Smith said. "Don't mention my name yet - me and Webber haven't always seen eye to eye in the past."

"I'll make the call then."

"There's something else I need," Smith said.

Fielding was finding it hard to hide his impatience.

"Yes, sir," he said.

"I need the names of the hikers who found Sophie Phoenix's body that morning."

"I've got them here somewhere," Wilkie took out a worn notebook from his pocket.

He tore out a page and handed it to Smith.

"Thanks," Smith looked at the piece of paper. "Looks like I'll be able to kill two birds with one stone, maybe three."

"Sir?"

"The hikers live in York," Smith said. "Not far from where I live actually. I need to go back there anyway to fetch my passport and I really ought to try and patch things up with a certain DC Whitton."

The most unusual cloud Smith had ever seen was forming in the sky over the moors as Smith drove back to Scarpdale. It looked like the mushroom cloud after a nuclear bomb had exploded. He slowed down and watched it grow in size in the sky. He didn't know whether it

meant good or bad weather was on the way. He parked outside the
Dove Inn and switched off the engine. As he got out, he noticed a
large lumbering figure coming towards him. It was Johnny Grouse. He
was pushing his chopper bicycle. The bicycle was far too small for him
and he had to bend almost double to reach the handlebars. Grouse
stopped when he spotted Smith. He spent a long time staring at the
tyres on Smith's car. He seemed confused because they weren't flat
anymore.

"Johnny," Smith said. "What are you up to?"

"Nothing," Johnny said in his unnaturally deep voice. "I was waiting for
Lewis but he didn't come. He said he was going to bring me some
videotapes for me but he didn't come so I thought I'd ride into town to
but some humbugs from Mrs Allen's shop. I like the brown ones
although Mrs Allen says I mustn't eat too many. They eat your teeth."

Grouse has obviously not heard about the murder, Smith thought.

"When was the last time you saw Lewis?" Smith asked him.

"This morning," Grouse stuck a large finger up his left nostril.

He made no effort to hide it.

"Where was this?"

"Mr Russell's farm. He looked nice. He said he was going to the
funeral. It's when people die."

"I see," Smith said.

Lewis Van Camp was planning on going to Sophie Phoenix's funeral
after all, he thought.

"What time was this?" Smith said.

"The sun was over the old oak tree. It was over the rooster's head.
When it's over the tail it's time for Sesame Street. I like Elmo - Elmo's
mad."

Smith didn't know what Grouse was talking about.

"Can you show me," he said. "Can you show me this rooster tree?"
"It's got a puncture," Grouse pointed to the old chopper. "It gets them all the time - Mr Russell says I'm too heavy for it."
"We'll put it in the boot of my car," Smith said. "I'll give you a lift back to the farm."

Smith had to drive very slowly up to the Russell's farm with the bicycle in the back. The boot wouldn't close properly and it kept banging up and down. Johnny Grouse sat crouched in the passenger seat. He didn't say a word. He had an inane grin on his face the whole time. He'd obviously forgotten about the humbugs he was going to buy. They reached the entrance to the farm and Smith drove towards Grouse's caravan. He spotted the old oak tree straight away. He had to agree that it did resemble a rooster. The clock on the dashboard said it was four thirty. The sun was far away to the west of the tree. Smith remembered that it was noon when Sesame street started the last time he was at the farm.

"Where was the sun when Lewis Van Camp was here yesterday?" He asked Grouse.

"There," Grouse pointed. "The highest spike on the tail."

Smith made a quick mental calculation. He figured that, from the position of the sun at noon to where Grouse had pointed, roughly two hours would have passed.

Lewis Van Camp was here at ten yesterday morning, he thought, an hour before the funeral.

Smith suddenly realised two things. Lewis Van Camp was killed between ten and eleven in the morning and whoever killed him probably wasn't at the funeral.

"Maybe he'll come later," Grouse interrupted his thoughts.

"What?" Smith said.

"Maybe Lewis will bring the videotapes later. I forgot to buy my humbugs."

CHAPTER THIRTY THREE

Smith realised his hands were tied until he could steal a look at the forensics reports. He was baffled - he hoped Webber would agree to help and he hoped even more he would be willing to divulge whatever information was on the report. Webber and Smith were not exactly on friendly terms. He parked outside the Dove Inn. It was still only five in the afternoon - the restaurant wouldn't be serving food for at least another hour. He decided he would pass the time by taking another walk to Whooton Tarn. He could work up an appetite and maybe he would find something there the local police had missed. He set off at a steady pace and reached the tarn in less than fifteen minutes. The sun was high in the sky and the peculiar cloud had mysteriously disappeared. He took a slow walk around the lake and came to the spot where he knew Sophie Phoenix's body had been discovered. It was as if nothing had ever happened - the lake was glimmering in the late afternoon sun.
Nature carries on, Smith mused, it always has and it always will.

Smith was about to leave when he spotted something out of the corner of his eye - a slight glint under the surface of the lake about two metres from the shore. He moved closer and bent down to get a better look. A silver coin was lying on a smooth grey rock under the water. Smith picked it up and held it in front of his face. He didn't know much about history but he knew that the face on the coin belonged to George Washington. It was an American quarter. He put the coin in his pocket and headed back to the village.

As he waited for the waiter in the Dove Inn, Smith took out the quarter he had found in the lake. It had been dropped close to where Sophie Phoenix had been found.

An American quarter, he thought, found in a lake in the middle of
Yorkshire. Surely that's more than just a coincidence.
He realised he couldn't put off the trip to New York any longer. He
decided that, after his meal, he would have a few beers in the Quail's
Arms, get a good night's rest and see what Webber could come up
with. After that, he would speak to Jimmy Phoenix and gauge his
thoughts on digging up a few things in New York.

The waiter arrived and eyed Smith suspiciously.
"Evening," Smith said. "What's on the menu this evening?"
"I didn't know you were still here," the waiter said. "After everything
that's happened and everything."
"Excuse me?"
"People are talking," the waiter looked anxiously around the empty
dining room.
"People will always talk. I'm hungry. What have you got?"
"Roast pork or Spaghetti Bolognese."
"I'll have the pork then, and a pint of Theakstons."
"I'll see to it," the waiter walked off, shaking his head.
He's definitely not getting a tip at the end of all this, Smith thought.
He wondered what he meant when he said people were talking.
Surely they can't think I had anything to do with any of this?

After the meal, Smith headed straight to the Quail's Arms. Jethro
was sitting in his usual place by the window. He was reading a
newspaper. His dog spotted Smith and rushed over to say hello.
"That little tyke has really taken a fancy to you," Jethro smiled. "What
are you, one of those dog whisperers?"
"I love dogs," Smith said. "They can sense it."
He approached the bar. A man and a woman were engaged in a
conversation at the table closest to it. Smith couldn't make out what

they were saying - they were talking so quietly but he was sure they both had American accents.

"Pint of Theakstons please," he said to the surly barman.

"You still here?" The barman turned on the tap. "I thought you'd be long gone by now."

He put the beer in front of Smith.

"Do you live around here?" Smith asked him.

"Have done all my life. Not that it's any of your business."

"What's it like living here?" Smith ignored his rudeness.

"Like living in a goldfish bowl."

His reply surprised Smith.

"What do you mean?"

"You know what it's like? Everybody knows everybody else's business. You can't fart around here without everybody knowing about it."

Smith took his beer to the table next to Jethro's. He took a long swig and leaned back in his seat. For some reason he suddenly had his doubts about flying across the Atlantic.

What's the point? He thought. If I can't find out anything in a place where everybody knows everybody else, what chance have I got in New York?

He finished his beer and stood up. As he reached the bar, the door to the pub opened and a familiar face stood in the doorway. It was Grant Webber. Smith was shocked.

What's Webber doing in here? He thought.

Webber closed the door behind him, walked up to the bar and stood next to Smith.

"Webber," Smith said. "It's actually nice to see you. Can I buy you a drink?"

"I thought I'd find you in here," Webber said. "Scotch. Make it a double."

They took their drinks back to Smith's table. Webber sipped his whisky and winced. He wasn't much of a drinker.

"Well," Smith came right to the point. "Have you got anything for me?" Webber looked at Jethro on the next table. He still had the newspaper in front of him but it was clear he wasn't really reading it - his eyes kept glancing over at Smith and Webber.

"Not here," Webber was now glaring at Jethro.

Jethro stood up. Webber's hint had been far from subtle.

"I'll be off then," he said. "Come on Fred."

He put on his hat, nodded at Smith and headed for the door. The repugnant dog followed after him.

"Why do you always do this to me?" Webber said when Jethro had closed the door behind him. "I don't know why I even agreed to this. I ought to be committed."

"What have you got?"

"Something very strange. I had to call in a few favours on this one, I can tell you that."

"Thanks, Webber," Smith said. "What did you find out?"

"The DNA - Sophie Phoenix and Lewis Van Camp share the same DNA."

"You mean Sophie's baby shares the same DNA as Van Camp?" Smith said. "So he was the father of the baby. I knew it."

"No," Webber looked around the room. "Sophie and Lewis share the same DNA."

"What does that mean?"

"What do you think it means? It means that something very disturbing is going on. It means they either have the same mother or the same father."

CHAPTER THIRTY FOUR

Smith lay awake thinking about what Webber had told him. It didn't make any sense. Sophie Phoenix and Lewis Van Camp were sister and brother. How could that be possible? Webber had returned to York and Smith planned on doing the same first thing in the morning. He would go back to York, speak to the two hikers who found Sophie Phoenix's body, pick up his passport and book himself on the first flight to New York.
New York, he thought, I wonder what I'm going to find in New York. He knew that Whitton would be furious. He was supposed to leave Scarpdale and come back home and now he was going to have to tell her he was flying to New York.

Smith closed his eyes and tried to sleep but it was no use. He sat up in bed and turned on his phone. It was still only nine thirty. He went to the bathroom and splashed some water on his face. He wondered if the Quail's Arms was still open.
There's only one way to find out, he thought.
He put some clothes on, left the room and wandered down to reception. There was nobody manning the desk but the door to the Inn was still open. He stepped outside and saw that the light was still on in the pub next door.

Smith went inside the Quail's Arms and looked around. The American couple were still sitting at the same table as before. Two young men were standing at the bar.
"Pint of Theakstons please," Smith said to the familiar barman.
"Can't stay away?" The barman said as he poured the beer.
"Must be the friendly service," Smith said.
The barman shrugged and handed Smith the beer.

"You're Australian aren't you?" A nasal American voice was heard. Smith looked across the bar. The man who had been sitting with the woman had stood up and was now holding out his hand.

"David Petrucci," he said.

Smith shook his hand and took his beer to Jethro's usual table.

"Are you here for the horses?" Petrucci had followed him and was about to sit down.

Smith sighed - he was really not in the mood for polite conversation.

"I'm on holiday," he said and hoped that would be the end of it.

"My wife and I are here to look at an Andalusian," Petrucci said. "One of the finest specimens on the planet if the photographs on the website are to be believed."

Smith nodded and took a long swig of his beer.

"I don't know much about horses."

"No, you're probably more into Kangaroos over there aren't you?" He started to laugh at his own joke. He was obviously very drunk.

"David," Petrucci's wife shouted. "Would you please leave the poor man alone. He doesn't want to listen to your nonsense. I think it's time we left."

"I just hope the whole thing hasn't been a total waste of time," Petrucci was showing no sign of leaving. "What with the terrible business of the suicide. Basil must be going out of his mind."

"Basil Van Camp?"

"What could make a young man want to do such a thing? Why would a man in the prime of his life want to end it all like that? Lewis had the whole world at his feet. Money, fame, everything. It's a terrible business and it's really put the sale of the Andalusian on hold."

"Do you know the Van Camps well?"

"As well as anyone could know them. We spent a bit of time with them over the summer in The Hamptons last year. We have the place across the bay from theirs. That was before the family crisis though."
"Family crisis?"
"You should see the place now," Petrucci shook his head. "You wouldn't believe what owns the place now. The Hamptons isn't what it used to be. New money, although you wouldn't think so to look at them - they look like they drove there on a bus or something."
"What happened there last year?" Smith asked.
"Nobody really knows. All I know is that poor Veronica couldn't cope. Last I heard, she was stuck in some nut house somewhere upstate."
"Veronica?"
"Basil's poor wife," Petrucci said. "And this business with Lewis will surely push her beyond the point of no return."
Smith was suddenly interested.
"Do you know what happened to Lewis' brother?"
"Sebastian?" Petrucci said. "He disappeared shortly afterwards. I heard he ended up in some commune down in Tijuana or somewhere. Probably frying his brains with the drugs that lot take down there. Matilda's still there though."
"Who's Matilda?"
"Lewis's sister," Petrucci said. "Sweet girl. She's nothing like the rest of them. She looks after the horses in the estate a few miles from our property. Poor girl - she went from rich kid to poor stable girl in the blink of an eye."
"I don't understand. I thought the Van Camps were still rich."
"Don't listen to a word my husband says," Petrucci's wife said. "He has a tendency to over exaggerate. Matilda is a rare breed in The

Hamptons. She couldn't care less about the money. I actually envy her for it."

"No you don't." Petrucci said. "You wouldn't survive a day without money. It's just the way it is. We can't help it - some people are destined to have money and some people aren't. It's actually not our fault."

David Petrucci was beginning to make Smith feel ill. His smug smile and arrogant banter was causing Smith to clench his fists under the table. Finally, Petrucci stood up. He teetered from side to side. Smith was afraid he was going to fall over.

"Enjoy your holiday," he said. "Are you staying in the quaint little inn next door?"

Smith nodded.

"Us too. We were supposed to be staying at the Van Camp place but after what happened we thought it would be best to leave poor Basil in peace. We should hook up for breakfast in the morning."

Smith shivered. He made a mental note to make sure he was up early the next day. He wanted to be checked out and on the road before this obnoxious man woke up.

CHAPTER THIRTY FIVE

Smith woke to the sound of rain pelting against the window. He got up, dressed and quickly packed his things in the small bag. He didn't want to bump into David Petrucci. The arrogant American had left him with a bad taste in his mouth. The man who normally worked as the waiter was sitting behind the reception desk when Smith walked down.
"Morning," Smith handed him his room key. "I'd like to check out please."
"You're making the right decision," the waiter tapped a few keys on the keyboard. "Better to get as far away from here as possible."
Smith wasn't in the mood for an argument. He handed the man his credit card.
"We won't charge you for checking out earlier. Under the circumstances I mean. I trust you won't be coming back to Scarpdale in a hurry?"
"You never know do you?" Smith signed the credit card slip and left the Dove Inn without saying another word.

The rain stopped as soon as Smith turned off after Skipton and headed south on the road to York. He slowed down and looked in the mirror. A dreary grey cloud appeared to hover ominously over Scarpdale. Smith pressed harder on the accelerator. He wanted to get as far away as quickly as possible.
Maybe I should just forget about this whole thing, he thought, it's really none of my business anyway.
He drove far too quickly back to York. He slowed down when he reached the turnoff that led to the hospital.
Why not? He thought.

Jessica Blakemore was in the day room. She was staring out of the huge window. Her hair had grown back slightly since Smith had seen her last. She appeared to have lost quite a bit of weight. The hospital gown she was wearing hung off her sloping shoulders. She didn't seem to notice than Smith had entered the room.

"Jessica," he said softly.

She turned round and Smith gasped. Her whole face was different. Her skin was a greyish yellow colour - her eyes were sunk into her head and there was very little of the spark Smith was used to left in them. Smith saw she had bandages on both wrists. She looked Smith up and down and finally their eyes met. For a brief moment, Smith wasn't sure if this really was Jessica Blakemore.

"Jessica," he said again. "What happened?"

She smiled and the hairs on Smith's arms stood on end. It was the most disturbing smile he had ever seen.

"Has it been two weeks already?" she said in a voice that Smith did not recognise.

"I came back early. What happened to you?"

"I can't go back out there," Jessica stared out the window again. "I have to stay in here. I'm safe in here. Do you know these windows are made from God-proof glass?"

"I don't understand," Smith said. "You seemed fine on Monday."

"Then Tuesday came," she snapped the words out so loud that Smith jumped.

"And then Wednesday," she said in a much softer voice. "Then Thursday. What day is it today?"

"Friday," Smith said.

"On Tuesday they told me I wasn't allowed to stay. There's nothing wrong with you, they said."

"So you can go home?"

"You're just like them," Jessica glared at Smith. "You're stupid. All of you."

"What happened, Jessica?"

She raised her arms in the air and started tugging at the bandage on her left wrist.

"Stop it," Smith said. "I get the picture."

"I opened them up for everybody to see during breakfast," she sighed. "They don't bleed as much as you would think."

Smith didn't know what to say. This wasn't what he had expected to find when he came here.

"What about you?" Jessica asked him. "Are you cured?"

"I'd better get going. Are you going to be alright?"

"Clozapine is my new religion," she said. "Clozapine clouds over the soul. What do you have to block out the blackness in your soul?"

"Good bye, Jessica, I'll come and visit you again. I promise."

Smith felt mentally and physically drained as he drove away from the hospital. In four days, Jessica Blakemore had turned into a completely different person. He followed the ring road around the city and turned onto the road that led to the river. The Minster was a welcome sight in the distance. The sun shone directly above it.
It's good to be back, he thought as he turned into his street.
He parked outside his house and turned off the engine. He sat there for a few minutes. Whitton's car wasn't there. Smith felt a pang of guilt when he realised he was glad Whitton wasn't there. After visiting Jessica Blakemore, he needed some time alone to process everything that had happened over the last few days.

Smith opened the door to his house and went inside. The house smelled different - there was still the slight whiff of dog in the air but

something was not quite the same. Smith realised what it was. The
house now smelled like a woman lived there. A faint smell of perfume
now lingered. He walked through to the kitchen and switched on the
kettle. Theakston ambled in from the living room and nudged his leg.
The dog ran to the back door to be let out.

"Morning, boy," Smith said. "I'm back for a day but I have to go away
again tomorrow. What's living with Whitton like?"

He noticed that the dog had lost a bit of weight since he had been
away.

He was getting fat anyway, Smith thought.

Smith opened the back door and Theakston ran outside. Smith made
some coffee and followed the dog outside to the back garden. He sat
on the bench and lit a cigarette. Theakston walked up and flopped at
his feet. For the first time in days, Smith felt himself start to relax. He
threw his cigarette butt over the fence into his neighbour's garden and
lit another one. He looked around the garden. He was sure the grass
had grown in the four days he had been away.

Everything's changing around me, he thought.

"Morning," Whitton appeared in the doorway.

Smith hadn't heard her come in the house.

"Are you finally back?" Whitton said. "I was getting worried when you
didn't phone."

"Sort of," Smith stood up and hugged her.

He felt her arms stiffen in his embrace.

"I ran out of milk," Whitton said. "And Theakston doesn't have much
dog food left. What's going on?"

"Are you off today?"

"Only a few hours this morning. There's not much happening at work but Smyth has got us all in this stupid new training course he's come up with."
"Let me guess," Smith said.
"Race relations," they said in unison.
They both started to laugh.
"I missed you," Smith said. "I tried to get away but something's going on and it's bugging the hell out of me. I'll make us some more coffee and I'll tell you everything."

CHAPTER THIRTY SIX

Smith told Whitton everything that had happened since he had set foot in Scarpdale - Sophie Phoenix's murder, the apparent suicide of Lewis Van Camp, the mysterious secret in The Hamptons. He even told her about Johnny Grouse and the enigmatic Jethro and his toad like dog. He finished off with the information Grant Webber had given him about Lewis and Sophie being brother and sister.
"Only you could stumble upon something like this in the middle of Yorkshire," Whitton said. "It sounds more like something from a bad American soap opera."
"I know, I'm still having a hard time taking it all in."
"What do you think? What does the great detective Smith's gut think?"
"New York," Smith said. "Somehow, all of this started in New York last year. I have to go to New York and bring back some answers. I'm sorry, I don't want to go but, you know me, I can't just leave it. I can't just forget about the whole thing. I've tried."
"I know, and I wouldn't expect anything else from you. That just wouldn't be you. When are you thinking of leaving?"
"As soon as possible, I'm sorry."
"I need to get ready for work," Whitton said.
"Race relations? What a bunch of crap. I'm glad I'm still on leave."
"Oh no," Whitton said. "You're not getting away with it that easily. Your time is coming. Nobody is immune - Smyth is adamant. Chalmers is spitting fire about it."
"I can imagine," Smith laughed.
"You look well," Whitton said. "Your face has some colour in it."
"You look pale," Smith kissed her on the lips. "I think you might be coming down with something. You should phone in sick."

"No chance," Whitton broke the embrace. "I've never phoned in sick before and I'm not going to start now. I'm sure you could do with a few hours rest after everything that has happened."

"I can't," Smith suddenly remembered he needed to speak with the hikers who had found Sophie Phoenix's body.

"I'm going to have a shower, and then it's the joys of police/immigrant relations for the rest of the day."

One of the hikers was out of town for the weekend but the other one had agreed to meet Smith at his place of work at lunchtime. Smith parked his car in the short stay car park next to the main shopping centre and got out. The hiker, a forty eight year old man by the name of Henry Joule ran an old book store just off the main tourist drag. Smith pushed past a clinically obese man who smelled like engine oil and made his way inside the shop. A thin, balding man wearing spectacles looked up from the book he was reading and stood up.

"Afternoon," he said. "What can I do for you?"

"I'm looking for Henry Joule," Smith said. "We spoke on the phone. DS Smith."

Joule frowned.

"DS Smith? Sorry, but you look nothing like your voice."

"Thanks, is there somewhere we can talk in private?"

"Sorry, it was the Aussie accent that threw me. You've lost a lot of it but you'll never lose it all. I was expecting someone more like the Crocodile Dundee type. Sorry, we can talk in my office."

He led Smith through to a tiny room that served as an office. Piles of books were stacked on the floor.

"Sorry," Joule said. "I haven't got round to putting these on our system yet. It's probably a waste of time anyway. I don't know how much longer we can survive. Nobody seems to have time for old books anymore. It's all these Kindles and e-reader things these days. I hate them - you can't beat the feel of a real book in your hands. Sorry, I'm rambling. Would you like some coffee?"

"No thanks," Smith wanted to get away from this apologetic man as quickly as possible. "You were up by Whooton Tarn on Tuesday morning?"

"That's right," Joule said. "Billy and I had set off early."

"Billy Laing?"

"That's right. We've been hiking buddies for years. Nothing serious. Gentle strolls really although we've been thinking of maybe tackling Ben Nevis later this year. It's not Everest but it's quite a challenging climb."

"What time did you come across the young woman?"

"Seven, zero, four," Joule said with a smile on his face. "Four minutes past seven. I like to look at my watch whenever I can."

"I see, and she was just lying by the lake?"

"Tarn," Joule said, "sorry, it's a common mistake but there is quite a difference between a tarn and a lake. Sorry, she was just lying on her back a few metres from the water's edge."

"Did you see anybody else around that morning?"

"Not by the tarn," Joule said, "but we'd almost reached the path that leads to it when a huge man barged past us in the opposite direction."

"What did he look like?" Smith said.

"Huge," Joule said, "like I said. I'm not one to exaggerate but he must have been seven feet tall. And big with it."

Johnny Grouse, Smith thought.

"And did you tell the police in Skipton all this?" He said.

"Of course," Joule said, "we told them everything I've told you. They seemed to have other things on their minds though. We were out of the station in nineteen minutes."

"That figures," Smith thought out loud.

"Sorry?"

"Nothing," Smith said, "thanks for your time. I'll let you get back to your books."

CHAPTER THIRTY SEVEN

Smith emerged into the sunshine and waited until his eyes had adjusted to the glare. The interior of the bookstore had been very dark. He took out his phone and dialed PC Fielding's number. He hoped Fielding was in an area covered by the cell phone masts.
"Fielding," Smith was in luck.
"Can you talk?"
"Hold on."
Smith could hear the crunch of gravel as Fielding walked.
"OK," Fielding said. "What's going on?"
"Do you remember the hikers who found Sophie Phoenix's body?"
"I didn't talk to them myself. Wilkie interviewed them."
"I've just spoken to one of them. Did Wilkie mention anything about Johnny Grouse being seen near the tarn the same morning Sophie's body was found?"
"No," Fielding said straight away.
"One of the hikers claims he saw a huge man shuffling along the road by the path to the tarn the day they found the body. He says he told Wilkie as much. It can only be Johnny Grouse."
"Why would Wilkie keep that to himself?"
"I don't know," Smith said. "Was Grouse ever interviewed in connection with Sophie's murder?"
"Not as far as I'm aware. What's going on here?"
"I don't know, but I don't like it one little bit."
"Do you want me to have a word with Johnny Grouse?"
"You're learning," Smith said. "But be careful. Wilkie mustn't find out you've spoken to him and don't let Grouse know what it's all about."
"The man's a total retard."

"Be that as it may, you have to know how to handle him to get him to talk."

"I think I know what you mean," Fielding said. "I'll just ask him about Whooton Tarn and see what crops up."

"Good," Smith said, "let me know what you find out."

"What about you? Are you back in York for good?"

"No, there's a flight to New York out of Manchester tomorrow at ten thirty. I've been putting it off but it can't wait any longer."

"Good luck," Fielding said. "Do you want me to let Mr Phoenix know what's going on?"

"No," Smith said rather too quickly. "Not just yet. Let's see what I can dig up over there first."

"The weather's nice in New York at this time of the year."

"I'll be in touch when I get back," Smith said and rang off.

Smith put the phone back in his pocket and looked around. A centipede of Chinese tourists were following a tour guide in a very orderly fashion. Tablets and I-phones had replaced the cumbersome cameras of old and the tourists were busy snapping away at anything that took their interest.

This is the best time of the year in York, Smith thought, late spring. In a month or two's time, York would be overrun with visitors from all over the world; the tourist shops would do a roaring trade and petty crime in the city would increase.

May, Smith thought, is definitely the best time of year to visit York.

Smith got in his car and started the engine. He wasn't sure what he was going to do for the rest of the day. He still had ten days of his leave left - he didn't feel like seeing any of his work colleagues and he didn't relish the thought of lounging around at home by himself until Whitton finished work. He drove out of the car park and turned right.

He followed the road for a few hundred metres and took the bridge over the river. Pleasure barges were already out in force. The river was getting busier and busier every year. He carried on for a while and stopped outside a modern building that seemed totally out of place amongst the older buildings surrounding it.

The new forensics building was a bone of contention amongst the men and women of the York police department. Nobody really knew for sure how the budget to build such an eyesore had been approved. Rumours were rife. Opinions were that some kind of shady underhand deal had occurred but nobody really knew for certain. The whole thing was shrouded in mystery. Smith made his way up to the second floor and approached the reception desk.

"Afternoon," he said to the unfamiliar face manning the desk. "Is Webber in?"

"He is," the woman said. "Who shall I say is looking for him?"

"Don't worry about it," Smith set off down the corridor before the woman had a chance to stop him. "I know the way."

Grant Webber was on his lunch break. For as long as Smith had known him, he had always eaten his lunch at his desk. He was halfway through a chicken sandwich when Smith walked in.

"Webber," Smith said. "How the hell are you?"

Webber swallowed what he had left in his mouth and smiled.

"I was wondering when you'd show up," he said.

Smith was confused.

"Are you sick?"

"On the contrary," Webber looked at his watch. "I've never felt better. In precisely four hours and ten minutes time I'm going to walk away from this building and not set foot in it again until eight o clock Monday morning. Bryony and I are heading to Wales for the weekend.

She's going to show me where she used to go sailing when she was small."

"Was Brownhill ever small?"

"Normally, I would rise to your taunts but today I'm going to take no notice whatsoever. What do you want? Time is ticking."

"I need a favour."

"Of course you do," Webber said. "Shoot."

"The forensics reports for Sophie Phoenix and Lewis Van De Camp. Can you get hold of them?"

"What is it with you," Webber said. "From what I can gather, this business has nothing to do with you. It's way out of your jurisdiction."

"Let me explain something to you, Webber, and I don't mean to talk ill of the dead but do you remember DS Thompson?"

"Of course I remember Thompson. He's only been dead a few months."

DS Alan Thompson had been a career detective sergeant and not a very good one at that. He had succumbed to cancer earlier in the year.

"Well," Smith said. "The sergeant leading the investigation, a sergeant Wilkie, makes Thompson look like a genius. The man's an idiot and I'm sure he's in someone's pocket. I have no choice but to step in."

"The moral high ground," Webber said. "Fair enough. I'll see what I can do."

"I need them today," Smith added.

"I wouldn't expect anything less from you. I'll e-mail them through to you."

"Send them to my home email. I have no intention of going into work today."

"Will there be anything else?"

"Just one more thing," Smith said. "This thing with you and the DI."

"What of it?"

"I hate to admit it, but it seems to be doing both of you the world of good."

"Get out," Webber said.

CHAPTER THIRTY EIGHT

"Twice in one day," Joe said. "She's not getting any better you know."
"I need her advice," Smith said. "Perhaps making her feel useful with be of some benefit."
"She's on a downward slide. I've seen it many times before. You know what to do."
Smith placed his belongings in the tray and walked down the corridor. All the security doors were wide open. A burly woman glared at him as he passed.

Jessica Blakemore was sitting on her bed in her room. She was gazing at a crack in the plaster on the wall. It was the shape of New Zealand.
"Jessica," Smith said. "I'm sorry to bother you again but I really need your help."
She continued to stare intently at the crack in the wall as if she thought if she stared for long enough she could make it disappear. She raised her index finger in the air and drew the outline of the crack in the air.
"Can I sit down?" Smith asked.
He detected a slight movement of her head and sat down on the chair next to the small desk. An unfinished drawing of what appeared to be a dragon with a spear through its eye lay on the desk.
"I wanted to thank you," Smith said. "Your advice has done me the world of good."
Jessica didn't say a word but Smith was sure he detected a subtle movement in her right eye - a spark of interest.

"Following the advice of my learned shrink friend," Smith said. "My two weeks of supposed peace and quiet has panned out something like this."

Jessica turned her head slightly.

"The first night I'm there, I almost get into a fight with one of the rich land owner's kids. The next morning I get woken up by three policemen who want to arrest me for the murder of this rich kid's girlfriend. Are you listening?"

She nodded her head.

Smith smiled.

"The sergeant in charge of the investigation," Smith carried on. "Got his stripes out of a Christmas cracker. Finally, I'm released without charge and ready to get the hell out of there when the father of the dead woman begs me to do some digging of my own."

"An offer DS Jason Smith simply cannot refuse," Jessica said.

"It talks," Smith said. "Right. An offer I can't refuse. I start asking questions and all the answers lead to the boyfriend."

"It's always the husband isn't it? But in this case it's the boyfriend."

"I was certain, but after the young woman's funeral, the boyfriend is found in his car, minus his head. Somebody killed him."

"They tried to make it look like suicide didn't they?" For the first time, Jessica made eye contact. "Boyfriend kills his girlfriend, the grief overcomes him and he can't take it anymore. Case closed."

"Welcome back."

"What else?" Jessica sat up straighter on the bed.

"Forensics will show it was murder," Smith said. "And I think the same person is responsible for both murders. There's something else. We compared their DNA. They were brother and sister. Either they had the same mother or the same father. And the woman was pregnant."

"Pregnant with her half brother's baby," Jessica said, more to herself than anyone else.

"What do you think?"

"I think it's time for my medication. My head is starting to clear - the mist is evaporating."

"Please, Jessica."

"You need to go," she gazed at the crack on the wall again.

Smith realised it was hopeless. He wasn't going to get anything else from Jessica Blakemore today.

Smith unlocked the door to his house and went inside. The smell of Whitton's perfume still lingered in the air. Theakston bounded up to him and then headed for his bowl. Smith filled the bowl full of dog food and turned on the kettle. While he waited for it to boil, he turned on his computer and opened up his emails. Webber hadn't yet sent through the forensics reports.

"Come on, Webber," Smith said out loud.

He made some coffee and took it outside to the back garden. His neighbour was busy lopping the dead heads off his roses.

"I want a word with you," he said.

Smith had lived next door to him for over ten years but he still didn't know the annoying man's name.

"You've been chucking fag ends in my garden again," he said. "I can report you for that."

"I've been away," Smith said. "It must've been the dog. I've been trying to get him to quit for ages but I'm afraid I'm fighting a losing battle. I'll have a word with him about it."

He took out his cigarettes and lit one. Right on cue, Theakston bounded out and sat at Smith's feet.

"No," Smith said to the dog. "It's time you quit."

The neighbour looked at Smith as if he were a serial killer and marched inside his house.

"Bloody arsehole, "Smith inhaled deeply and breathed out a cloud of smoke.

People are suffering all around the world, he thought, and this idiot it making a fuss about a few cigarette butts.

Smith went back inside and checked his emails. The reports from Webber were busy coming through. When they had been delivered, Smith opened the first one up. There was a short message from Webber informing him that this was the very last time he would be sticking his neck out for him.

It won't be the last time, Smith smiled to himself.

He opened up the forensics report for Lewis Van Camp. The time of death had been between ten and ten thirty in the morning. Cause of death was obvious. Smith scrolled down the screen. The shotgun had been fired only once. There was still one cartridge in the chamber. The gun was registered to Van Camp. Towards the end of the report, Smith found what he was looking for. Lewis Van Camp hadn't fired the weapon himself. There was no sign of any cartridge discharge residue on his hands. Also, measurements had been taken and the results showed that it would have been physically impossible for Lewis Van Camp to have pulled the trigger while the barrel was pointed at his head - the barrel was simply too long. Lewis Van Camp was murdered.

Smith carried on reading. There had been no fingerprints other than Van Camp's found inside or outside the vehicle. The tyre tracks around the car were from the Range Rover only. The passenger side window had been shattered and the driver's window was open. There was no sign of a struggle - Van Camp had no defensive wounds on his body.

"You know who killed you," Smith said out loud. "You know them very well. You'd arranged to meet someone up there on Maggie's Moor before the funeral and whoever it was blew your brains out."

Smith went to the kitchen and took a beer out of the fridge. He opened it and sat in front of the computer again.

Lewis Van Camp had every intention of going to Sophie's funeral, he thought, Johnny Grouse had said he was wearing a smart suit. I doubt he was in the habit of carrying his shotgun around with him which means whoever killed him somehow managed to get hold of the gun. Smith took a long swig from the beer bottle and opened up the forensics report for Sophie Phoenix. He wasn't expecting anything different from the report Jimmy Phoenix had pushed under his door in Scarpdale and as he read on it appeared to be an identical report. She had drowned - water was found in her lungs. Her blood, alcohol level was very high and the time of death was thought to be around three in the morning.

"Shit," Smith said. "I'm an idiot."

Johnny Grouse was seen close to the tarn at around seven, he thought, if Sophie Phoenix was killed around three, why did Grouse wait around for a further four hours after he killed her?

Sophie's body had been found on the shore but the cause of death was drowning.

Johnny Grouse didn't kill her, Smith thought, Johnny Grouse moved her body out of the water much later.

CHAPTER THIRTY NINE

The Hog's Head was quite busy when Smith and Whitton went inside. Smith had decided to take Whitton out for a meal before he flew off to New York the next day. Marge, the landlady beamed at them when they walked up to the bar.
"Where have you two been hiding?" She said. "I haven't seen you in ages."
"Sorry, Marge," Smith said. "It's been a bit busy recently."
"Well it's nice to see you're still together," Marge said. "Drink?"
"Two pints of Theakstons please."
"And a couple of pies?"
"That would be great, Marge," Whitton said.
"We'll be over there," Smith pointed to one of only a few free tables left in the place.

"What have I missed?" Smith said to Whitton when they sat down. "Anything exciting happening at the moment?"
"You won't believe old Smyth," Whitton said. "Today we had to sit through three hours of the proper procedures while dealing with illegal immigrants. If you robbed a house, you'd be arrested, interviewed and charged but let one of these illegals be up for burglary and we have to be careful not to upset them. This country's gone soft."
Marge arrived with the drinks.
"Pies'll be about forty five minutes I'm afraid, "she said. "We're a bit rushed off our feet at the moment."
"No problem, Marge," Smith said. "We'll just have a few drinks in the meantime."

"Bridge's new girlfriend dumped him," Whitton said. "But he's already got his eye on somebody else."

"That guy never ceases to amaze me. How's Chalmers doing?"
"Regretting the day he agreed to the DCI job. Smyth's trying to persuade him to take up golf."
Smith started to laugh.
"Can you imagine it? Chalmers hitting a little ball around a golf course? He'd smash every window in the clubhouse."
"How long are you going to be in New York for?" Whitton's tone turned serious.
"I'm not sure. I don't even know where to start looking once I get there. New York's a big place."
"Do you want me to come with you?"
"I don't think that would be a good idea," Smith leaned over and kissed her on the neck. "You'd be too much of a distraction."

They sat in silence for a while. Smith looked around the room. He realised he didn't recognise anybody in the pub.
"Thanks for looking after Theakston," Smith said eventually. "He really likes you."
"I like him too. Do you still think we're doing the right thing?"
"What do you mean?"
"I don't know. I can't help wondering whether we'll still be doing stuff like this in a year's time. Where are we going with this thing?"
"We'll be here doing this in ten years time," Smith said. "These past few months have been crazy - it won't always be like this. It'll get back to normal after this horsemen thing."
"Will it?" Whitton looked him in the eyes. "How can you be so sure?"
"It will."
The food arrived and they ate without saying a word. Whitton left half of her pie untouched.
"What's wrong?" Smith said. "You normally finish before me."

"I'm just not that hungry. I haven't had an appetite for a few days now. It must be the stress from that race relations thing at work."
"We can go home if you want. We can just curl up in front of the TV and do what any other normal middle aged couples do on a Friday night."
"Middle aged?" Whitton slapped him on the shoulder. "You're the one that's knocking on for thirty."

Smith took two beers out of the fridge and took them through to the living room. 'The girl with the dragon tattoo' was showing on television and Whitton was watching it intently.
"I love this film," she said.
"I don't get it," Smith handed her a beer. "Some Swedish journo hooks up with a tattooed freak and together they save the day. It's not very realistic is it?"
"It's not supposed to be realistic," Whitton sipped the beer slowly. "It's what's known as escapism."
"Whatever you say. Give me 'The life of Brian' any day."

Smith's phone started to ring in the kitchen.
"I'll leave you to your escapism," he said but Whitton was so engrossed in the film, she didn't hear him.
Smith answered the phone.
"Sir," it was PC Fielding. "Sorry to bother you so late but I thought you'd like to know. I had a little chat with the village idiot."
"Johnny Grouse?" Smith said. "And?"
"He was by Whooton Tarn the morning Sophie Phoenix was killed sir," PC Fielding said. "It took me a while but I managed to get him to admit what he did."
"What did he do?"

"He says he saw Sophie Phoenix lying in the water, and something made him drag her out. He said she shouldn't have been lying in the tarn like that so he picked her up and carried her to the shore. He could be lying."

"He's not lying. That's exactly what I thought. Thanks, Fielding."

Smith rang off and took another beer out of the fridge. He went back to the living room. Whitton was now so engrossed in her escapism, she had dozed off and was now snoring quietly.

CHAPTER FORTY

Smith sat in the departure lounge and read the message on his phone for the fifth time. It was from Whitton.
'Sorry for fading on you so early last night,' it read. 'Come back soon. I love you.'
Smith put the phone in his pocket and smiled. He decided he would try and spend as little time as possible in New York and get back to his life in York. An announcement came over the loudspeaker informing him that the British Airways flight to New York was going to be delayed - they had encountered some technical problems and the repairs were likely to take at least two hours.
"Great," Smith said. "Another two hours in this dreary place."
"It happens all the time," a familiar voice was heard behind him.
Smith turned round. It was Charlotte Phoenix.
"Once," she said. "We were told we'd have to wait two days to catch our flight from New York. It was snowing so badly, the planes couldn't take off. We ended up driving down to Miami in the end - it was quicker."
"What are you doing here?"
"Nice to see you too. I'm here to help you."
"Help me?"
"What do you know about New York? In case you've forgotten, it's a rather large place."
"I'll be fine," Smith said. "I don't need any help. How did you even know I was here?"
"PC Fielding," Charlotte sat down next to him.
She smelled of jasmine.

"Then PC Fielding is in for a bollocking when I see him next," Smith said. "I really don't need any help."
"Just hear me out. From what I gather, you're going to try and find out what happened last summer in The Hamptons. How are you planning on doing it? Are you going to just ask some stranger why the Van Camps ran back to England in a hurry? You'll meet with silence everywhere you turn."
Smith thought hard. Charlotte was right. He didn't even know where to start digging.
"What is it you're suggesting?" He said.
"I know a lot of people on that side of the pond. Influential people. People who can give you answers."
"What would you want to help me?"
"In case you'd forgotten, my sister was murdered a few days ago. I want to find out who's behind this as much as you do."
"Does your father know you're here?"
"Dad?" Charlotte said. "God, no. He'd be furious if he found out. He thinks I'm spending a few days in London with some friends."
"Good, let's keep it that way. I just hope that big mouthed PC can keep his trap shut."
"You don't have to worry about that," Charlotte said. "I can be very persuasive. He promised not to say a word."

The flight took off two hours later and Smith found himself squeezing the arms on the chairs on either side of him as hard as he could as the plane left the tarmac of Manchester airport behind.
"You don't like flying do you?" Charlotte asked him as they reached cruising altitude over the Irish Sea.
"Is it that obvious? It's just not natural. If we were meant to fly, we'd be born with wings."

"Your knuckles are white," Charlotte said. "You can let go of the arm rests now."

"I need a drink, it's past midday."

"It's half seven in the morning in New York," Charlotte said. "But then again, it is supposed to be the city that never sleeps. I'll try and flag down one of the semi-conscious flight attendants. I'd forgotten how tedious it was in peasant class."

Three hours and four beers later, Smith felt slightly more relaxed. The constant drone of the engines was making him feel drowsy. His head kept lurching forward as he drifted in and out of sleep. Charlotte Phoenix was not in her seat - she had spotted someone she knew a few rows in front of them and was now engaged deep in conversation. Smith looked out of the small window. The sky above the clouds was a dazzling blue colour. He leaned against the window and drifted off to sleep.

CHAPTER FORTY ONE

Smith opened his eyes and immediately felt wide awake. Charlotte Phoenix was asleep next to him. Somehow, in mid sleep, she had managed to rest her head on Smith's shoulder and now it was a dead weight. Smith looked at his watch. It was seven thirty - two thirty, New York time. He knew they would be landing in an hour or so. Charlotte started to stir next to him. She was mumbling something in her sleep. Smith couldn't make out the words but he was sure one of them was 'Sebastian'.

"Would you like anything, sir?" A short fat flight attendant asked Smith. "Only, we'll be landing in New York shortly. We've had a good tail wind the whole way."

"No thanks," Smith said.

He watched as the squat woman shuffled down the aisle. There was barely enough room to accommodate her hefty hips.

"I've just had the weirdest dream."

Charlotte was awake.

"I know it was weird," she rubbed her eyes. "But now I can't remember any of it."

"You're lucky," Smith said. "Sleep well?"

"It helps with the time difference. You've just gained an extra five hours of your life. You'll lose it on the return trip of course but right now, it's two thirty on a Saturday afternoon in the greatest city on earth and I intend to be awake for it."

Smith shuddered. He wasn't sure he was ready for the greatest city on earth.

Two hours later they were in a taxi heading east on the Montauk highway towards the eastern tip of Long Island. The Atlantic Ocean stretched out before them on the right hand side. The driver of the taxi was driving far too quickly for Smith's liking.

"I paid him a bit extra," Charlotte said. "To get us there before the fun starts. East Hampton on a Saturday night is something you have to see to believe."

The road was busy. Smith was amazed at the driver weaved in and out of the traffic at ninety miles an hour.

"You should see the highway in July and August," Charlotte said. "It can sometimes take six or seven hours to get here from the city."

"Where are we going?"

"An old friend of mine is out of the country for a while. We can stay at her place for as long as we like. Don't worry, I won't let anything happen to you."

The driver was forced to slow down as the landscape around they became more built up.

"It's not far now," Charlotte said.

Smith looked out of the window and saw a sign for Wainscott. They drove past golf estates and huge beach front properties and Smith gazed in awe at the mere size of these mansions. Most of them appeared to have been built and, as though the owner didn't think them grand enough, they had been extended and now new wings spread out in all directions.

"You're looking at some of the most expensive real estate in the US," Charlotte said. "If not in the world. They say that if you own property in The Hamptons you've made it."

"Who owns all these places?"

"Things have changed," Charlotte said. "A few years ago this was all old money. Generations of it but after the crash, billions of dollars were wiped off the stock exchange, almost overnight. A lot of people lost everything. There are still a few of the old crowd around but a lot of what you see here now belongs to foreigners - Russian oil billionaires, Arab Sheiks and, most recently, Chinese tycoons. New money."

Smith suddenly realised he was out of his depth. He had encountered wealth before but never on the scale of The Hamptons.

"This is Phoebe's house here," Charlotte said.

The driver slowed down and turned onto a driveway that had to be over three hundred metres long. The road meandered between landscaped gardens and elaborate water features. They stopped outside a huge double storey house that had to contain at least thirty rooms.

Smith got out of the car and looked around. The late afternoon sun was beating down on the lawns. A huge swimming pool sparkled in the sunlight.

"Let's go inside," Charlotte said. "I want to freshen up a bit. There's a massive party up at Sagaponack tonight. At the Hartford's place. Sophie and I spent a lot of time up there last summer.

She seemed lost in thought for a moment.

"I miss her you know," she said. "Sophie. We didn't always get on but I suppose sisters don't. I still miss her though."

"We'll get to the bottom of all this," Smith didn't know what else to say.

"I'm going to have a shower. There's always beer in the fridge in the bar. It's American but it's not that bad."

Smith watched her as she walked up the wide wooden staircase. She walked slowly - head bent as if she bore the weight of the world on her shoulders.

All the money in the world, he thought, and it still can't make the pain go away.

Smith walked through the enormous open plan living room and came to the entertainment area. A long marble counter took up one side of the room. Smith had been in smaller pubs in York that the room he stood in now.

Everything in America is totally over the top, he thought.

He found the fridge and took out a Becks. It was not his favourite beer but it would have to do. The bar opened out onto a large patio that looked out onto the Atlantic Ocean in the distance. Smith opened up the sliding doors and went outside. There was a slight offshore breeze and Smith breathed in deeply. He smiled - once upon a time he wouldn't have been able to even look at the Ocean, he would've been thrown into a terrible panic but now his phobia was all but gone.

"It's beautiful isn't it?"

Charlotte emerged from the house. She was wearing a pair of cut off jeans and a black T shirt. Her hair was wrapped in a towel. She was holding a glass of wine in her hand.

"We've got a few hours to kill," she said. "Before the party. Is there anything you feel like doing?"

"This," Smith pointed to the Ocean in the distance. "I could pass a few hours just breathing in the sea air."

Charlotte sat down on a very expensive looking cane chair.

"Everything changed after last summer," she said. "We didn't realise it then but everything changed and now Sophie's dead."

'What is it that happened here last summer?"

"It's all a bit of a blur. Everything seemed to happen at once. I remember it was a scorching summer. July and August were hotter than anything I've ever experienced before. We spent a lot of time down on the beach. Me, Sophie, Lewis and Sebastian. Lewis and Sophie were inseparable."

"And you and Sebastian?"

"We were just friends. Sebastian was more like a brother to me than anything else. The days went by in a whirl. Days on the beach followed by nights outside, drinking and dancing. Then one night, Lewis and Sebastian just didn't show up. We thought nothing of it until they didn't show up for the next few nights. They seemed to just vanish into thin air. It turns out they had left The Hamptons in a hurry and we later found out that Lewis and Basil had returned to England."

"What about Sebastian?"

"That's the strangest thing," Charlotte said. "He didn't go with them. Nobody really knows what happened to him. Some say he went north to Canada and others reckon he's in Mexico somewhere but I know one thing - nobody has seen him since."

"This is all very odd," Smith said. "What about the mother? What happened to her?"

"Veronica? She was found walking barefoot down the highway one night. She'd lost her mind completely. She's in some nut house somewhere upstate."

"There was a sister too wasn't there?"

"Matilda, she's much younger than us. I heard she was living with her Grandmother in Vermont somewhere."

"And nobody knows what happened that ripped the whole family apart like that?"

"I think Dad knows what it's all about," Charlotte finished the wine in her glass. "But he never wants to talk about it."

"Are you sure? Jimmy told me he didn't know anything about last summer."

"He knows. He was here and he knows. Jimmy Phoenix didn't get to where he is today by being honest with people. I need another drink."

CHAPTER FORTY TWO

The party at the Hartford's place in Sagaponack was already in full swing when Smith and Charlotte arrived. It was a windless, balmy May evening and an enormous marquee had been erected on the lawn outside the house. Smith took a deep breath and followed Charlotte along the path towards the crowd of people. A string quartet were playing an unusual version of a song Smith recognised next to a huge table laden with bottles of alcohol. It was a song that wasn't normally played by a string quartet.

"Charlotte," A woman with unnaturally full lips said. "Where have you been hiding my dear?"

She looked Smith up and down as if he were a specimen in a zoo. Smith was wearing an old pair of jeans and a faded Jimi Hendrix T shirt.

"I've been busy with the horses in Yorkshire," Charlotte said. "But I've missed this place."

She looked at Smith.

"Let's get a drink," she said.

"What the hell was that?" Smith said. "What's the story with those lips?"

"That was Mary Flanders. She's famous for being famous if that makes any sense and those lips are an example of what happens when Botox goes horribly wrong."

"I feel a bit underdressed. I don't think I actually own any smart clothes."

"Don't worry about it. I doubt anyone will even notice - they'll just think you're some eccentric billionaire and I forgot to say anything earlier but it may be better not to mention anything about you being a police detective."

"I wasn't planning on it," Smith said. "Does anybody drink beer around here?"

He scanned the table. There were plenty of bottles of wine, whisky, vodka, gin and brandy but Smith could not find any beer.

"People don't drink beer at these things. Beer is seen as vulgar in the evening."

"I brought a crate with me," a man roughly the same age as Smith was standing listening in. "You're welcome to share. You're Australian aren't you?"

"You've got me there," Smith said.

"Brandon," the man held out his hand. "Brandon Leach."

He nodded to Charlotte. Smith got the instant impression they knew each other but they weren't exactly close friends.

"Jason Smith," he shook Leach's hand. "I'll take you up on the offer of beer. I can't handle wine or spirits."

"Will you be OK?" Charlotte said to Smith. "I'd quite like to catch up with some old friends."

"I'll introduce you to some of the guys," Leach gestured with his arm for Smith to follow him. "And I'll organise that beer."

Smith followed Leach past the string quartet. They were now performing their own rendition of Metallica's 'Enter Sandman'.

"Pretty cool hey?" Leach noticed Smith was very interested in the music. "We found them in the city. They're going to be famous - they're all over You Tube."

He led Smith to a table next to a swimming pool that hadn't yet been filled with water. Three other men of roughly the same age stood up when they approached.

"What do we have here?" The shortest of them looked at Smith. "Born again hippy?"

Smith was confused.

"The T-shirt," the man said. "Hendrix was overrated if you ask me. If he hadn't died young nobody would have even bothered about him."

Smith was in no mood for an argument.

"Take a seat," Leach said. "And pay no attention to Thomas. He's a Philistine. Beer?"

"Thanks," Smith said.

Leach leaned back and took a Budweiser from a huge tin bath tub filled with ice. He flipped the top off and handed the bottle to Smith.

"How do you know the Hartfords?" The man named Thomas asked Smith.

"I don't," Smith said. "I'm here with Charlotte Phoenix."

"You don't look like one of her horsemen."

"Looks can be deceiving," Smith finished the beer in one go.

It tasted terrible - more like beer flavoured water but he figured he needed to be at least a bit tipsy to be able to tolerate the likes of Thomas.

"Terrible thing about Sophie," Leach handed Smith another beer. "I heard that she drowned."

"She was murdered," Smith said without thinking.

This information caught the attention of one of the other men at the table - a blond man with a tiny button nose.

"Murdered? Who would want to kill Sophie?"

"Nobody knows," Smith said. "Do you all live around here?"

Button nose started to laugh.

"Sorry," he said. "Nobody lives around here. Not permanently anyway. No, we have a modest summer house further down the coast. Closer to the city."

"The cheap seats," Thomas educated him. "The further east you get, the more expensive the real estate."

"Do you know the Van Camps?" Smith addressed the whole table. Nobody said a word. Smith could hear the string quartet in the distance. They were now playing some traditional classical piece.

"It's just that Lewis was killed too," Smith said. "He was on his way to Sophie's funeral but he never made it."

"Lewis was a real asshole," Thomas said. "A thug. It was bound to happen eventually. How did he die?"

"He had his head blown off with a shotgun," Smith said.

"Excuse me," the blond man stood up.

He looked like he was going to be sick. He rushed inside the house.

"Daniel is a bit of a wet," Leach said. "His folks have babied him his whole life. He's probably puking right now. What really brings you to The Hamptons?"

"Charlotte invited me," Smith lied.

"Are you and Miss Phoenix an item?" Thomas said. "You know, like a couple."

"No," Smith said. "I'm friends with her father."

"The great Jimmy Phoenix? He's a real bastard if you ask me."

"Thomas doesn't like anybody," Leach said. "I think he has some kind of inferiority complex."

Two hours later, Smith had ingratiated himself enough with this Hamptons clique to be invited for lunch on Brandon Leach's father's boat the next day. Smith had declined at first - he was not overly fond of boats but Leach had been very insistent. The blond man with the button nose had recovered from his bout of nausea and Thomas had drunk too much and was now becoming maudlin and musing over failed relationships. The fourth man at the table had still not uttered a word since Smith had joined them. Smith stared at him. His eyes were glued to a lap top computer on the table in front of him.

"I don't mean to be rude," the man said as though he could feel Smith's eyes on him. "But I have until tomorrow afternoon to submit the final draft of my book and it's far from ready. I'm not sure if I'm going to be able to make the deadline."

"You're a writer?" Smith said.

"Poetry," Thomas scoffed. "It's not proper writing. It's more romantic nonsense than anything else."

"Romance is only nonsense to those who know nothing of romance," the man smiled at Smith.

"My name is John," the poet said to Smith. "John Dunn, but I write under another name. Emilio Wyatt. John Dunn is a bit close to John Donne don't you think?"

"I don't think I've ever read any poetry," Smith admitted. "I don't seem to get the time to read anything anymore."

Their conversation was cut short by the sound of an ear-splitting scream. A crowd of people had run up to the edge of the swimming pool.

"Someone's fallen in again," Thomas said. "I don't know why old Hartford doesn't just fill it up. Somebody's going to sue his ass one day."

Luckily, the pool wasn't very deep and the clumsy woman who had slipped in was now being helped up the stairs by two men. She seemed to be alright.

Smith stood up.

"I'm going to look for Charlotte," he said. "Thanks for the beer."

"Don't forget the boat trip tomorrow," Leach said. "Charlotte knows where it is. Bring your swimming costume."

Charlotte was talking to the cello player from the string quartet. They appeared to have packed up for the night.

"Having fun?" Charlotte said to Smith. "You were gone for ages."

"I couldn't get away, those friends of yours are very strange."

"They're no friends of mine. They're just always around that's all."

"Well, Leach has invited us both to lunch on his dad's boat tomorrow. I couldn't get out of it."

"I've got plans," Charlotte said.

"What plans?"

"Secret plans," she smiled at him. "Do you want to get out of here? I'm tired - it's six in the morning in England right now."

CHAPTER FORTY THREE

Smith opened his eyes and for a moment he didn't know where he was. The curtains in the guest room were so thick, he wasn't sure if it was day or night. He got out of bed and opened them. The sunlight poured in and Smith flinched. He looked out of the window at the Atlantic Ocean in the distance. From where he stood, the blue ocean looked calm and flat. There wasn't a puff of wind in the air. He put on a clean T-shirt and a pair of old shorts and went downstairs. Charlotte Phoenix was nowhere to be seen. Smith spotted a note stuck to the huge double door fridge in the breakfast room.
'Gone to do a bit of digging myself. Enjoy the boat trip. Charlotte. X.'
Smith was on his own. He rummaged around until he found some coffee and took it outside onto the patio.

The Hamptons was eerily quiet on a Sunday morning. The roads were deserted. Smith lit a cigarette and looked down onto the beach below. He spotted some tiny figures in the sand. They looked like ants, scurrying back and forth.
What am I doing here? Smith thought.
From what Charlotte had told him, the only person who seemed to know what happened last summer was Jimmy Phoenix and he was back in Yorkshire. Smith tried to think hard about everything that had happened.
Sophie Phoenix is killed, he thought, she was pregnant with Lewis Van Camp's baby. Just before her funeral, Van Camp is also killed. Van Camp was her half brother. Did Jimmy Phoenix know Sophie wasn't his daughter? Did he know she was pregnant? Who else knew about it?

Smith's thought process was interrupted by the sound of a car door slamming. He looked down and saw a black beach buggy parked outside the house. Brandon Leach was walking up the stairs towards the patio.

"Morning," Leach said. "It's a beautiful day for a cruise. Charlotte left me a message this morning. She asked me to come and pick you up."

"Where's the boat?" Smith couldn't recall seeing any marinas or yacht clubs when they had driven from the city.

"It's a few miles further up the coast. Are you ready?"

Fifteen minutes later, they were on the Montauk Highway heading east. The mansions seemed to get grander the further up the coast they went. Leach was driving very slowly.

"It's something else isn't it?" he said. "It's just a shame that most of this now belongs to foreigners. Uncle Sam has gone crazy."

"Where's the Van Camp place?" Smith asked.

"We passed it a few miles back. They don't own it anymore. Some trailer trash from Buffalo or somewhere snapped it up. Lottery money I think. They won't last long, you mark my words. Why are you so interested in the Van Camps?"

"I'm just curious. I wonder what happened last summer that could have been so bad they had to leave everything behind in such a hurry."

"I reckon there's only two people who really know for sure. Apart from Basil Van Camp himself - Sebastian, but he's disappeared off the face of the earth and Van Camp's wife Veronica. She doesn't even know who she is anymore. We're almost there."

He slowed down and turned right onto a road that led to the Ocean. Smith spotted a huge sign for the Montauk Yacht Club.

"My father has had boats here for over forty years," Leach bragged. "He's just bought a real beauty - a sixty four footer imported from Sweden."

He drove through the security gate, waved to the guard manning the boom and carried on towards the water. Smith was in awe. Masts of all sizes rose high into the air. As they got closer to the boats he could see flags from all corners of the earth hoisted up the back stays.
"This is a popular stop off point for the round the world guys," Leach said proudly. "En-route to The Caribbean or onto Panama and into the Pacific."
Who would want to travel round the world on a boat? Smith thought. The mere idea repulsed him.

Leach stopped the beach buggy on a grassy verge overlooking the walk on moorings.
"We'll have to walk from here," he said. "My father's yacht is at the far end of the walk on jetties. It's quite a trek but it makes docking much easier."
They walked along a wide, wooden gangway. Sailing vessels and motor boats of all shapes and sizes bobbed up and down on either side. Names such as 'Free Spirit' and 'Wandering Albatross' were painted on the hulls. Smith couldn't help but notice that a lot of the boats had obviously not been used in a very long time. Green algae seemed to thrive below the waterlines of most of them - bird droppings were everywhere and one boat appeared to be a nesting ground for a flock of gulls.
"It's still quite early in the season," Leach said. "Come late June and most of these boats will have been hauled out, cleaned and ready to go. Then, in early September, those who have the foresight to do so will haul them out again before the hurricane season arrives."

A few people had already gathered by Leach's father's boat at the end of the jetty when they got there. The boat was called 'Dreamer' and she really was a beautiful vessel. The woodwork had been

meticulously maintained. The American flag was raised at the stern. Smith recognised a few of the people from the party the night before. He spotted Thomas straight away. He was wearing a ridiculous captain's hat and he looked like he needed some more sleep - his eyes were puffy and his face was a disturbing, sickly-grey colour. Daniel, the blond man with the button nose was standing next to him. He'd already put on a life jacket. The poet was nowhere to be seen.
He must be fighting against his deadline, Smith thought.

More people started to arrive. Most of them were young women - hangers on, Smith thought, but one man stood out from the rest. He was a short, muscular man in his late forties. His hair was thick and black and he had the rugged good looks of a swashbuckling hero from the movies of the forties and fifties. Smith noticed there was something strange about the expression on his face. He appeared distant - lost in thought.
"Are we all set then?" A young man said to Leach in an accent Smith recognised at once.
It was the unmistakable Sydney nasal whine.
"Forecast is for a steady four to five knots off shore," he said. "That ought to make it easy to cast off but I'm afraid it's dying down to one to two for pretty much the rest of the day. We're not going to be setting sail today. We'll have to use the motor."
"Get on to it then," Leach said.
Smith watched as the young Australian jumped on board, lowered the gang plank and helped everybody onto the boat. Smith and Leach were the last to board. The diesel engine was started and, after a signal from the skipper, two men on the jetty undid the ropes from the cleats fore and aft. There was a click as forward gear was engaged and 'Dreamer' slowly chugged out to sea.

"Who's the captain?" Smith asked Leach when they were well underway.

"Some Australian," Leach said. "We have a different one each summer but this guy seems to know what he's doing."

The yacht was about two miles off the coast when another, smaller boat approached them. It was a thirty foot motor boat with two huge outboard engines on the back. As it moved closer, the sound of giggling girls could be heard. They'd obviously started drinking early. Smith looked closer and realised that Charlotte Phoenix was sitting at the back of the boat. She was holding a glass of champagne in her hand. The Australian skipper put the engine in neutral and allowed the yacht to drift towards the motor boat. He quickly attached fenders to the starboard side and let the motor boat rest against the hull.

"Tie her up," he shouted to Smith just as a rope was thrown from the motor boat, narrowly missing Smith's head.

Smith tied a crude half hitch on the cleat at the stern. His fellow countryman did the same at the bow.

"Morning," a young woman shrieked at Smith.

She was obviously very drunk.

"We seem to have run out of alcohol," she screamed. "Could you please help a boat in distress."

Her friends seemed to find her very amusing. Charlotte Phoenix didn't look impressed.

"Come on board," Leach offered. "We're fully stocked. There's plenty to go around."

Smith found it hard to watch as the three intoxicated ladies made their attempt to board the yacht. One of them lost her footing and if it weren't for the quick reactions of the captain, she would surely have ended up in the ocean.

"They can't handle their drink," Charlotte sat next to Smith with her back to the huge wooden mast. "I suppose we were all young and stupid once."

"Words of wisdom from an old lady," Smith said. "How do you put up with these people?"

"All this is for show. Deep down they're the same as everybody else really. Only much more miserable."

One of the young women was now emptying the contents of her stomach over the side. Her friend was holding her hair as she retched.

"They joys of youth," Smith said. "Who owns the other boat?"

He pointed to the motor boat rafted up next to them.

"William Hartford junior," Charlotte said. "It was a gift for his eighteenth birthday."

"Some birthday present, I think I got a pair of socks for my eighteenth."

"Have you found anything yet?" Charlotte's tone turned serious.

"Nothing - and I don't think I'm going to find anything. Everyone here is so secretive. They don't seem to trust anybody."

"You're dead right there. I suppose it's been drummed into us from an early age. The paranoia - always assuming everybody is out to get their hands on our money."

"Who's the man over there?" Smith pointed to the well built man with the thick black hair.

He had deftly hopped onto the motor boat and was heading down the steps into the cabin. Charlotte looked shocked - she looked like she was going to be sick.

"That was Basil Van Camp," she said. "Lewis Van Camp's father."

CHAPTER FORTY FOUR

"What's Basil Van Camp doing here?" Smith said. "I thought he was in China."

"He was," Brandon Leach was leaning against the safety rails opposite the mast. "He's on his way back for the funeral. Apparently he took the long way round. He had some business to attend to with Hartford senior that couldn't wait."

"I thought he had left The Hamptons for good," Smith said. "I didn't think he was welcome any more."

"Not all of us are animals. Van Camp has done me and my family no harm. When he phoned me this morning and asked if I would take him to Hartford's boat I agreed straight away."

"A business deal in the middle of the ocean?" Smith's detective brain was working overtime. "What's that all about?"

"It is what it is. Van Camp needed to speak with Hartford - most of the people here will be so drunk later they won't even remember he was here. Hartford's guests will return to the yacht club with me and Hartford will drop Van Camp somewhere nobody knows. He's just lost his son. Cut him a bit of slack."

"Fair enough," Smith said although he wasn't convinced.
This wasn't a simple business deal, he thought, something else is going on here. Nobody flies from China to a funeral in England via the Pacific Ocean - no business deal is that important.

The sun was high in the sky and loud screams could be heard from the stern of the yacht. Those bold enough to brave the cold of the Atlantic had stripped off and were taking the plunge off the diving platform at the back.

"Are you going in?" Charlotte asked Smith.

"I don't think so," Smith replied. "I didn't bring my swimming shorts."
"Those'll dry quick enough," Charlotte pointed to Smith's old shorts. "Come on, don't be a chicken."
She took off her T-shirt and shorts and threw them on the deck. She was wearing a one piece bathing suit underneath.
"It's a bit cold, but its fine once you're in."
Smith had no choice but to follow her. He took off his T-shirt and realised how pale his chest was. It hadn't seen the sun in a very long time. He made his way to the stern and watched as Charlotte elegantly dived off the platform. She broke the surface and wiped her eyes.
"Come on in," she shouted up to Smith. "It's not as cold as I thought."
Smith stepped carefully onto the diving platform, held his breath and dived into the water. The cold hit his head straight away - it was like diving into a brick of ice. He swam down and the water got colder. He swam back towards the sunlight, broke the surface and gasped a lungful of air.
"I thought you said it wasn't cold," he said through chattering teeth.
"You weren't supposed to dive to the bottom of the ocean," Charlotte laughed. "Stay on the surface where it's warmest."
Smith lay back and let the ocean's natural buoyancy hold him up. The sun on his face felt very pleasant and he closed his eyes. Charlotte swam over to him and they lay side by side in the water.
"You need more sun," she said. "For an Australian, you're as white as a ghost."
"I live in Yorkshire. We're lucky if the sun comes out three or four times a year."

The sound of powerful engines starting up could be heard and Smith watched as Hartford Junior's boat eased away from the yacht and powered off at full speed towards the shore.

No doubt Basil Van Camp is on board, Smith thought.

"Lunch is served," the Australian skipper shouted from the yacht.

Smith waited until everybody was on board and then climbed up the ladder at the back. The dip in the ocean had stirred his appetite and he was starving. Brandon Leach had spared no expense. The spread of food inside the cabin was enough to feed an army. Smith filled his plate with shrimps, oysters and a selection of meats and breads and went back up on deck. William Hartford Junior's boat was now a mere speck on the horizon. They hadn't gone back to the Montauk Yacht Club, they were heading further east. Smith made a mental note to find out where they had ended up.

"Can you stop being a detective sergeant for one day?" Charlotte whispered in Smith's ear.

She was so close that her lips almost touched his skin. Smith shivered. He could feel goose bumps forming on his arms.

"Sorry," he said. "This food is delicious."

Charlotte handed him a beer.

"There's going to be a huge bonfire on the beach tonight," she said. "There'll be music and plenty of alcohol."

"Doesn't anybody work around here? Tomorrow's Monday. I thought everybody would be wanting to get back to the city."

"Tomorrow's Memorial Day, or Decoration Day as some people still call it. It's a federal holiday. Come on, you can have one day away from detective work. You are on leave aren't you?"

Smith realised she was right - he was officially on leave. Even so, he still felt a pang of guilt nipping away at his stomach. He had promised Whitton he would try and get home as soon as he could and all he'd done since he had stepped off the plane was attend party after party.

"One more party," he took a long swig of the beer. "And then it's back to the real reason I came here. I'm not sure how much more my liver can take."

CHAPTER FORTY FIVE

"Why do you think Basil Van Camp came back to New York?" Smith asked Charlotte.
Brandon Leach had dropped them off and they were now sitting on the patio at Charlotte's friend's house.
"You never know with Basil," Charlotte said. "He's always been a bit of an enigma."
"How long did he have his place in the Hamptons? Before he had to sell it I mean."
"Years. Long before I was born anyway. We've been coming here for as long as I can remember. Before Sophie was born even."
"I don't mean to be personal, but where's your mother now? You never talk about her."
"Your guess is as good as mine," Charlotte shrugged her shoulders. "She left us when I was five years old. Sophie was still a baby then. No, it was just me, Sophie and Dad when I was growing up and we were just fine. I heard her latest hook up was some oil baron from Texas. Good luck to him - it won't last. I love my dad but he's always had crap taste in women."
"What do you think of your father's new wife? Just tell me to shut up if I'm asking too many questions."
"No, I don't mind. Davina? What is there to say about Davina? She's only a few years older than me for God's sake. I don't even know what dad was thinking. I suppose he was lonely but that's all over now isn't it?'
"Just one more question," Smith said. "And then I promise I'll shut up."

"Shoot," Charlotte turned her head so she was looking straight into Smith's eyes.

Smith hadn't noticed before what an unusual shade of blue her eyes were. Rings of emerald green surrounded the pupils.

"Is there any more beer in the fridge? I'm parched."

Charlotte slapped him on the shoulder and burst out laughing. She stood up and kissed him playfully on the forehead.

"Detective," she said. "I could quite easily fall for you. Too bad you're taken."

Smith could see the light from the bonfire long before the taxi had reached the road down to the beach. The driver stopped behind the longest stretch limousine Smith had ever seen.

"We'll make our own way back," Charlotte handed the driver a hundred dollar bill and did not wait for change.

"Remember what we agreed," Charlotte linked arms with Smith. "No more work. At least not until tomorrow"

"I'll try," Smith said.

They made their way along the beach towards the fire. Smith could hear the sound of acoustic guitars playing and people singing.

This isn't too bad, he thought, this is more my kind of thing.

They passed a circle of young women sitting on the sand. Smith could feel their eyes on him as they walked past.

"Bees," Charlotte whispered. "Led by the biggest queen bee of them all. They're so bewitched by her - she can get them to do anything she wants. Even murder."

They stopped next to another group of young women. Smith recognised them as the drunk women who had been on Hartford junior's boat. John Dunn, the poet was talking to one of them - a slightly chubby woman with dyed red hair.

"John," Smith said. "Did you make the deadline?"

"By the skin of my teeth," Dunn said. "And now I'm letting my hair down a bit. It's all in the hands of the Gods now. Would you like a beer?"

"That would be great."

They walked towards the bonfire. Brandon Leach and Thomas were talking to a man Smith didn't know next to a table set up on the beach.

"The Australian," Thomas said. "You survived the cruise on Leach's old tub then?"

"It was fun," Smith said.

Dunn handed him a beer. Smith looked at the stranger. Nobody had bothered to introduce him.

"Sorry," Thomas said. "I'm terribly rude sometimes. This is William Hartford the third. Or is it the fourth? There's been so bloody many of them."

"Call me William," Hartford said.

He made no attempt to offer his hand.

"Jason," Smith said. "Nice to meet you."

"The skinny dipping is due to start in a couple of hours," Thomas said and the tension in the air lifted. "I got my hands on a special night vision camera with one hell of a zoom lens specially for the occasion."

"You're such a pervert," Leach said.

"What? It'll be something to remember the night by."

A couple of hours later, Smith sat in a circle with the musicians. There were four of them - three men playing acoustic guitars and a woman on the bongo drums. A circle of people had gathered around them and the pungent scent of marijuana mingled with the smell of the bonfire.

"You guys are good," Smith said when they had finished their version of Rodriguez's 'Sugar Man'.
"Do you play?" A bald man asked him.
Smith was sure he once saw him playing bass with Joe Bonamassa.
"It's been a while," Smith admitted.
The man handed him his guitar. It was an old Gibson. Smith held it carefully. He knew how valuable it was. He played the opening chords to 'Stairway to heaven' and stopped.
"Just kidding," he said.
The other musicians started to laugh. Smith realised that the classic Led Zeppelin intro was a universal joke amongst musicians.

The man sitting next to Smith started to play the opening bars to 'Shine on you crazy diamond'. It had always been one of Smith's favourite songs. He placed his fingers on the fret board and tried to remember the chords. It soon came back to him and he closed his eyes. The smell of marijuana was getting stronger and before Smith knew what was happening, someone had placed a joint between his lips. He inhaled deeply and resisted the urge to cough.

The song ended and everybody cheered.
"That was bloody brilliant," John Dunn shouted.
Smith handed the guitar back to the bald bass player and stood up. His vision went black for a few seconds and he had to take a deep breath to stop himself from falling over.
"Are you alright?" Charlotte asked him.
Smith didn't recognise her voice. He realised he was quite stoned - whatever was in the joint was very strong.
"Let's go for a walk along the shore," Charlotte suggested. "It'll clear your head a bit."
She took his arm and led him down the beach.

"I haven't smoked that stuff in quite a while," Smith said when they reached the surf. "I'm a bit out of practice."

"You're a dark horse Jason Smith. Top detective and guitar player. Is there anything else you're keeping quiet about?"

"No, that's it. What you see is what you get from now on."

"I see it," Charlotte took a step closer to him.

Smith could smell the champagne on her breath.

"Now it's just a question of how to get it."

She leaned forward and kissed him on the lips. Smith didn't move. She put her hand on the back of his head and moved him closer to her. Smith closed his eyes and kissed her back.

CHAPTER FORTY SIX

Jethro turned off the light in the kitchen and walked through to the room that served at a living room cum bedroom. The two rooms upstairs in the small stone house hadn't been used for a very long time. Jethro slept on a firm mattress on the floor in the middle of the room. During the day, the mattress was stored out of sight behind the three seater sofa. Jethro was about to make up his bed when a car headlight shone through the window. A car had pulled up outside the house. The headlights were switched off and the sound of a car door being slammed could be heard. Jethro stared at the clock on the wall. It was two minutes to midnight.
Who's coming calling at this hour? He thought as the sound of the doorbell was heard in the hallway.
He pushed the mattress back behind the sofa and went to answer the door.
Jimmy Phoenix was standing in the doorway. His face was very red from drink. He was holding a bottle of Laphroig single malt whisky in his hand.
"Mr Phoenix?" Jethro said. "Come in. What's wrong?"
Phoenix stepped inside. Jethro peered outside. There was nobody else around.

Phoenix made himself comfortable on the single armchair in the living room.
"Sorry for troubling you so late at night," he said. "Let's have a drop of this shall we?"
He set the whisky bottle down on the coffee table. Jethro went through to the kitchen and returned with two glasses. Late as it was, he wasn't

going to pass up the offer of free single malt. Phoenix poured two
large measures and handed one of the glasses to Jethro.

"Here's to Sophie," he said.

"To Sophie," Jethro obliged him.

"Jethro," Phoenix's face turned serious. "How long have we known
each other?"

"I don't know, Mr Phoenix. My memory isn't what it used to be."
"Nonsense, there's nothing wrong with your memory. It was just
before Sophie was born. Janie had a rough pregnancy. They always
say the second one is easier but Janie had a hard time with Sophie."
"I don't mean to sound rude," Jethro said. "But what are you doing
here in the middle of the night?

"I had to talk to someone. I suddenly realised something. I have no
friends - my first wife left me, my second wife is more than likely
going to spend the next few years in jail, my youngest daughter is
dead and Charlotte... God knows where Charlotte is at the moment.
She told me she was going to London to visit some friends but when I
spoke to them, they said they hadn't seen her in months. Drink up."
Jethro finished what was left in his glass and handed it to Phoenix.
"You're the only one I can talk to Jethro," Phoenix refilled both glasses.
"What about Keith?" Jethro asked.

"Keith is loyal, I'm not denying that but he has far too many morals.
I'm not saying that it's not admirable but that's why I can't talk to
him."

"This is about the Van Camps," Jethro stood up and went over to an
oak sideboard.

He opened it, took out an envelope and placed it on the table in front
of Phoenix. Phoenix slid the photograph out and gasped. It was a

photograph taken just after Sophie had been born. Phoenix was
holding her in his arms. His wife Janie was not in the photograph.
She must have taken it, Phoenix thought.

Charlotte was standing by his legs. Basil Van Camp was also in the
photograph. Lewis and Sebastian were standing on either side of him.
"We were inseparable back then," Phoenix put the photo down and
stood up. "But I knew of course. I knew as soon as I set eyes on
Sophie. I'd best be off. You've been a good friend over the years
Jethro."

He took out a thick brown envelope and placed it over the photograph.
"Thank you," he said. "I'll see myself out."

CHAPTER FORTY SEVEN

Smith was finding it impossible to sleep. This kiss with Charlotte Phoenix was troubling him. He was trying to convince himself that it was nothing - a spur of the moment drunken mistake, but it was still eating away at his conscience.
How could I have been so stupid? He thought, I'm an idiot, I'm supposed to be working on a murder investigation and all I've done since I got here is drink and enjoy myself.
After the kiss, Smith had turned round and made his way back along the beach without saying a word to anybody. He'd managed to find his way back to Charlotte's friend's house, and had gone straight to bed.

Now, Smith lay wide awake, staring at the thick curtains as they moved back and forth. The wind had picked up in the night and they were being blown by the breeze coming in through the open window.
What am I actually doing here? he thought. Nobody wants me here - nobody wants to talk about what happened here last summer. Nobody wants a stranger coming in and stirring things up again.
He was torn between getting on the first flight back to England and sticking around for a few more days to see what he could find out. He looked at the clock on his phone. It was three thirty in the morning. Eight thirty in York, he thought.
There was a telephone on the bedside table. Smith picked it up and was relieved to hear the dialing tone. He dialled the number. He hoped he had remembered the correct dialing code.
"Hello," Whitton answered after a short pause.
She sounded suspicious. Her voice was perfectly clear - it was as if she were in the room with Smith.

"Whitton," Smith said and straight away wished he had used her first name for once.

"Hi," Whitton said. "I didn't recognise the number."

"I'm phoning from The Hamptons. This place is starting to make me lose my mind. I've just done something really stupid."

He regretted saying it immediately.

"What did you do?"

There was a hint of mockery in her voice.

"Nothing you do surprises me anymore."

Smith realised that telling Whitton about the kiss wouldn't be a good idea. He tried to think quickly.

"I think I've just opened up a whole can of worms here," was the best he could come up with. "About last summer in The Hamptons."

"Is that all? I thought you were going to tell me you'd killed someone. I have to go. We've got another one of the Super's dumb lectures to look forward to. When are you coming back home?"

"Soon - hopefully in a few days. I love you."

"I'll see you in a few days," Whitton said.

Smith replaced the handset and frowned.

"I'm such a chicken," he said out loud.

He thought about what he was going to do next. The mere fact that Basil Van Camp had turned up again was gnawing at his insides. What was he doing back here? He thought. Has it got something to do with the reason Sophie Phoenix and Lewis Van Camp were killed? He lay back on the bed and closed his eyes. The wind was still howling outside. Smith was sure he could hear the sound of the waves breaking on the beach in the distance.

When Smith woke up a few hours later it was light outside. A slice of sunlight cut the curtains in two. The curtains were now still. Smith got out of bed and opened them. He was met by an eerie mist that rose up from the sea and shrouded the road below in a haze. He got dressed and went outside onto the balcony. The fog had drenched everything it had come into contact with.

"You're up early," Charlotte Phoenix appeared behind him.

Smith turned round. She looked like she'd had even less sleep than he had. Her eyes were still half closed.

"It didn't mean anything," she said and yawned. "The kiss I mean. It was just one of those drunken spur of the moment things. It's not as if I'm going to fall in love with you because of it."

"Good," Smith said.

"You didn't have to run away like that though."

"Did anything exciting happen after I left?"

"John Dunn and Hartford junior had a bit of a flare up," she smiled. "Poets really shouldn't fight. Hartford floored him with one punch."

"What was it all about?"

"Basil Van Camp. I'm afraid your coming here has stirred up a few bad memories for a lot of people. They had been happy to put it all behind them."

"What do you mean?"

"Your poet friend had a bit too much to drink, and he started laying into Hartford about Basil Van Camp. What was he doing here, that sort of thing. He basically accused poor Hartford of associating with a criminal. In league with the devil was how he put it. Poets can be so melodramatic some times."

"I need to speak to him," Smith said.

"Hartford junior? That's a bad idea; you're not exactly his favourite person at the moment."

"Not Hartford, the poet, John Dunn. The least I can do is apologize for all of this."

"He went back to the city," Charlotte said.

"Then I'll need his address."

"You're way out of your depth here. You know that don't you. I've realised that this was a huge mistake. I think it would be safer for you to get on the first plane home and forget about the whole thing."

"Why the sudden change of heart? Has somebody got to you?"

"No," she said.

Smith could tell at once that she was lying.

"What good is it going to do?" she added. "Whatever you find out is not going to bring Sophie and Lewis back is it?"

"You're right," Smith said. "I'm going to head back to the city this morning but I might as well have a word with the poet before I catch my flight."

CHAPTER FORTY EIGHT

John Dunn lived in a two bedroom apartment in Brooklyn's Sunset Park district. When Smith had got the address from Charlotte he thought she'd made a mistake. He'd seen Brooklyn portrayed on television before - all gang related crimes and ethnical clashes. Why would an affluent New Yorker want to live in a place like that? The reality was nothing like what he'd seen in the films. Dunn's apartment was situated above a neat little bakery on Fifth Avenue. Smith paid the taxi driver and stepped out into the sunshine. There were very few people on the streets - Smith had expected Brooklyn to be teaming with people from all corners of the world but then he realised it was a holiday. Most of them would be making the most of the time off.

Smith hadn't told John Dunn he was coming and he hoped he would be at home. He rang the bell on the door next to the bakery.
"Hello," the poet's voice was heard on the speaker above the bell.
"John," Smith said. "It's Jason Smith. We met in The Hamptons. Can I talk to you?"
There was a long pause. Smith wondered if Dunn would agree to talk to him after the trouble he had caused.
"I'll come down," Dunn said eventually.
A minute later the door opened and Dunn stood there in a green T-shirt and a pair of red jeans. He had a bump the size of a small egg over his right eye.
"We can go to the park," he said. "I need some fresh air."
They walked for two blocks and turned right onto the path that led to the park the district was named after.
"That's quite a view," Smith said.

He looked out across the harbor towards Governor's Island. The sky line of Manhattan rose above everything in the distance.

"I thought you'd own one of those fancy Manhattan penthouses."

"What for?" Dunn sat down on a wooden bench.

Smith sat next to him.

"I'm a poet," Dunn said. "I write about real life. What happens out there is mere make believe."

He pointed to the skyscrapers of Manhattan to the north of them.

"New York is a crazy place," Smith said.

"What do you want?"

"What happened between you and William Hartford last night?"

"Nothing, things got a bit heated that's all. It happens sometimes when alcohol is involved. Opinions turn to violence. I'm on the verge of hooking a really great agent for my work and I let my hair down a bit too much. It was nothing serious."

"So it wasn't anything to do with Basil Van Camp's sudden reappearance?" Smith said. "And Hartford junior's involvement in that?"

"Of course not," Dunn said although Smith wasn't convinced.

"Do you know what Van Camp was doing back here in New York?"

"Horses," Dunn said. "What else? I heard the Chinese are going ape for Mustangs at the moment and Hartford knows Mustangs. Van Camp is just the middleman. It's as simple as that."

"As simple as that? So why all the cloak and dagger crap on the boat?"

"In case you haven't realised, Van Camp isn't exactly popular in these parts."

"I believe you accused Hartford junior of being in league with the devil," Smith said. "And then that happened."

He pointed to the lump over Dunn's eye. It was starting to turn a bluish black colour.

"Hartford has a bit of a temper. It was something over nothing."

A man in his seventies approached. He was dressed in a black suit and his shoes were polished so perfectly that the sunlight reflected off them as he walked. A row of medals hung from his jacket. He nodded to Smith and Dunn as he walked past.

"It's Memorial Day," Dunn said. "Not that any of those leeches in The Hamptons will give a damn. All it means to them is another excuse to get wasted on the beach. I don't know what you expected to find over here."

"Why do you hate Basil Van Camp so much?"

"Who said I hated him?"

"I'm not stupid."

"I've noticed that, and neither am I. You're lucky the rest of them in The Hamptons are so hung up on themselves not to notice the York detective sergeant amongst them."

Smith was shocked.

"Is it that obvious?"

"Not at first. You don't look like any police detective but you ask way too many questions and I looked you up on the internet. You have quite an impressive resume"

"OK," Smith said. "Why do you hate Basil Van Camp so much."

"Sebastian and I were friends," Dunn said. "Not friends like William Hartford and Lewis were. We don't share that old fraternity bond bullshit. Till death do us part and all that crap, but we were buddies."

"Go on," Smith felt he was finally starting to get somewhere.

"Sebastian wasn't like Lewis, he was quite sensitive. That's probably why we got on so well and, before you ask, no, we're not gay. We just shared a lot in common, that's all."

"What do you think happened to him?"

Dunn started to fidget. He locked the fingers of both hands together and looked around the park.

"Sebastian didn't tell me he was thinking of leaving. He would have let me know. Also, he hated Canada with a passion and he would never dream of going to Mexico."

"Where did he end up then?"

"This is just my opinion, and if you mention this to anybody, I'll deny it. The Van Camps used to own a boat - a small fishing vessel. They sold it when they left. Lewis and his father used to go out all the time but Sebastian wasn't keen. He seemed to hate the water for some reason. That's why it surprised me when he told me he was going out with his father that day."

"They went out on a boat?"

"Fishing," Dunn said. "That's what Sebastian said. Basil and Sebastian set off but only Basil returned.

"And you think it's suspicious?"

"I wasn't the only one. Basil Van Camp's story is that the fishing trip was a ruse. Sebastian wanted to head off somewhere on his own - he wanted to find himself or some bullshit like that. Basil dropped him off further up the coast and came back without him."

"What did you mean when you said you weren't the only one to think it suspicious?"

"There was this cop," Dunn looked around as though he was afraid somebody might be listening in. "A man not unlike you in a way. I wasn't the only one to doubt Basil's version of events. Veronica,

Sebastian's mother was worried and she filed a missing person's report. Basil tried to stop her of course but in the end he humored her - passed it off as some kind of mother's anxiety. Anyway, there was an investigation and this cop was sent out."

"What did this detective find?"

"Nothing, but he wasn't convinced that Sebastian simply ran off like that."

"What happened?"

"In the end, the case was dropped. There was no evidence to point to any kind of foul play and they passed it off as a rich kid who wanted to be alone for a while. The cop wouldn't let it lie though. He carried on snooping around afterwards. Big mistake. You don't mess around in the lives of the folk of The Hamptons. The cop wasn't a cop for much longer. That's just how it goes."

"What about Mrs Van Camp? Did she stop asking questions too?"

"What happened to Veronica was far worse than what happened to the cop," Dunn said. "She started drinking heavily to forget. Then it was the pills. Old Van Camp and Lewis had already run away by the time they found her, half naked walking along the highway at night. Basil Van Camp then made damn sure she was shipped off to the nut house and she's been there ever since. Are you starting to understand why I hate Basil Van Camp so much? He's pure evil - he has no conscience whatsoever."

"So Van Camp and Lewis ran away because of the mystery surrounding Sebastian's disappearance?" Smith said. "I still don't get it. If there was no proof of foul play, why didn't they just stay in New York?"

"Rumours are often worse than facts, especially in communities like The Hamptons. Van Camp's reputation was shot. It galls me that he can still set up somewhere else and ply his foul trade. What are you going to do now? I've told you all I can."

"I need the name of that police detective, and I need the name of the psychiatric hospital Veronica Van Camp was sent to."

CHAPTER FORTY NINE

Detective James McGuiness had been a detective in the Long Island police department. John Dunn had heard that he had since been transferred to some hell hole precinct in Queens.

"Watch your back," the driver of the taxi pulled up outside the 105th precinct in Queens Village. "And keep your wallet close. Even the cops around here can't be trusted."

Smith paid him and stepped out onto the pavement. The police station was like nothing he had ever seen before. The whole building looked like it may fall to the ground at any moment. It was early afternoon but the neon light above the department sign was still flickering on and off. Smith walked through the revolving door and emerged into what could only be described as hell on earth. The noise was unbearable. Everybody seemed to be speaking at the same time. A large man with red hair was arguing at the top of his voice with the woman behind the front desk. Smith could hear every word of the conversation.

"Just go home, Frank," the woman screamed. "Go sleep it off. It's over."

Before the red headed man had a chance to argue, two stocky men in uniform grabbed his shoulders and frog marched him, past Smith and out of the building. A Latin American man was sitting next to a young woman by the front desk. They were both handcuffed. The whole room smelled of stale alcohol and vomit. There were blood stains on one of the walls.

Smith approached the front desk and thought about what he was going to say.

"Are you lost, honey?" The woman in handcuffs asked him.

Smith ignored her.

"Afternoon," he said to the tired looking woman behind the counter.

"My name's detective sergeant Jason Smith. I'm looking for James McGuiness."

"Jimmy?" She said. "Jimmy aint here."

"Jimmy don't work here anymore," a small bald man said appeared behind them.

He was wearing a suit that was far too big for him. An unlit cigarette hung from the side of his mouth.

"What's he done?" The man asked. "What do the English police want with him?"

"I just need to talk to him," Smith said.

"What did you say your name was again?"

"Smith, I'm a detective sergeant with the York police department."

"You're a long way from home. Captain Wilder. This dump is my responsibility."

He held out a small clammy hand and Smith was forced to shake it.

"Do you know where Jimmy is now?" Smith wiped his hand on the back of his jeans.

"He's got a place down on Thirty Fifth Street. Last I heard. That's if he's kept up with the rent. That's where you'll find him - probably drunk out of his mind."

"What happened? Why did he quit his job?"

"The job quit him," Wilder sighed. "Jimmy was one of the best but you know how it goes. Wife can't hack being married to the job, she clears off and the drink takes over. Isn't that how it always pans out in the movies?"

Smith knew it all too well. He'd read somewhere that the divorce rate in the police department was considerably higher than in most other professions. He suddenly realised how unusual the people he worked with were. Bob Chalmers had been married for over thirty years - the late DS Thompson had also been married for as long when he died.

"Do you have an address for me?" Smith said.

"I'll give you a lift - I'm heading out that way anyway and, if you don't mind me saying you seem pretty green for a cop. That accent aint British is it?"

"No," Smith said.

Captain Wilder's car smelled of stale cigarette smoke. Wilder lit up before he had even started the engine.

"Smoke?" He pointed to a packet of Chesterfields on the dash board. Smith took out a cigarette and lit it. It was much stronger than the cigarettes he was used to.

"Thanks," he resisted the urge to cough.

"New York City's gone to the dogs," Wilder pulled in front of a yellow taxi.

The driver of the taxi honked his hooter but Wilder seemed unperturbed.

"When I started on the force, we could smoke anywhere," he continued. "In the offices, in the John, even in the Goddamn interrogation rooms. Now we don't even have a Goddamn smoking room. We have to step outside and risk being shot at. No, New York's not what it used to be. It's not the smoking that'll do you in - it's the drive by shooting you get caught in when you're outside for a smoke. What's the deal with Jimmy McGuiness?"

"I need to ask him a few questions," Smith said. "About the time he worked in The Hamptons."

Smith decided to tell Wilder the truth. His gut was telling him he could trust this police captain.

"That was a strange one," Wilder threw his cigarette out the window and lit another one. "Anybody who gives up a gig in The Hamptons to come to Queens needs putting away in a nut house."
"Did Jimmy ever mention what happened in The Hamptons?"
"Nope, all I know is he came back here and within a few months his wife had skedaddled, he started drinking and the big chiefs wouldn't tolerate it anymore. I tell you, New York is not the good old NYC I remember. In the old days, my captain practically encouraged alcoholism - it was part of the job."

Wilder parked the car outside what looked like a converted warehouse. It was a double storey building that had been turned into apartments. Washing lines hung from the tiny balconies above their heads.
"You don't mind if I don't stop?" Wilder said. "Around here, they steal your wheels as soon as you turn off the engine."
"Thanks for your help," Smith said. "If you're ever in York, look me up."
Wilder was about to drive away when he appeared to have thought of something.
"Where are you staying tonight?"
"I have no idea," Smith hadn't thought that far ahead.
"If you can make your way back to the precinct by five, I'll put you up for the night. You don't want to see the inside of a Queen's hotel."
He drove off before Smith had a chance to say anything. A cloud of smoke oozed out of the driver's window.

CHAPTER FIFTY

Jimmy McGuiness was not at all what Smith was expecting when he stood in the doorway. He answered the door almost immediately. He was a tall thin man with a receding hairline. His eyes were bright and intelligent looking. He reminded Smith more of a college lecturer than a New York detective.
"Can I help you?" his voice was soft and slightly high pitched.
"Sorry to bother you, Mr McGuiness," Smith said. "My name is Jason Smith. I'm a detective sergeant from York, England."
"Yorkshire? You don't sound like a Yorkshireman."
He looked Smith up and down.
"You'd better come in," he said. "Excuse the mess. This is about Basil Van Camp isn't it?"
He led Smith inside to a tiny room that served as living room, dining room and bedroom all in one. A door to the side led to what Smith assumed was the bathroom.
"I'll make some coffee."

Smith sat down on a worn leather couch. There was a stale smell in the room. The windows had obviously not been opened for a while. McGuiness placed two mugs of coffee on the table next to the couch.
"How did you know I was here about Basil Van Camp?" Smith came straight to the point.
"A Yorkshire cop in New York? What else could it be about?"
"I'm sort of investigating two murders in Yorkshire, and I have a feeling that what happened in The Hamptons last year is at the heart of it."
"Sort of?" McGuiness was sharp. "Nobody knows you're here do they?"

"You've got me there. You were working in Long Island last year weren't you?"

"It seems like a lifetime ago now," McGuiness sighed. "We felt like we'd won the lotto. Me and Martha, that is."

"Martha's your wife?"

"Not anymore. The transfer to the two twenty second was a God send to her. She always hated the city."

"What happened?"

"I was second in charge at the two-two-two, as we called it. Nothing much happened down there. It was like another world. The worst we had to deal with was drunken kids - Ivy League brats crashing their cars. Nothing serious. I got bored pretty quickly. When the missing person report came in I thought I'd finally found something to get my teeth into."

"Veronica Van Camp filed the missing person report," Smith said.

"That's right," McGuiness said.

A strange noise could be heard from somewhere in the room. It sounded like an electric alarm clock. McGuiness stood up and opened up the sideboard standing against the wall. He turned off the alarm and took out a bottle of Jim Beam. He placed it on the table with two dirty glasses.

"I may be an alcoholic," he said. "But I'm a civilised one. The alarm signals that it's an acceptable time to start drinking. Will you join me?"

"Sounds great," Smith said.

McGuiness poured two double measures.

"All in moderation," he handed one of the grubby glasses to Smith. "Where were we?"

"Veronica Van Camp, she filed a missing person report."

"She was convinced something had happened to her son," McGuiness took a sip of the bourbon then a sip of coffee. "And my gut told me a mother's instinct is not something to ignore."

"So you took her seriously?"

"Like I said, a mother's instinct is not something you underestimate and it was different from the usual stuff we had to deal with. I started doing some digging around."

"What did you find out?"

"I found out straight away that my presence wasn't welcome in The Hamptons. Basil Van Camp made that quite clear. His story was this: Sebastian had suffered some kind of minor crisis and wanted to be alone to work through it. He wanted some time to be by himself."

"But you didn't believe him?" Smith took a sip of the Jim Beam. It tasted similar to Jack Daniel's.

"I'm a cop," McGuiness said. "At least I was then. I didn't believe anybody and it was my job to follow through on a missing persons report. I don't care how much money Van Camp has, he wasn't going to stop me doing my job. Sebastian Van Camp vanished into thin air. Even if he wanted to disappear, there would be some trace of him somewhere - credit card transactions, cash withdrawals, phone calls. I checked to see if he had left the country. There were no records to suggest he exited the States by car, bus or airplane."

"What do you think happened to him?"

"I know he left The Hamptons on a boat with his father. That was common knowledge. What wasn't common knowledge was Sebastian Van Camp hated the water and he hated boats. I spoke to some of his friends. I also learned that Sebastian had a huge fight with his father the night before they set off on the boat. More Bourbon?"

"No thanks," Smith said.

McGuiness poured himself another, much larger measure.

"Are you saying that something happened on the boat?" Smith said.

"I am. Two people set off but only one of them returns. You're the detective in the room, what do you think?"

Smith's head was starting to spin. He wasn't sure if it was the effects of the whisky or all the new information his brain was trying to digest.

Even if Basil Van Camp did kill his son, he thought, it still doesn't explain why Sophie Phoenix and Lewis Van Camp were killed.

"Of course I couldn't prove a thing," McGuiness was starting to slur his words. "There was no evidence of foul play and Van Camp stuck to his story. Sebastian had merely wanted to get away from it all for a while and he didn't want anybody to know where he was."

"And the case was dropped?"

"The case was dropped, but I couldn't just leave it alone. The whole think reeked. I carried on digging - I spoke to all of Sebastian Van Camp's friends again, I even spoke to the coastguards to see if any bodies had been washed up but I found out that, even if Sebastian Van Camp had gone overboard, the currents would have pushed him further out. His body would never be found. Then, just as I thought I'd found the evidence I needed, Basil Van Camp stopped me in my tracks. Somehow, he made damn sure I would never work on Long Island again. Van Camp is a very powerful man - he has friends in very high places. I was shipped off to the worst precinct in Queens, Martha left me soon afterwards and I started hitting the bottle on a regular basis. All because of one man."

"I'm sorry," Smith was quickly learning how the world really worked. "You said you found evidence?"

"It wasn't so much evidence that would hold up in court, it was more proof that I'd been right all along. The Van Camps are typical of The Hamptons folk. They don't lift a finger if they can help it. They'd rather pay someone to do the tedious work. They get on their boats and everything is done for them - the vessels are cleaned, stocked with food and booze and the fuel tank is filled up. One of the people I spoke to was the guy who maintained the Van Camp's boat. He'd filled up the fuel tank for them before they set off that morning. He helped them launch and watched them head out to sea. They went straight out according to him. They told him they were going to do a bit of fishing. Basil Van Camp claims he dropped Sebastian off further up the coast but according to the boat guy, the fuel they'd used would only have been enough to get them a few miles out. The nearest place to stop was at least ten miles further up the coast."

"Maybe they had extra fuel on board," Smith suggested.

"I thought of that. The guy who looks after the boat said they've never kept spare fuel on the boat and even if they did, neither Van Camp nor his son would even know where the fuel tank was. No, Basil Van Camp somehow dumped his son in the ocean knowing full well the body would never be found."

CHAPTER FIFTY ONE

With time to kill before he was due to meet Captain Wilder, Smith sat in the diner across the road from the police department. He tried to digest everything Jimmy McGuiness had told him. The diner was obviously a favourite haunt of the police officers who worked across the road. Old photographs depicting policemen in uniform from times gone by hung on the walls. Smith had believed Jimmy McGuiness. He was a drunk but there was clearly nothing wrong with his mind. Everything he'd said had made sense.
Basil Van Camp killed his son, Smith thought, all I have to do now is figure out why and what has it got to do with the murders in Scarpdale. Did Sebastian discover something? Something so terrible that his father had to kill him to prevent anybody else finding out?

Smith finished his coffee and left the diner. He walked across the road to the police station. He could hear the sound of a brass band somewhere in the distance. Captain Wilder was reprimanding a young woman in uniform when Smith walked in. Smith waited until he had finished and approached him.
"Do I look like an idiot?" Wilder said to Smith.
"No," Smith said. "You don't look like an idiot."
"The kids in this place think I'm a Goddamn idiot," Wilder headed for the door without further explanation.

Wilder lit a cigarette and started the engine of his car. The brass band seemed to be getting nearer.
"Memorial Day procession," Wilder said. "It looks like we might be stuck here for a while."
He turned the corner and drove right into the heart of the procession. A marching band dressed in the colours of the American flag was

walking slowly towards them. A crowd of people had joined in and now the procession was at least five hundred strong.

"Bunch of bullshit," Wilder turned off the engine. "We'll have to wait for them to pass."

Smith watched as the marching band came closer. The sound was deafening. Men and women in various uniforms were walking behind them. Onlookers waving American flags were cheering as they walked past.

"Look at them," Wilder said. "Bunch of idiots. Honoring their brothers in arms. Men and women who died without knowing what the hell they were fighting for in the first place. Liberty and justice for all. Bunch of bullshit."

Smith was taken aback by Wilder's outburst. He'd always thought that Americans were the most patriotic nation on earth.

"It's all about the money isn't it?"

"You're not as stupid as you look," Wilder lit a cigarette and started the engine.

They arrived at Wilder's house just as it was starting to get dark. Wilder parked the car in the driveway next to a house Smith was surprised a police captain could afford. It was a large double storey building in what appeared to be a very affluent neighbourhood. Huge sedans and luxury SUVs were parked on either side of the road.

"Money," Wilder got out of the car. "Is not always what it seems to be."

He led Smith up the path to the house and opened the door. The interior of the house took Smith by surprise. He was no expert on home décor but he knew the furniture and fittings inside must have been very expensive. Wilder switched on the lights in what appeared to be an entertainment room.

"Take a seat," he gestured towards a very old looking table. "I'll get us a few beers."

Smith looked around the room. There was an oak bar counter in the corner with six bar stools next to it. A coin slot pool table took up another corner of the room and an old fashioned juke box stood next to the wall.

"What do they call it these days?" Wilder handed Smith a beer. "A man cave, that's it although I've never been married so I suppose this whole place is one big man cave. Cheers."

He raised the bottle to his lips and drained it in one go.

"Let me put your mind at ease, before you put two and two together and come up with five. No, I'm not on the take."

"Excuse me?" Smith said.

"You're probably wondering how I can afford a place like this on a captain's salary."

"It had crossed my mind," Smith admitted.

"I know all about money. Not Basil Van Camp sort of money - not summer in The Hamptons money, my mother and father were both attorneys. I grew up with money. They both died before I joined the force and me being an only child meant I ended up with this place. My old man must be turning in his grave knowing his only son ended up joining the opposition."

Smith started to laugh - he was starting to warm to this eccentric police captain.

"I'll drink to that," he had always hated lawyers.

Wilder ordered pizza and they sat at the table eating straight from the boxes. Smith had selected a Led Zeppelin song on the juke box and 'Black Dog' was playing quietly in the background.

"How's McGuiness holding up?" Wilder asked him.

"He seems OK," Smith said. "He's sharp enough."

"Too sharp - he should never have joined the police."

"Why did you join up?"

"It seemed like the natural thing to do," Wilder popped the cap off a bottle of beer. "In the greater scheme of things I mean. Yin and Yang - good Karma and bad Karma and all that crap. My folks were attorneys so I figured I'd reset the balance a bit. What about you?"

"Pretty much the same. I did a few years of law, got a bit disillusioned and decided I'd rather be the one catching the bad guys than the one who gets them off."

"I'll drink to that. Can you play pool?"

"I haven't played since I was at school," Smith said.

"No problem, I'm useless anyway. I'll rack em up."

Two hours later, Smith was five games down. Captain Wilder hadn't been entirely honest about his pool playing skills.

"I think I've had enough humiliation for one night," Smith said.

"What are your plans?" Wilder put the pool cues back in the glass cabinet. "Did you find the answers you were looking for?"

"Some of them, but there's still a couple of loose ends I need to tie up before I go home."

"Let me know if I can be of help," Wilder drained yet another beer. Smith had never met anybody who could drink so much beer before.

"You can point me in the right direction," he said. "I need to get to a place called Peekskill."

"Peekskill? That's upstate, almost in Connecticut. What are you looking for in Peekskill?"

"I don't know yet. Do you know how to get there?"

"It's about an hour's drive north," Wilder opened them both another beer. "I'll drive you up there myself if you want. I have a couple of days owed to me. It's been a while since I took a trip upstate."

CHAPTER FIFTY TWO

Lewis Van Camp's funeral was a much smaller affair than Sophie Phoenix's. Lewis had obviously not made himself very popular in the years he had been in Scarpdale. His father Basil had flown in from New York and was now speaking to the vicar at the front of the small church. Johnny Grouse was sitting two rows back, his eyes streaming with tears. Lewis had been one of his only friends. Jimmy Phoenix entered the church and the vicar stopped his conversation with Van Camp, mid sentence. Van Camp turned to face his old rival. The other members of the funeral party braced themselves for what was about to happen. It was common knowledge that Jimmy Phoenix and Basil Van Camp hated each other.

"Basil," Phoenix spoke first. "I'm sorry about Lewis. He didn't deserve that."

"Thank you," Van Camp nodded.

A collective sigh was heard throughout the church. The tension inside seemed to ease. Jimmy Phoenix took a seat next to Johnny Grouse. Jethro came in and sat on the other side. He put his hand on the babbling giant's arm.

"Get a grip, lad," he said. "Lewis wouldn't have wanted to see you like this."

Jethro's words seemed to have the desired effect. Grouse wiped his eyes with the sleeve of his shirt and took a deep breath.

Phoenix checked his watch. It was eleven on the dot. He looked around the room and counted the people. A grand total of nine people had come to pay their last respects to Lewis Van Camp. Basil was the only family member in attendance.

This is what it all comes down to, Phoenix thought. This is how many lives Lewis Van Camp has touched in a positive way.
He suddenly felt emotionally drained.
All the money in the world, he thought, and this is how it ends - nine people at your funeral.
He wondered how many people would be at his own funeral.

"Lady and gentlemen," the vicar nodded at the only woman in the room. "Thank you all for coming."
He looked at all the empty pews.
"I appreciate that not everybody was able to attend at such short notice," he continued. "Mr Van Camp has matters to attend to so he had to arrange it as soon as possible, but to those of you who are here, let's begin."
The whole service lasted less than twenty minutes. Even the vicar seemed to want to get it over with as quickly as possible. It was obvious he found it hard to come up with many positive things to say about the short life of Lewis Van Camp. He'd been on the earth for almost thirty years and nobody could think of anything good to say about him.

When the vicar had finished, Basil Van Camp stood up and walked to the back of the church. Jimmy Phoenix followed him outside into the sunshine.
"You'll take a drink?" Phoenix asked him. "The Quail ought to be quiet today."
"I have urgent matters to attend to," Van Camp said. "Matters that can't wait."
"Let them wait - you'll take a drink."
This time it wasn't a question. They walked through the church yard and headed towards the centre of the village. It was a sombre sight -

two men dressed in suits, both with their heads bowed in sorrow. The two most powerful men in Scarpdale now looked utterly lost.

Phoenix had been right, the Quail's Arms was empty when they walked inside. A new barman was cleaning the pipes that fed the beer tap.

"Two double scotches," Phoenix said to him. "We'll be sat over there." He pointed to the table furthest away from the bar. The barman shrugged and poured the drinks. Phoenix and Van Camp sat down opposite each other. The barman placed the drinks in front of them.

"Here's to Lewis and Sophie," Phoenix drained his glass in one go.

"I have to go," Van Camp stood up. "I have to be back in China the day after tomorrow."

"Sit down," Phoenix said, much louder than he intended.

Van Camp glared at him and sat down.

"This can't go on," Phoenix said. "It's been going on for far too long and it has to stop."

"I'm tired of talking, and right now I have nothing to say to you."

"Sophie's dead, Lewis is dead - are you so bloody cold that it doesn't affect you in the slightest?"

"Emotions are a weakness. My father drilled that into me and I did the same for my children."

"How's that working out for you?" Phoenix stood up and walked up to the bar.

He returned with a bottle of Glenfiddich.

"How's Sebastian?" He filled up both their glasses. "And how's Matilda doing? Your eldest son didn't even have his brother and sister at his funeral. Don't you get tired of it all?"

"You don't have a clue do you? You don't know anything. What was Charlotte doing in The Hamptons last weekend?"

Phoenix didn't know what to say. He could not hide his surprise.
"You see," Van Camp smiled. "What do you know? What do any of us know about what goes on in our children's lives?"
"You're lying," Phoenix said. "Charlotte never mentioned anything about going to New York."
"We bring them into the world, we try to raise them as best we can but we have no control. It's the world around them that moulds them into what they become, not us."
"I know more than you give me credit for. I know about what happened in The Hamptons last summer."
Basil Van Camp started to laugh.
"Jimmy," he said. "What happened last summer is history - it's all been forgotten. The past is the past."
"The past never stays in the past. You mark my words."

CHAPTER FIFTY THREE

"Are you sure you don't want to see a few of the sights of the city while you're here?" Captain Wilder said.
They were heading north on Interstate eighty seven.
"That's the Yankee stadium on the right," Wilder slowed down and a pickup truck almost drove into the back of them.
"Baseball," Wilder saw the look of confusion on Smith's face. "I don't suppose they play much baseball in the UK?"
"I don't follow sport."
"The George Washington Bridge is coming up. You tend to take it all for granted when you live here."
Smith was inclined to agree with him.
Familiarity does make you take things for granted, he thought.

The countryside became less built up as they headed further north and left the city behind. Patches of green were becoming more and more frequent.
"What are you going to do when you get to this nut house?" Wilder asked. "What if they won't let you see this fruitcake? She might not even want to talk to you. What if she's so spaced out, she doesn't know what she's saying anyway?"
"You ask a lot of questions. I'll think of something."
"Spontaneous type are you? Me, I always prefer to have a plan."
"Plans have a habit of changing - I'll think of something."
He knew that Wilder was probably right - the staff at the psychiatric hospital may not even let him see Veronica Phoenix - he didn't have his ID with him and he wasn't family.

"You're going to help me," Smith said to Wilder as they drove past the botanical gardens. "Do you have your ID with you?"

"Of course I do, I never go anywhere without my badge and my gun. What do you expect me to do?"

"A New York police captain should be able to get us in the door. At least I hope so. You've got more chance than an Australian DS who doesn't even look like a policeman."

"I should've known this would be a bad idea," Wilder slowed down and stopped next to a row of shops.

"What's wrong?" Smith said. "Have you changed your mind?"

"I forgot to buy more smokes. I've got a feeling I'm going to need them."

Wilder got back in the car, lit a cigarette and threw the packet on the dashboard.

"Help yourself," he said to Smith.

They carried on through the semi-countryside. Smith saw signs for towns with names like Pleasantville and Valhalla on the side of the road. The Hudson River flowed to their left.

"Did you know," Wilder said. "Over eight million people live in and around New York?"

Wilder's statement made Smith feel claustrophobic and he shivered. Eight million people, he thought, a third of the population of Australia living on top of each other.

Wilder looked in the mirror and frowned.

"We've got company," he said. "Don't look now but that black Buick has been with us since we left upper Manhattan."

Smith turned round. An expensive looking black sedan was driving about fifty metres behind them.

"Are you sure? Are you sure it's the same car?"

"The guy who's driving is wearing a White Sox cap. You don't see many of them in New York. It's the same car."

He slowed down and the Buick was forced to overtake. It sped off into the distance.

"Maybe you were wrong," Smith said.

"He was following us alright. He was behind us when I stopped for smokes."

"Why would someone want to follow us to Peekskill?"

"You tell me," Wilder took out a cigarette then realised he already had one in his mouth. "This filthy habit will be the death of me."

Wilder drove through Peekskill and turned right onto the Bear Mountain Parkway.

"We're almost there," he said. "What's the plan?"

"Plan?" Smith said.

"I assume you're not going to tell them the truth?"

"Why not?" Smith said. "Sometimes the truth works better than anything else."

"Because they won't let you anywhere near her if you tell them what you're working on. From what you've told me, this Van Camp guy wanted his wife out of the way for a reason. We've got to be careful that's all."

He approached the grounds of the hospital. Well maintained lawns led to a building that was painted the most disgusting colour Smith had ever seen. It was a blend of bright orange and green. The result was a sickly frog like colour that resembled the colour of bile.

"That colour alone is enough to make you go nuts," Wilder parked the car in the large car park opposite the entrance.

A large black Buick drove towards them and parked about twenty metres away.

"We've got trouble," Wilder threw his cigarette on the ground and patted his shoulder holster although he knew his gun was there.

They watched as three men got out the Buick and started to walk towards them. One of them was wearing a Chicago White Sox baseball cap.

"What do you want to do?" Smith said.

"Nothing," Wilder said. "They look like hired muscle to me. Bullies. The badge usually scares them off."

"What if it doesn't?"

"What are you like in a fist fight?"

"It's been a while. Do you think they're Van Camp's men?"

"Probably," Wilder said.

The three men approached. Two of them held back and the third calmly walked up to Wilder. He was short with thinning black hair. He was using far too much hair gel. His face resembled a rat's - his eyes were far too close together and his nose seemed to grow out of his forehead.

"It's a beautiful day," he said. "Are you guys lost?"

"Nope," Wilder took out a cigarette and lit it.

He blew a cloud of smoke into the air.

"Those things will kill you," rat-face said.

"We're here to see a friend," Smith said.

"You aint from around here," rat-face smiled at Smith. "I suggest you go back to where you came from and there'll be no trouble."

He turned round and looked at the two men behind him.

"Is that supposed to be a threat?" Smith said. "Because if it is, I have to be honest, I've heard much better ones than that before."

Wilder smiled.

"Nobody's threatening nobody here," rat-face turned back to Smith. "We don't want any trouble. Why don't you go back home and forget all about this? It really don't concern you."

"OK," Smith said. "I've come a long way. I have something I need to do and when I'm finished I'll go back home. The people around here are starting to get on my nerves anyway. Gentlemen."

He turned and smiled at rat-face's reinforcements.

"You aint hearing me," rat-face took a step closer.

Smith braced himself for an attack – it'd been a while since he'd fought anybody.

Wilder took out his badge. Rat face took a step back.

"Take your friends," he said. "Get back in your fancy car and go tell Mr Van Camp he's not the law around here."

Rat-face appeared to think hard for a minute. His tiny eyes became even smaller.

"You're going to regret this," he said.

"Really?" Wilder put his badge back in his pocket. "What's the great Basil Van Camp going to do to me? Ship me off to Queens? Get out of here."

Smith watched with relief as rat-face turned round and walked back to the car. His two thugs followed closely behind.

CHAPTER FIFTY FOUR

'The past never stays in the past,' Jimmy Phoenix's words were still ringing in Basil Van Camp's ears as he drove to his stables, 'you mark my words.'

What the hell did he mean by that? Van Camp thought.

He was exhausted. When he'd received word about Lewis's death he had caught the first flight out of China via New York. He'd come straight from the airport to the funeral and now he was physically and mentally exhausted. Phoenix's words had unnerved him.

What does he know? He thought.

He turned on to his property and drove down the road towards the main house. He noticed that the fields on either side of the fence appeared to be more overgrown than they had been the last time he was here. He realised he couldn't even remember when that was. He slowed down when he spotted a woman riding what looked like an Appalachian on the road ahead of him. He stopped the car in front of her and wound down the window.

"Mr Van Camp," she seemed surprised to see him.

Van Camp didn't recognise her.

"Who are you?"

"Susan," she said. "I've been working here for a few months."

Has it been that long? Van Camp thought.

"We're all so sorry about Lewis," Susan said. "Will you be coming to check on the horses? I can arrange to have them ready to ride if you like."

"I'm tired of horses," Van Camp rolled up the window and carried on towards the house.

Van Camp had built a huge cottage style house with a thatch roof. He hated staircases and he had plenty of land to build on so he had opted for a single storey building. He pressed the remote control and the door to the six car garage opened slowly. Van Camp parked next to a Land Rover he had last driven over six months ago. The garage door closed behind him and he opened the door that led into the house. He breathed in deeply. The air inside the house was stuffy and slightly stale. The windows had obviously not been opened in a long time. He tried hard to remember the last time he spent a night at home. Since March that year he had been travelling to China, Russia and the Middle East in search of horses. He shuddered when he realised he'd spent the best part of a quarter of a year in hotel rooms.

Van Camp walked through to the lounge and poured a large measure of brandy from a crystal decanter. He took it to a chair a Russian billionaire had given him - an ostrich leather arm chair that claimed to be the most comfortable chair in existence. He sat down and finished half the brandy in the glass. The chair was positioned to offer the best view from the room - a view over the whole estate with the fells in the distance. Clouds were forming over the higher ground. Van Camp put the glass down on the coffee table and closed his eyes. The clouds were still swirling in his mind.

Van Camp's mobile phone started to ring in his pocket. He opened his eyes and for a moment he didn't know where he was. He wasn't sure how long he had been asleep but he still felt exhausted so he knew he hadn't slept long.

"Van Camp," he never ignored his phone.

"Basil," a familiar voice said.

It was William Hartford Junior.

"We have a problem," Hartford came straight to the point. "That Australian detective is still digging around. He's not giving up and I think he might be close to finding something."

"He won't find anything," Van Camp rubbed his eyes. "There's nothing to find in The Hamptons."

"He's not in The Hamptons anymore. Last I heard, he was snooping around in the city. He knows about that cop you had transferred."

"You keep your mouth shut about that," Van Camp stood up and opened the window.

A cool breeze wafted in. The clouds over the moors had drifted off to the east.

"That cop can't prove a thing," he added. "And anyway, Who's going to believe a washed out alcoholic?"

"That Australian won't give up."

"Then deal with it, I'm sure you know a few people who can stop him digging around."

"I'll see what I can do."

"Make sure you do," Van Camp said. "And remember, you have just as much to lose as I do if any of this gets out."

He rang off.

Van Camp finished the brandy in the glass and poured himself another one. All hope of sleep had now disappeared. Hartford Junior's phone call had unsettled him. He remembered the day on the boat with Sebastian like it was yesterday. Not a day had gone by without thinking about that day. Van Camp and Sebastian had argued the night before the boat trip. There had been a party at their house - a typical Hamptons' affair with drinking and live music. Sebastian had too much to drink and was starting to get loud and obnoxious. Van Camp had pulled him to one side and told him to calm down. Van

Camp shuddered when he thought about what Sebastian had said to him that night.

"How dare you lecture me about my behavior?" He'd said.

Even though Sebastian was roaring drunk, the words were spoken clearly.

"How can you lecture me after what you've done? I was three years old and I didn't know what was happening back then but I do now."

Van Camp remembered he didn't sleep that night. He got up early and the idea of the boat trip had come to him. A father, son bonding experience. He knew that Sebastian hated boats and it took some persuading to get him to agree but Sebastian finally gave in and they set off early that morning. Van Camp headed straight out to sea. The waves were choppy that morning and they had the whole bay to themselves. He'd turned off the engine and they bobbed around in the ocean with no other boats in sight.

The argument from the previous night soon fuelled up again. Sebastian once more accused his father of being the biggest bastard on the planet.

"I was three years old," he said. "I saw you."

"What did you see? You were barely out of nappies - you can't remember that far back."

"I saw you and Jane Phoenix," Sebastian said.

The words hit Van Camp like a punch in the face.

"You're wrong," it was all he could think of to say. "You were just a child."

"I didn't know back then," Sebastian continued. "But I know now. I know everything."

"It was a mistake," Van Camp finally admitted. "A silly drunken mistake."

The argument had started to get out of hand after that. Sebastian went on and on about the consequences of his silly drunken mistake. Van Camp had to listen. He sat in the cockpit of the boat feeling like his whole world was collapsing around him.

"Mother knows," Sebastian had said. "I told her last night. She knows everything."

Van Camp was still unsure as to what had happened after that. He remembered standing up and facing his son. He looked at the smug smile on his youngest son's face and something had happened deep inside him. Sebastian hadn't been expecting the first blow. It hit him under the chin and he was dazed for a few seconds. He couldn't defend himself.

When Van Camp was finished, his son was left slumped in the cockpit of the boat, all bloody and bruised. He was barely alive. Van Camp had removed the life jacket Sebastian always wore on the rare occasions he joined them on the boat, and tipped his battered body over the side. He had watched as Sebastian slowly sank out of sight.

"I had to be done," Van Camp had said to himself afterwards.

He'd tried to convince himself it had been the only way out. He'd grabbed the bailing bucket and washed Sebastian's blood off the boat. He'd watched as the blood stained brine disappeared through the drain holes in the stern. The story about Sebastian's breakdown had come to him as he returned to shore alone. He knew everybody would believe him. The only problem he had now was how to ensure the silence of his wife, Veronica. Miraculously, that problem had sorted itself out after Van Camp and Lewis had left The Hamptons. They'd sold up everything, gone to the UK and Veronica and Matilda had stayed behind. Veronica had suffered her own breakdown a few weeks after they had left. They'd found her walking half naked down the highway in the middle of the night. When Van Camp had found out, he felt like all the tension in his body had suddenly been released. Nobody would believe the words of a madwoman. He'd got away with it - everything had worked out in the end.

Until now. Van Camp was dragged back to the present. Until that Australian detective arrived and started stirring everything up again.

CHAPTER FIFTY FIVE

"You can come and work for me any time," Wilder said to Smith. They watched as the black Buick turned out of the car park and sped off into the distance.
"It always confuses the hell out of them," Wilder said. "When they're not sure which one's the good cop and which one's the bad cop. They don't know what to do."
"Do you think they'll be waiting for us when we're finished here?"
"You bet your life on it, but we'll figure that one out when it happens. What's the plan?"
"I have no idea," Smith admitted. "Let's see if they'll let us speak to Basil van Camp's wife shall we."

The interior of the Peaceville psychiatric hospital was as equally garish as the outside. The walls were a pastel green colour and the windowsills were black. Smith thought that whoever decided on the colour scheme must have been colour blind. Two men in hospital uniform eyed them suspiciously as they walked past to what looked like an information desk. The ugliest man Smith had ever seen was manning the desk. He was bald apart from a few thin wisps of hair behind his ears. Two unfortunately long yellow teeth stuck out beneath his top lip. His eyes were black and one of them had heavy lids and was set much further back in his head than the other one. He reminded Smith of the vampire Orlock in the twenties film Nosferatu.
"Afternoon," Smith said. "We're here to see a patient. Mrs Veronica Van Camp."
The man seemed to find this highly amusing.
"Is something funny?"

"Sorry," Orlock licked his teeth with an unusually long tongue. "Are you family?"

"Yes," Smith lied. "Distant relative. I've come all the way from the UK to see her."

"I'm afraid you're wasting your time here," Orlock said.

"I really need to see her," Smith wasn't going to give up.

"Mrs Van Camp hasn't seen anybody for months. Her daughter was here about three months ago but Mrs Van Camp doesn't talk anymore."

"Can I please see her? This is extremely important."

A tall man in a grey suit approached the desk. He looked at Smith and Wilder with obvious disapproval.

"Doctor Young," Orlock said. "These men would like to speak with Mrs Van Camp."

"What's this all about?" Young asked Smith.

"It's very important that I speak to her," Smith said.

"Who are you?"

"Is there somewhere we can speak in private?"

"Follow me," Young lollopped off down a corridor.

Smith and Wilder had to run to keep up. They followed him through a wide door that led out to the hospital gardens. A thick mossy lawn led down to a small lake surrounded by trees. Wooden benches were dotted around the grass. Young sat down on a bench close to the lake.

"Who are you?" He asked Smith again.

"My name's Jason Smith. I'm a detective sergeant with the York police department. Mrs Van Camp may have some information regarding an investigation I'm working on."

"And who's that?" Young pointed to Wilder.

He'd lagged behind. He sat down on the bench and took out his cigarettes.

"Do you mind if I smoke?" He asked Young.

"That's Captain Wilder," Smith said. "New York city. He's helping me out here."

"Do you mind if I smoke?" Wilder said again.

"Feel free," Young shook his head.

Wilder lit up a cigarette, inhaled and started to cough.

"I'm afraid you're wasting your time here gentlemen. Mrs Van Camp hasn't uttered a word in months."

"Why was she brought in here?" Wilder said.

"She wasn't brought in, this isn't a prison - she was admitted here almost a year ago. She'd suffered a complete mental breakdown."

"What caused her to flip?" Wilder blew a cloud of smoke in the doctor's face.

"Forgive my friend," Smith said. "He's used to questioning hoodlums in Queens. Do you know what caused Mrs Van Camp's breakdown?"

"When she was admitted, she was extremely paranoid. I'll never forget the look on her face that day. Her eyes darted from side to side like a hunted animal's. She was found walking along the highway in the middle of the night. She was half naked and she kept babbling about her baby boy."

"That'll be Sebastian," Smith said.

"She was given treatment - we've tried everything but her condition has never improved. I've seen it plenty of times before. She's withdrawn inside her mind and she's not going to come out. I'm afraid you're wasting your time here detectives."

"Where is she now?" Smith said.

"She sits by the lake most of the time," Young pointed to a small figure huddled on a bench next to the lake.

"She sits for hours," Young added. "Just staring at the water."

"Do you mind if I talk to her?"

"It won't do you any good," Young said. "Like I said, she hasn't spoken a word in months."

"Let me try. What harm can it do?"

"You're wasting your time, but you're welcome to give it a go."

"Thank you," Smith said.

"One more thing, it might be best if you talked to her alone. Captain Wilder here might just push her over the edge for good."

CHAPTER FIFTY SIX

Smith walked along the path round the lake. An odd looking duck was being followed by a group of ducklings on the surface of the water. They were struggling to keep up. The path took Smith through a copse of trees and ended at the far side of the lake. Veronica Van Camp was sitting by herself on a bench close to the water's edge. It reminded Smith of Whooton Tarn in Scarpdale where all of this had started with the discovery of Sophie Phoenix's body. He approached the bench and stood in front of her.
"Veronica," he said softly. "Do you mind if I sit down?"
Veronica continued to stare across the lake. A small frog surfaced, took a breath and dived back down again.
"Veronica," Smith sat down next to her.
He looked at her face. She was a very slight woman. Her green eyes were sunk into her face. Smith stared at her for some time but she didn't blink.
"Veronica," he said again. "My name's Jason. I'm from Yorkshire. I know your son Lewis."
If Smith was expecting some kind of spark of recognition it did not materialise.
Maybe Doctor Young was right, he thought, maybe I am wasting my time here.
Veronica coughed and Smith jumped but when he looked at her, she was still staring blankly across the lake.

Smith thought about something Jessica Blakemore had said, something about the mad people being in the outside world while the sane ones are all locked up in institutions.

"It's nice here," he said. "I could quite easily live here. It's peaceful. Do you come down here every day? I bet it's nice when the pond freezes over in the winter."

He was sure he detected a slight change in Veronica's face. The lines around her mouth had moved; she was trying to smile.

"Veronica don't talk," a man younger than Smith had emerged from the trees.

He had a tattoo of an armadillo on his neck. It was very badly drawn.

"Veronica don't talk," he said again. "Veronica don't talk. I have half a chicken sandwich if you're hungry."

"No thanks," Smith said.

"What's wrong with it?" The young man's face turned aggressive.

"I'm not hungry. Would you mind leaving us alone?"

"Veronica don't talk," the man said and continued on his way.

Smith watched him as he skipped up the lawn towards the hospital.

"That was a terrible tattoo," Smith said. "I bet the guy who did it has never seen an armadillo before. Can I ask you a question about Sebastian?"

Veronica didn't stir.

"Basil killed him didn't he?" The words shocked Smith as soon as they left his lips. "Basil took him out on the boat and killed him. He pretended that Sebastian had run away somewhere but he didn't did he? I know all about it Veronica. I know what happened."

Veronica started to rock back and forth slowly. Smith wasn't sure what it meant.

"Why did Basil kill Sebastian?" He didn't know what else to say.

"They'd had an argument the night before hadn't they? Do you know what the argument was about? Can you remember that night?"

Veronica stopped moving and closed her eyes. Another frog plopped into the water and she opened her eyes again.

"Basil killed Sebastian. You know. I believe you Veronica. I believe you."

Smith could see the grey suit of Doctor Young's at the top of the lawn. Young was striding towards them.

"I believe you," Smith said again. "Can you tell me what happened?"

Doctor Young had now stopped to talk to a group of people who were sitting on the grass.

Veronica's mouth opened. She ran her tongue over her cracked lips.

Smith's heart started to beat faster. Doctor Young was now nowhere to be seen.

"Sebastian," Veronica whispered.

Smith shivered - her voice was much deeper than he had expected.

"Sebastian," she said again.

Smith waited for her to continue.

"Jane was my friend," she turned her head slightly.

Her eyes were still fixed on the lake.

"Sebastian was a baby and he found them. Jane and Basil. Jane was supposed to be my friend. Do you believe me?"

"I believe you," Smith said.

He heard the sound of footsteps in the undergrowth. Doctor Young emerged from behind the trees.

"Time's up," he said. "You're not supposed to be here. Nobody in York even knows you're here. I checked."

Veronica Van Camp continued to stare across the lake.

"You were right anyway," Smith said. "It was a waste of time. I don't think she's ever going to talk again."

CHAPTER FIFTY SEVEN

The band in the Quail's Arms had finished their second set and were now taking a break. The pub was much busier than usual on a Tuesday night and Jethro had to wait twice as long to get served at the bar.
"Better give me two pints," he said to the stressed looking barman. "These bloody tourists and their Bacardi and cokes are making me feel like getting drunk."
The barman poured the beers and put them on the bar counter. Jethro took them back to the table next to the door where Fred, his ugly pug was waiting for him. Jethro's usual table was occupied by some strangers sipping Pimms.
"Bloody southerners," Jethro said to the dog. "Horsemen probably."
The door to the pub opened and Keith, Jimmy Phoenix's sidekick and Johnny Grouse walked in. Keith nodded to Jethro in acknowledgement and sat down next to Grouse at the only free table left in the pub. Jethro took a long sip of his beer and stared over at them. He wondered where Jimmy Phoenix was - Keith was seldom seen without Phoenix and what was he doing associating with the village idiot?

The band started up again and the tourists in the pub started to cheer. The three piece band, consisting of a guitarist, a violinist and a banjo player, launched into their own rendition of 'Helter Skelter'. Jethro finished one of the beers in one go and made a start on the second one. He remembered there was still over half a bottle of Jimmy Phoenix's whisky at home. He decided to drink up and go home - he hated it when the Quail's Arms was so full of strangers.

The band stopped playing halfway through the song. They stopped so abruptly that Jethro jumped. A man walked past his table. It was Basil Van Camp.

Here comes trouble, Jethro thought.

Van Camp wasn't very popular in Scarpdale.

"Carry on," Van Camp screamed at the band.

He was obviously very drunk.

"Don't stop on my account," he added. "All the drinks are on me tonight."

He took out a huge wad of notes and dropped them on the floor.

"Drinks are on me," he stooped down to pick up the money, lost his balance and tumbled to the ground.

After a short while, Johnny Grouse stood up and offered Van Camp his hand.

"Come on, Mr van Camp," Grouse picked him up. "Come and sit at our table."

"Play," Van Camp screamed at the band.

They started the song from the beginning again. The barman came round and picked up the money Van Camp had dropped.

"Worth sticking around a bit longer, hey boy?" Jethro said to his dog. "Free drinks and entertainment you certainly don't get on TV."

He finished almost a whole pint in one go and went to the bar to get another one.

An hour later, the band had packed up and only a few of the locals remained in the pub. Seven empty pint glasses stood in front of Jethro on the table and he was feeling very drunk. Basil Van Camp was still sitting with Johnny Grouse. Keith was nowhere to be seen.

That's odd, Jethro thought.

He hadn't seen him leave. The barman called last orders and Jethro stood up. He steadied himself and made his way to the bar. He realised he was more drunk than he thought and a dull pain had now spread from his shoulder down to the base of his back.

"Another pint," he said to the barman. "I assume it's still free."

The barman shook his head and poured the drink. Jethro took a long sip and headed back to his table. The pain in his lower back was getting worse. His whole body was starting to tingle. The weakness spread to his hands and he could no longer grip the beer glass. It fell to the floor with a dull thud. Jethro looked at his dog and collapsed in a heap on the floor.

CHAPTER FIFTY EIGHT

"Did she tell you anything?" Wilder asked as they drove out of the hospital car park. "The Doc was pretty sure she wasn't going to talk again."
He turned left and took a different road to the one they'd taken to get there.
"Scenic route," he lit a cigarette. "Those goons won't expect us to be going this way."
"She spoke to me," Smith still couldn't believe it. "But she didn't give me much to go on. The doctor showed up before she had a chance to really open up. I never got the chance to ask her anything else."
"That's something," Wilder said. "At least it wasn't a complete waste of time."
He drove across a short bridge and gazed at the Hudson River below. He seemed lost in thought for a while.
"I love this place," he said. "Have you got your passport ready? We'll be in Jersey soon."
"Sebastian Van Camp saw something when he was three years old," Smith said. "But he only brought it up last summer at The Hamptons."
"What did he see?"
"I don't know. Veronica said it was something about Basil and her friend Jane. Sebastian said he saw something and when he told his father about it he was killed."
"It must've been something pretty bad then," Wilder said. "Shit."
"What's wrong?"
"Looks like I was wrong," Wilder looked in the rear view mirror. "That damn Buick is following us again. They must have waited for us round the corner from the hospital."

"What are you going to do?"

"I don't know," Wilder put his foot down on the accelerator. "I can't outrun them - that Buick has much more power than this old thing and from what I remember, there's no roads running off the highway for quite a while. We'll just have to keep going. Maybe they'll run out of gas before we do."

"Great," Smith said. "What do you think they're going to do?"

"I don't know," Wilder increased his speed further. "But I'm not going to stick around to find out. Once we get past the state park we'll have a few more options."

Smith looked at the speedometer. They were travelling at almost a hundred miles an hour.

They drove on for a few miles. The black Buick stayed close behind them the whole time. It remained a constant fifty metres behind. It was showing no sign of giving up. Smith was starting to get agitated. The countryside on either side of them was becoming more and more built up.

"Why don't we just stop?" He suggested. "See what they want. They don't know if I found anything at the hospital - I told the doctor that Veronica Van Camp didn't speak to me."

"I don't think they'll take the chance," Wilder lit his fifth cigarette in half an hour. "Our best bet is to keep going until we reach the city."

They carried on driving south. Smith could hear his heart beating in his ears. Occasionally he glanced behind them. The Buick seemed to be getting closer and closer. The skyline of New York City appeared in the distance. An eerie orange haze clouded the higher skyscrapers.

The approach to the George Washington Bridge meant that Wilder had to reduce his speed. Smith saw a line of slow moving traffic on the road ahead.

"Don't you have a siren we can use?" He asked Wilder. "Maybe then, these cars will have to get out of the way."

"In the glove compartment, but I haven't used it in months. I'm not sure if it still works. I try to leave the high speed chases to the younger guys."

Smith rummaged around in the glove compartment. Captain Wilder was a bit of a slob - it was full of empty cigarette packets and old polystyrene coffee cups. Smith found the siren at the back and plugged it into the cigarette socket. He switched it on and nothing happened.

"I thought so," Wilder said. "It's busted. I can't actually remember the last time I used it."

The flow of traffic had slowed right down. The three lanes of the Palisade's Interstate Highway had now turned into two. The black Buick was still hot on their tail. Smith could now see the rat like eyes of the man in the passenger seat. He stared menacingly ahead.

"They wouldn't try anything in this traffic," Smith hoped.

"Don't fool yourself," Wilder swerved behind a red pickup truck and deftly put the pickup between them and the Buick. "This is New York City. People are used to this kind of thing."

Smith turned round. The Buick had somehow managed to get onto the outside lane and was quickly approaching alongside them.

"That guy can drive," he said. "I don't like this."

The Buick was almost next to Wilder's car. They had almost reached the George Washington Bridge.

"Once we're on the bridge," Wilder said. "There's nowhere to go but into the Hudson. Why the hell did I agree to help you with this crazy scheme?"

Smith was about to reply when Wilder spun the steering wheel far to the left and the car swerved onto the other side of the road, narrowly missing a bus full of wide eyed school children. They stared at the car as it just missed them. Wilder quickly steered the car back to the right and increased his speed. The Buick was now three cars behind them.

They drove through the huge archway and onto the bridge towards Upper Manhattan. Smith picked up Wilder's packet of cigarettes and lit one. He wasn't sure how much more of this his nerves could handle.
"Once we're safely across the bridge I can lose them," Wilder said. "Hold on."
He slowed down, got the car behind a small truck and stayed put for a few seconds. Smith could see the Buick approaching quickly behind them.
"What the hell are you doing? They're catching up."
"Just wait," Wilder smiled at him.
The Buick was now less than twenty metres away on the other side of the road. Wilder waited until it was almost alongside them. He pulled in front of it and slammed his foot on the accelerator. The car shot forwards and just before it slammed into the back of a taxi cab, Wilder swerved and overtook it on the left. The road ahead of them was clear. Smith looked behind them. The Buick was stuck behind the taxi. The truck on the other side of the road was preventing them from overtaking.

"Nice driving," Smith said as they reached the other side of the bridge and headed south towards Manhattan.
"I need a drink," Wilder slowed down and turned into an alley in a particularly seedy looking part of town.
He lit a cigarette and turned off the engine.
"Come on," he opened the car door. "You're buying."

CHAPTER FIFTY NINE

Captain Wilder led Smith through a black door next to a Fenix grocery store. The stench of stale alcohol and cigarette smoke hit Smith straight away. They walked through a dark corridor that led to a small room with a bar in the corner. The cigarette smoke formed a permanent haze in the top half of the room. Three pool tables stood to the left. Two men who looked like heavyweight wrestlers were playing at one of them. Wilder nodded to the bigger of the two.

"Harry," an old man standing behind the bar shouted as Wilder approached. "Long time no see."

He looked at Smith and smiled.

"What'll it be?" He said.

"Just two beers, Al," Wilder said. "We're working."

The man called Al took two Becks from a rusty refrigerator behind the bar and placed them on the counter.

"Thanks, Al," Wilder handed Smith one of the beers. "Let's get to work then."

Smith followed him to a table away from the pool tables and sat down.

"Cheers," Wilder opened the beer and took a long sip. "Tell me what you've got so far."

"What do you mean?"

"Well," Wilder finished the rest of his beer in one go. "The way I look at it is like this. As much as I like your company, you're a real pain in the ass to be around. The sooner we find out what the hell is going on the sooner you can get back on that plane and back to God knows where you came from. I'll be waving you off from the ground."

"Thanks."

"Al," Wilder shouted. "Two more beers."

Smith started at the beginning. He told Wilder everything from the day Sophie Phoenix was found by the lake up to the information he had gleaned from Veronica Van Camp. Wilder seemed to hold on to his every word. He finished his fourth beer.

"Give me a minute," he stood up. "I need to pee. I always think best in the John."

He returned a few minutes later with two fresh beers.

"Right, the way I see it is this. You're been looking at things in the wrong order."

"What do you mean?"

"You started your thinking from when that young lady was found by the lake."

"Sophie Phoenix."

"Right, and that's what's confusing you. I reckon this all stems from what that young lad saw all those years ago."

"Sebastian Van Camp?" Smith said. "His mother was rather vague - we don't exactly know what he saw."

"And he's fish food right now so we can't exactly ask him can we?" Wilder said. "But it seems to me that it can only be one thing. Young kid walks in on his dad having his way with someone who's not his mother. He doesn't know what's happening at the time - he's too young, but as he gets older, he put's two and two together. That sort of thing can really mess with a young man's mind."

"Shit," Smith said. "I'm an idiot."

"You're far from an idiot," Wilder signaled to Al that two more beers were in order. "You've just been confusing the sequence of events."

"Sebastian Van Camp walks in on his father with another woman," Smith said. "Years later he realises the significance of it all and confronts his father about it. His father can't have this kind of information getting out so he kills his son and disposes of the body. He makes up some story about Sebastian wanting time by himself. Basil then leaves New York and takes his eldest son with him. The only other person who knows what happened conveniently ends up in a nut house and the secret is dead and buried."

"There's no such thing," Wilder said. "Secrets have a habit of surfacing in the end."

"What about Sophie Phoenix and Lewis Van Camp? All of this still doesn't explain why they were killed. Basil Van Camp wasn't in the country when they died."

"That's your problem. I think you know as well as I do the answer to that one doesn't lie in New York. I think it's time you went back home. I need to get back to the peace and quiet of Queens."

CHAPTER SIXTY

When Smith drove out of the car park at Manchester airport into the grey drizzle, he was exhausted. He hadn't slept at all on the eight hour flight from New York and the five hour time difference was now catching up on him. He left the airport far behind him and joined the M62 towards Leeds. The few days he had spent in the city that never sleeps had been a blur. So much had happened there, he hadn't had time to process it all. He was starting to feel drowsy so he opened all the windows and inserted an ACDC tape into the cassette player. The introduction to 'Whole lotta Rosie' blasted out of the speakers.

The drizzle cleared as Smith drove further east. It was still early in the morning but the air drifting in the open windows felt warm. Smith lit a cigarette and tried to think about everything that had happened in the past week or so. Captain Wilder had made some sense of the sequence of events in New York but Smith was still unsure how it all tied in with the murders in Scarpdale.

Basil Van Camp killed his youngest son, Smith thought, and his eldest son is killed a year later across the Atlantic Ocean. Van Camp was out of the country when Lewis was killed.

He saw a sign that told him York was ten miles away and smiled. He still didn't know what he was going to do. He hadn't even told Whitton he was on his way home and the more he thought about it, he realised he didn't particularly want to see her. The feeling disgusted him - he didn't know what it meant.

I'm losing it, he thought, I'm losing my mind completely.

With that thought in mind, Smith took the turn off a few miles before the city centre and continued along the familiar road that led towards the hospital. He parked his car in the car park and turned off the engine. He sat in the car for quite some time.

What am I doing here? He thought. Why do I always seem to end up here? Why do I feel most comfortable in the company of a woman who spends her time within the four walls of a psychiatric hospital?

Jessica Blakemore was in her room when Smith walked in. Her hair had grown back slightly. The wisps of hair she had missed when she had shaved her hair off were barely noticeable. She was frantically sketching the outline of a map of the world with a pencil at the desk in the corner of her room.

"Knock knock," Smith said. "Is this consultation room free?"

Jessica continued to draw. She finished the southern tip of South America and turned around. Smith was shocked. Her eyes were bright and much more alive than they had been the last time he had seen her. Her short hair made them appear much bigger.

"You look terrible," she said.

"I've just flown in from New York," Smith said. "You look great, although that crew cut makes you look like GI Jane. What are you drawing?"

"Dreams," she smiled softly. "Dreams of places I want to go. I can tick New York off now. I can go there through you. That would be right here."

She raised her finger in the air and brought it down on the map. It was closer to Mexico than New York but Smith didn't tell her.

"You look happy. Have they finally admitted you're a bona fide whack job?"

"Oh yes, I'm not going anywhere anytime soon. Sit on the bed. You look troubled."

"I'm exhausted," Smith sat down. "In five days time, my leave is over and I have to go back to work. I feel more drained than ever."

"You said you've just flown in from New York," she put down her pencil and turned her chair so she was facing Smith. "That means you haven't been home yet. You chose to come here first rather than face what waits for you at home. Why is that?"

"I don't know. My head is all foggy - I can't seem to think properly. You're the shrink, you tell me."

"Do you want to go for a walk? The fresh air will clear your head a bit. This building is clouded with the obscure thoughts of the people who stay here."

They sat outside on a bench looking out towards the city in the distance. Smith could just make out the highest tower of the Minster. He took out his cigarettes, lit one and offered the packet to Jessica.

"No thanks," she said. "I'll just inhale what you breathe out, "do you know what your main problem is?"

"You mean I have more than one?"

"You're too hard on yourself. Your expectations are way too high. Take it from me - you're going to spend the rest of your life disappointed unless you lower the bar a bit. A lot, actually."

"I don't set the bar too high."

"You're not even aware of it. When was the last time you failed to crack a case?"

"Before now you mean?"

"Before now. When was the last time a murder investigation stumped you?"

"Never," Smith said. "It's never happened before. I always seem to get to the bottom of it."

"That's because you don't stop. You have to carry on until you've figured it out without any regard for the consequences."

"Consequences?"

"Are you happy?" Jessica stared deep into his eyes.

"No, I mean yes. Is anybody really happy?"

"Plenty of people are happy. Why do you keep coming to see me?"

"I have no idea. I like it here and I like your company."

"Go home. Go home and talk to Miss Whitton. That woman loves you, God help her and if you carry on along this path you're going to lose everything. Go home and enjoy the last few days of your holiday."

"Is that doctor's orders?"

"No," Jessica stood up. "It's what any fool can see. You're your own worst enemy, Jason Smith."

"Can I come and see you again?"

"Not for a while," she said. "You're starting to drive me crazy."

CHAPTER SIXTY ONE

For once, Smith decided to follow the advice he had been given. He drove slowly towards the city centre.
Maybe Jessica Blakemore is right, he thought, maybe I do expect too much.
It was not yet ten in the morning but the air was already thick and muggy. Smith was hoping that Whitton had a day off - there was so much he wanted to tell her. He wondered if he ought to tell her about the kiss with Charlotte Phoenix but he decided it wouldn't be a good idea. He parked his car next to his house and got out. Everything was exactly as he remembered it. He was sure he detected a movement in the curtains in the house next door as he walked up the path. His neighbour was spying on him.
"Arsehole," he whispered to himself.

Theakston was all over him as soon as Smith stepped inside. The dog jumped up and tried to lick his face. He'd lost quite a bit more weight in the few days Smith had been away but he looked good for it. The smell of coffee coming from the kitchen told Smith that Whitton was at home. Smith could hear the sound of the shower running upstairs. He put his bag down in the hallway, went through to the kitchen and turned on the kettle. Theakston nudged the back door open and Smith followed him outside to the back garden. He was amazed at how much the grass had grown. His neighbour's roses were starting to flower. Smith lit a cigarette and sat down at the garden table. Theakston lay by his feet and within seconds he was snoring loudly.

For the first time in a very long time, Smith felt content. Jessica Blakemore's words were still fresh in his ears.

'You're your own worst enemy.'

Smith knew that things had to change. He couldn't carry on like this anymore.

"You're back," Whitton appeared in the doorway.

She was dressed in a pair of shorts and a T-Shirt. Her hair was wet. Smith could smell her shampoo from where he sat.

"You look tired," she said. "Do you want some coffee?"

"Right now," Smith stood up and walked over to her. "All I want is a few hours to forget about everything else in the world apart from this."

He wrapped his arms around her and rested his head on her shoulder. He held her tightly and breathed in her scent. Before long, his shirt was drenched from her wet hair.

"Are you alright?" Whitton asked when Smith finally let go of her.

"I am now. Please tell me you have a day off today"

"I've got two days off actually. I was planning on doing some washing."

"Washing can wait. We've got two days off together. Washing can wait."

"When did you get back?"

"This morning," Smith said. "I came straight back here from the airport."

He decided not to mention he had been to see Jessica Blakemore first.

"How was New York?"

"Weird," Smith said. "I'll make us some coffee and I'll tell you all about it."

    Smith told Whitton everything - about the mysterious secret Basil Van Camp had been carrying around with him since the previous summer and the destruction that secret had caused on both sides of the Atlantic. He told her about the people at The Hamptons, the car chase and the help he had received from the eccentric Captain Wilder.

"They sound like a horrible bunch of people," Whitton said when he had finished.

"Money," Smith said. "Money brings evil with it."

"So what now? What about the two murders in Scarpdale?"

"What about them? I've realised that it's none of my business. The local guys can figure that one out."

Whitton looked at him like he had grown another head.

"What?" Smith said.

"Who are you? And what have you done with my boyfriend?"

"It's time I took a step back. For the sake of everybody in my life."

"I don't know what happened to you in New York," Whitton kissed him on the forehead. "But I think I like it. What do you want to do today?"

"First I need to have a shower," Smith said. "To wash the past few days away. That's if you've left me any hot water. And after that, how does a day in bed sound?"

"I think I'd rather do my washing," Whitton laughed.

Smith started to laugh too. He walked back inside the house. Whitton followed him.

CHAPTER SIXTY TWO

Smith woke up to the sound of rain pelting against the window. It was coming down at quite a rate of knots. Whitton was breathing heavily next to him. Somehow, Theakston had managed to get onto the bed and was now making loud grunting noises between them. Smith stretched his arms and smiled. The rain was coming down even harder now - it was drowning out Theakston's snoring. Smith got out of bed quietly and went downstairs. The message light on his phone was flashing. He ignored it and opened the fridge. He took out a beer and went outside to the garden dressed only in his boxer shorts. He sat down at the table and let the warm rain wash over his whole body. It felt invigorating. In less than a minute he was totally drenched. He spotted his neighbour staring at him from the window next door, raised the beer in the air and waved at him.
"Stupid fool," Smith said.
Theakston appeared in the doorway. He ran outside and ran straight back in again. The dog hated the rain.
"What are you doing?" Whitton shouted from the kitchen. "Are you mad?"
She was wearing one of Smith's old T-Shirts and nothing else.
"Come outside," Smith said. "It's great out here. I can't remember the last time I stood out in the rain."
Whitton shook her head and stepped outside. She shivered as the rain soaked her hair and T shirt. She sat down next to Smith. He handed her the beer and she took a long swig.
"This is great," Smith said. "Wave to old what's his name next door."
Smith's neighbour had now taken a sudden interest in what was going on in Smith's back garden.

"You're crazy," Whitton wiped the rain water from her eyes. "I don't know what's got into you. I'm going inside; I'm drenched through."

"I'm starving," Smith said.

He and Whitton were drying each other off in the kitchen. The message light on Smith's phone had now disappeared.

"I'm taking you out for something to eat," Smith said.

"Not the Hog's Head," Whitton said. "I feel like something different. Something hot and spicy."

"Let's go then," Smith said.

"Give me ten minutes to get ready."

"No woman on earth can get ready in ten minutes."

Twenty minutes later, Smith and Whitton closed the door behind a begging, pleading, Bull Terrier.

"You've been spoiling him," Smith said.

The look on Theakston's face had been pitiful - pathetic even.

"You've already ruined him," Whitton said. "I used to think all that stuff about a dog taking on the traits of its owner was a load of rubbish but I can see it in Theakston."

"I'm nothing like Theakston," Smith insisted.

"You are. He's stubborn. Bull headed, sweet sometimes and he has no social skills whatsoever."

"What? I can be perfectly sociable when the occasion deserves it."

"You and that dog are so alike sometimes. It's scary."

"Well he loves you - at least that's one thing we have in common."

"You old romantic," Whitton got in the passenger side of Smith's car. "Where are we going?"

The Lantern was one of the less tacky Indian restaurants in York. It didn't have the gaudy interior and clichéd ambience of most of the other curry houses in the city. Its menu was also not restricted to Indian cuisine - they also offered a variety of Western dishes.

"Best of both worlds, "Smith said when they had parked outside. "You can get your painful, torture food and I can have a decent steak and chips."

"Chicken," Whitton got out of the car.

"I'm not chicken," Smith said. "I just can't see the attraction of food that hurts. Food shouldn't attack you after the first mouthful."

"I'm having a Madras," Whitton said. "A nice hot one."

They were shown to their table by a young blond woman. The restaurant was surprisingly full considering it was still early on a Wednesday evening.

"Can I get you something to drink?" The waitress asked Smith.

"Two pints of Theakstons," he said without thinking.

He'd been looking forward to a decent beer after enduring the beer flavoured water the American's seemed to enjoy.

"Coming right up," the waitress said. "I'll bring you a couple of menus too."

"What's come over you?" Whitton asked when the waitress was gone. "You're a totally different person to the one who left for New York last week."

"I don't know," Smith said. "Spending time in The Hamptons has made me see things differently. You should see the place, Erica."

Whitton was shocked. Smith had used her first name for once.

"It's sickening really," Smith continued. "The houses, the cars and the boats. They're like something you only see on TV and yet, with all of that money, none of the people there are really happy. They're all miserable actually."

"It doesn't make sense. Most people dream of having a load of money. I wonder if rich people secretly dream of being poor."

"Very philosophical," Smith said. "I sometimes think it's the dream itself that's the exciting part. When the money does come it's a bit of an anticlimax."

"Now who's being philosophical?"

The waitress arrived with their drinks and two menus.

"I think we know what we want," Smith said. "A hot Madras and a steak and chips. Medium to well done."

"It'll be about half an hour," the waitress informed them.

"Since when did you eat hot food?" Smith said.

"I used to hate it, but I'm really starting to crave the stuff I used to turn my nose up at. I'm starving. I hope it's not going to take too long."

CHAPTER SIXTY THREE

"That was delicious," Smith put his knife and fork on the plate.
"How was the Madras?"
"Hot," Whitton said. "But just what the doctor ordered. Can I ask you something?"
"Anything."
"Don't take this the wrong way, but I don't understand. This isn't like you."
"What isn't like me?"
"Leaving an investigation in the air - leaving it half finished. From what you told me, the mystery of what happened in The Hamptons last summer is cleared up but it still doesn't explain why those two young people were killed in Scarpdale."
"It's not my problem/ I was a fool to get involved in the first place."
"Is all this for my benefit?"
"All what?"
"Don't act dumb. This all this is not my problem rubbish, because if it is, I'm flattered but it's not you, and I know you well enough by now. It's going to eat you up inside after a while."
"It's not," Smith said. "I've put it all behind me."
The waitress arrived with the bill and Smith and Whitton were quiet for a while.
"Let's go home," Whitton said when the waitress had gone. "Let's go through it together."
"Through what?"
"How many murder investigations have we worked on together?"
"Too many," Smith sighed.

"In case you've forgotten," Whitton said. "I'm not just your girlfriend, I also happen to be a detective constable. A bloody good one at that."

"Do you mean it?"

"Well I've been told I'm a bloody good detective."

Smith laughed.

"Thanks, Whitton," he said. "After this we can get back to normal."

Smith and Whitton sat at the kitchen table in Smith's house. Smith took out two beers and put them on the table.

"OK," Whitton said. "Let's go back to the start. The murder of Sophie Phoenix."

"I don't think that was the start of all this," Smith said. "Captain Wilder made me look at it all from a different perspective. Sophie's murder was the result of something that happened years earlier."

"What happened?"

"When I spoke to Veronica Van Camp, she mentioned something Sebastian witnessed when he was three years old. He was too young to realise the significance at the time but he grew to understand it. He confronted his father and Basil van Camp killed him because of it."

"What did he see? What can have been so terrible he had to die because of it?"

"Veronica said Sebastian saw Basil and Jane, her best friend. I think he found them in bed together."

"An affair?" Whitton said. "Surely that's no reason to kill your child."

"No, unless the consequences of Van Camp's actions run much deeper than that."

"What do you mean?"

"The Van Camps and the Phoenix's go back years. Over twenty years from all accounts. They didn't always hate each other. I think what happened when Sebastian was three years old caused this rift."

"Who is this Jane woman? Veronica's friend. Who is she?"

"I've thought about that," Smith said. "Jimmy Phoenix talked about his ex wife Janie. I think Basil Camp was having an affair with Jimmy Phoenix's wife."

"So Basil had an affair with Jimmy's wife," Whitton said. "It still doesn't explain why three young people had to die."

Smith popped the caps off the beers and handed one to Whitton. "Why would the exposure of Basil Van Camp's affair be worth killing for?" He said.

"Get me a piece of paper and something to write with," Whitton suddenly seemed animated.

Smith rummaged in the draw but couldn't find anything.

"Quickly," Whitton said. "Before I lose my train of thought."

Smith found an old notebook and a pencil. He handed them to Whitton.

"Basil Van Camp," Whitton started to write, "and Jimmy Phoenix. Van Camp had two sons, Lewis and Sebastian."

"And a daughter," Smith said. "Matilda."

"That's not important," Whitton said. "Jimmy Phoenix had two daughters. Charlotte and Sophie."

She wrote all the names on the notepad.

"Do we know how old the children are?" She asked.

"Charlotte's twenty three," Smith said. "And Sophie was eighteen when she died."

Whitton wrote their ages next to their names.

"And the Van Camp children?"

"Lewis was about my age, and Sebastian was quite a few years younger than him. He was twenty one or twenty two when he disappeared last year."

"There's your answer then," Whitton pointed to the scribbles on the notepad.

Smith was none the wiser.

"I think I've had too many beers," he said. "Please explain."

"Sebastian Van Camp was around four years older than Sophie Phoenix," Whitton said. "Which means Sophie was born less than a year after Sebastian found his father in bed with Sophie's mother. Are you starting to get the picture?"

"Shit," Smith said. "I'm such an idiot. Webber even told me that Sophie and Lewis shared the same DNA. I'd forgotten about it. I should have known that Jimmy Phoenix wasn't Sophie's father. Basil Van Camp killed his son in case he blabbed and somebody put two and two together."

"We still have a problem though," Whitton said. "It still doesn't explain who killed Sophie and Lewis in Scarpdale."

"I'd forgotten how much I enjoyed working with you," Smith raised his bottle and took a long drink. "I've got an idea about that."

"Who was it?"

"I'll let you know when I've figured it out."

CHAPTER SIXTY FOUR

Smith and Whitton were about ten miles from Scarpdale when the heavens opened. Smith's windscreen wipers were finding it hard to keep up.

"It's nice around here," Whitton said. "Or at least it would be if I could see anything. Why on earth did you pick this place of all places to come on holiday?"

"It seemed like a good idea at the time," Smith slowed down as the rain came down harder.

"You think Jimmy Phoenix killed Sophie and Lewis don't you?"

"No," Smith said. "I don't think Jimmy Phoenix has it in him. I think Jimmy knew all along that Sophie wasn't his real daughter but he still thought the world of her. He loved her like she was his own."

"Who then? Basil Van Camp was out of the country at the time of both the murders."

"Basil Van Camp is a monster, but it would serve no purpose to kill two more of his children. Neither Sophie nor Lewis knew they were half brother and sister. Sophie was pregnant with Lewis' child remember. They would never have started a relationship if they knew the truth."

The rain came to a sudden halt as they drove into the village of Scarpdale. It was as if some divine force was trying to tell them something.

"Who would have thought it," Smith said. "Who would have thought a tiny peaceful village like this could hold such sinister secrets?"

He stopped outside the Quail's Arms.

"Quail's Arms?" Whitton said. "What a strange name for a pub."

"What is a quail? I've never heard of it before."

"It's a small game bird - a bit smaller than a grouse."

A police car approached as Smith and Whitton got out the car. Smith sighed. Sergeant Wilkie was driving. A nervous looking PC Fielding was sitting next to him on the passenger side. Wilkie got out first.

"Morning," Smith said to Wilkie. "Beautiful day."

More rain clouds were gathering over their heads.

"What are you doing back here?" Wilkie said. "Don't you think you've done enough damage around these parts?"

"Not yet," Smith said.

PC Fielding got out the car. He smiled sheepishly at Whitton.

"Whitton," Smith said. "This is PC Fielding. A detective in the making."

Fielding first shook Smith's hand and then Whitton's. Wilkie glared at all of them.

"It's quiet around here," Smith said. "Quieter than usual I mean."

"Old Jethro took a turn for the worse last night," Fielding said. "I sent you a message to let you know. Odd bugger that he was - he was well liked around here. Most folk are in Skipton saying their goodbyes. They're saying he won't last out the night."

The news hit Smith for a six. He'd become quite fond of the loveable rogue.

"Skipton you say?"

"That's right. He's in the small hospital there. They wanted to ship him off to Leeds but Jethro was having none of it. Stubborn old bugger. I think he knows the ends near and he wanted to die close to home."

Smith felt a lump in his stomach.

"Where's Jimmy Phoenix?"

"Skipton," Fielding said. "Everybody's there. Keith, Johnny Grouse, Charlotte Phoenix. Even Basil Van Camp promised to make a trip out there. I didn't realise he had a heart."

"This is none of your business," Sergeant Wilkie chipped in. "I suggest you go back to York and never come back. This is none of your concern. This is village business."

"You're right," Smith said. "I'll be heading back to York after I've finished up at the hospital in Skipton. I strongly advise you to come with me. I'll take no satisfaction in clearing up this investigation. It's all yours."

Wilkie looked confused.

"What on earth are you blabbering on about?"

"Follow me to Skipton, and you'll find out."

"What did you mean by that?" Whitton said as they drove towards Skipton.

"By what?"

"You taking no satisfaction in clearing up the investigation," Whitton said. "What's going on?"

"If I'm right, this case is going to leave a bad taste in my mouth for a very long time."

They drove in silence. The rain that had threatened had now drifted off to the west. The sun made an appearance and cast an eerie glow over the heather on the moorland. A strange bird darted out into the middle of the road and Smith had to swerve to avoid hitting it.

"That was a quail," Whitton said. "Strange birds. Some people like to eat them."

Smith didn't say a word. He had a peculiar expression on his face. Whitton could tell that something was clearly troubling him.

Smith parked his car in the car park outside the small hospital in Skipton. He spotted Charlotte Phoenix immediately. She was standing outside the entrance. Fred, Jethro's ugly Pug was lying at her feet. Smith and Whitton got out the car and walked up to her.

"Charlotte," Smith said.

She had obviously been crying. Her eyes were red and puffy.

"Hi," Charlotte said.

She looked at Whitton and smiled.

"So you're the one who waits for Jason Smith back in York?" She said. "You're pretty."

Whitton didn't know what to say.

"Erica," Smith said. "This is Charlotte Phoenix. Jimmy Phoenix's daughter."

He turned to Charlotte.

"How's Jethro doing?"

"Not good, but he says he's made his peace. I don't think he's got long."

The grotesque dog suddenly woke up and stared at Whitton. Its eyes bulged out of its head like a chameleon's.

"What an ugly dog," Whitton said.

The dog walked up to her and sniffed her legs. It then started to run in crazed circles around her. It did this a few times, stopped and jumped up at her belt, all the time globs of drool flew out of its mouth.

"Fred," Smith said. "That's enough."

"What a strange dog," Whitton said as they made their way to Jethro's room in the hospital.

"Ugliest thing I've ever seen," Smith said.

Jimmy Phoenix was leaving the room as Smith and Whitton approached. Keith, his sidekick was standing next to him.

"Detective," Phoenix shook Smith's hand. "I know everything. I just wanted to thank you."

"How's he doing?"

"He's made his peace. He won't last the night."

"What happened?"

"You'd better talk to him. I've got a few of my own demons I need to exorcise right now. It's been a privilege knowing you."

He shook Smith's hand again and walked down the corridor.

Jethro was sitting up in bed when Smith and Whitton walked in. There was a tube attached to his left arm feeding a saline solution into a vein. He smiled when he saw Smith.

"I'm surprised to see you here," he said.

His voice was very weak. He seemed to find it hard to talk.

"I couldn't keep away," Smith said.

"And who's this pretty young thing?" Jethro nodded at Whitton. "Don't tell me she's fallen for your feeble Australian charms?"

Whitton smiled.

"This is Erica," Smith said.

"Pleased to meet you, Erica," Jethro said. "If you ever get tired of this idiot, you know where to find me."

He looked at Smith. His gaze turned serious.

"You hold onto her. Don't make the same mistake I made and start taking her for granted. Nowt lasts as long as you think it will, you know. Take a seat."

"Can I talk to Jethro on my own?" Smith asked Whitton. "I'll be out in a few minutes."

"I'll grab some coffee," Whitton stroked his shoulder and left the room.

Smith closed the door behind her and sat on the chair next to the bed.

"The Big C," Jethro growled. "In case you were wondering. I've known for quite a while. They tried to get me to go for treatment but what's the point? You tell me that."

Smith didn't know what to say.

"I'm an old man," Jethro said. "I've had a good life."

He started to cough. Smith wondered if he should call for help.

"I'm alright," Jethro calmed down a bit. "You couldn't arrange a pint of Theakstons for me though could you."

Smith smiled.

"I don't think they'd allow it."

"It's the only thing that's helped with the pain over the last few months," Jethro said. "The pills don't work. I stopped taking the pills weeks ago. How long have you known?"

"Known what?"

"Don't act the fool, detective," Jethro sat up further in bed. "You and me both know you're no fool. I'm not sorry you know. Jimmy was like the son I never had. I couldn't let him be tortured like that for the rest of his life. It wasn't right."

"Why?" Smith said. "Why did you kill them?"

"You first," Jethro now had a pained expression on his face. "How did you figure it out?"

"I had some help. First from a New York police captain and then from my girlfriend last night. They made me look at things differently."

"Smart lass that one," Jethro said. "I could tell that the minute she walked in the room."

"Basil Van Camp is Sophie's real father," Smith said. "He killed his son in New York last summer because he knew about the affair Van camp had with Jane Phoenix. I figured that Jimmy knew all along but he still treated Sophie like his own."

"Jimmy would, Jimmy's a good man. Most folk don't see it but Jimmy's not like the rest of those horsemen. He's decent - he still has morals. He came from nowt and he hasn't forgotten it. He's always treated me as an equal, not like that bastard Van Camp. No, Jimmy is one of the good ones. That's why he didn't deserve this."

A young nurse entered the room and checked Jethro's blood pressure.

"How are you feeling, Mr Jamison?" She said.

"All the better for having you leaning over me love," Jethro smiled.

The nurse shook her head and left the room.

"I had no choice," Jethro said. "I knew that bastard Lewis Van Camp was Sophie's half brother. I also knew she was pregnant with his child. I couldn't let Jimmy wake up every day knowing the bastard child of Van Camp incest was breathing the same air as him. Oh, I know Jimmy would've loved the kid like his own but it would've destroyed him in the end."

Smith felt sick. He wanted to get as far away as possible.

"You still haven't told me how you knew it was me," Jethro said.

"You were in the pub that night," Smith said. "That night when I asked Lewis Van Camp to leave. You were still there when I left and every time I was at Whooton Tarn you were hanging around. You were always asking questions. On the day of the funeral, when Lewis van Camp was killed, you arrived late. You were red in the face. I didn't think anything of it then. I realised how much you thought of Jimmy Phoenix and I put two and two together. You were the most unlikely suspect in a murder investigation but somehow everything fitted."

"What's going to happen to me? Are you going to arrest me?"

"No, I don't think that will do any good. I'll have to relate all of this to the retarded village sergeant of course but I doubt you'll see the inside of a jail cell."

"I've seen plenty," Jethro smiled. "I'll not make it out of this room. I'm not stupid - I'll be lucky to see another sunrise. I'm not sorry you know."

"No," Smith mused. "I don't doubt you are."

He stood up and patted the dying man on the shoulders.

"I like you," Jethro said. "I liked you from the first moment I spoke to you in the Dove Inn and there's not many folk I can say that about."

"There's just one thing I don't understand," Smith said. "How did you know Sophie was pregnant? Nobody knew about that. I doubt if Sophie even knew herself."

"Fred," Jethro said. "He may be the most offensive looking dog on the planet but he has this gift. He's got this odd way of behaving around pregnant women. He spots it a mile off. I don't know how he does it but he's never wrong. I've seen it plenty of times. He acts all peculiar and he won't stop. I don't know what'll become of him when I'm gone."

CHAPTER SIXTY FIVE

Jethro died later that night. Jimmy Phoenix phoned Smith to tell him the news. Smith stood with the phone to his ear long after the phone had gone dead. He walked outside to the back garden and lit a cigarette. Whitton was playing with Theakston on the grass. Fred, the repulsive Pug was finding it hard to understand what was going on. The dog was obviously not used to playing games. Theakston darted towards him and Fred jumped out of the way. Theakston thought this was a great game and moved in for another attack. Fred sought solace on Whitton's lap. The Pug settled on her stomach and within seconds, loud snorting sounds came out of its mouth. Smith sat down on the lawn next to them.

"Jethro's dead," he said. "He died half an hour ago."

"Poor guy," Whitton said. "In spite of what he did, I still feel sorry for him."

"He killed two people. I still don't understand it."

"He decided on what he thought was the lesser of two evils I suppose," Whitton said.

"When did you become so wise?" Smith slapped her on the shoulder.

Fred woke up and started to growl.

Whitton started to laugh.

"He may be ugly," she said. "But I'm getting to like him. He's protecting me. I think it's sweet."

"He has another talent too," Smith said.

"What's that?"

"You'll see," Smith smiled. "We'll both just have to wait and see."

Printed in Great Britain
by Amazon